It felt as if the ground had shifted beneath Jordan's feet.

Just enough to catch his attention.

He regarded Paige with a hint of wonder and wariness. A week ago he would have claimed that he was accustomed to adapting to new circumstances. Yet in a brief time, she had altered something he'd thought was immutable.

Maybe it was Paige's innocent idealism that cut through everything else. Idealism could be dangerous...and compelling. She was young and fresh and untouched by the horrors he'd seen around the world. But that was the biggest reason he should have little to do with her.

People like him weren't good for someone like Paige.

He was too cynical, too aware of the darkness that existed, and he knew his hard edges would just damage the idealism he found so intriguing.

Dear Reader,

My first Harlequin Heartwarming novel, *Twins for the Rodeo Star*, takes place around Shelton, Montana. Though fictional, Shelton holds a special spot in my imagination, so I wanted to set more stories there. No community is perfect, and from the start I had in mind a series of novels pivoting around a harsh grandfather who drove his grandsons away from Montana. Now bitterly regretting his choices, Saul Hawkins hopes to bring these Navy heroes home again by offering a challenge—prove yourself as a rancher and receive a third of the Soaring Hawk Ranch.

Family relations are complex and even if you've forgiven someone for the past, returning can open old wounds. Jordan Maxwell is no exception. A decorated Navy SEAL, he accepts Saul's challenge, yet his biggest challenge may be the idealistic young woman who has befriended "Sourpuss Hawkins."

Classic movie alert: *Angel and the Badman*. This 1947 Western is about a notorious gunman transformed by love—a theme I cherish as a romance author.

Please visit my website at sites.google.com/view/juliannamorris--author/home, where I share information on my books and other news. I'm also on Twitter @julianna_author and can be contacted on my Facebook page at julianna.morris.author. If you prefer writing a letter, please use c/o Harlequin Enterprises ULC, 22 Adelaide Street West, 41st floor, Toronto, Ontario Canada M5H 4E3.

Best wishes,

Julianna Morris

HEARTWARMING

The Cowboy SEAL's Challenge

Julianna Morris

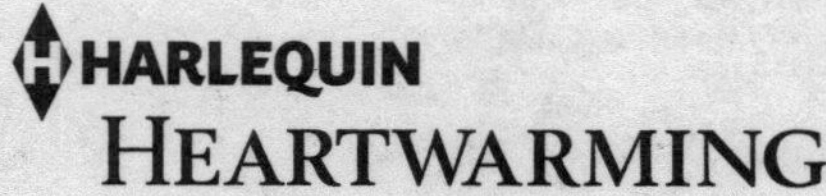

Recycling programs for this product may not exist in your area.

ISBN-13: 978-1-335-42674-1

The Cowboy SEAL's Challenge

For questions and comments about the quality of this book, please contact us at CustomerService@Harlequin.com.

Harlequin Enterprises ULC
22 Adelaide St. West, 41st Floor
Toronto, Ontario M5H 4E3, Canada
www.Harlequin.com

Printed in U.S.A.

Julianna Morris barely remembers a time when she didn't want to be a writer, having scribbled out her first novel in sixth grade (a maudlin tale she says will never ever see the light of day). She also loves to read, and her library includes everything from history and biographies to most fiction genres. Julianna has been a park ranger, program analyst and systems analyst in information technology. She loves animals, travel, gardening, baking, hiking, taking photographs, making patchwork quilts and doing a few dozen other things. Her biggest complaint is not having enough hours in the day.

Books by Julianna Morris

Harlequin Heartwarming

Hearts of Big Sky

The Man from Montana
Christmas on the Ranch
Twins for the Rodeo Star

Harlequin Superromance

Bachelor Protector
Christmas with Carlie
Undercover in Glimmer Creek

Visit the Author Profile page at Harlequin.com for more titles.

In memory of my parents. Always in my heart.

PROLOGUE

JORDAN MAXWELL DROPPED onto the floor and did fifty push-ups, waiting for his brothers to connect on the video conference call.

He was in top condition—fifty push-ups was nothing to him—yet he couldn't do anything about his age. At thirty-eight he was considered an old man by the ranks. Being a Navy SEAL was for young men. He could pass every physical test thrown at him, but they were still making noises about wanting him behind a desk.

The computer bleeped to say someone was waiting on the conference link. Jordan jumped to his feet and swung the laptop around. He pressed a button.

"I'm here, Dakota. Just waiting for Wyatt."

"He texted that he'll be a few minutes late. He and Amy had to make another run to the hospital."

Jordan tensed. Soon after getting pregnant, his sister-in-law had been diagnosed with an autoimmune disease. It was bringing back memories of their own mother, who'd died after a viral infection damaged her heart.

The computer bleeped again and Wyatt came on the screen. He looked exhausted and worried, nothing like his usual easygoing self. "Hey, guys."

"How is Amy?" Jordan asked.

Wyatt made a vague gesture. "As well as can be hoped. We're in a wait-and-watch mode. They said she—she could lose the baby. I'm guessing you want to talk about the letter we received from Grandfather's attorney." He obviously wanted to change the subject.

Jordan nodded and picked up the letter, looking at the most significant paragraph.

> Mr. Hawkins proposes you spend a year on the Soaring Hawk Ranch. If you prove yourself to the satisfaction of a mutually agreed upon third party, one third of the ranch will be placed in an irrevocable trust in your name. If you or one of your brothers does not accept this offer within the next six months, the land will be left to the University of Montana in Missoula. However, if one

of you accepts and succeeds, the offer will remain open to the remaining two brothers.

"To be honest, it sounds like a practical joke," Dakota said.

"You're the one who likes to kid around," Jordan reminded him. "I don't think Saul has a sense of humor. I'm not even sure I've ever seen him smile."

A strained look crossed both of his brothers' faces and Jordan wondered what it meant. After their mother died, Saul had taken them away from their hard-drinking father. But life on the Soaring Hawk had been cold and harsh, their grandfather believing they needed to be taught hard work and responsibility to make up for their father's "bad" genes. The situation had improved after Jordan enlisted and was out of the house, but Saul had remained a gruff, grim man who rarely spoke except to give orders. Ultimately they'd all gone into the navy as the fastest means to get away from him.

"Even if this isn't a joke, I can't resign," Wyatt said, breaking the silence. "With Amy's health being uncertain and the baby coming, we have to be near a major hospital."

Jordan nodded. It was what he'd expected. Wyatt was a family guy, through and through. Going into Special Forces like his brothers had appealed to him, but he'd resisted, knowing how rough it would be for his wife and on his marriage. They'd tried for years to have a child, yet now that Amy was pregnant, she was facing a serious health condition. As for the possibility she could lose the baby? That was a nightmare over and above the one they were already living.

"Dakota, I already know you can't do it, either," Jordan said and his brother nodded on the screen.

"Yeah, I've been training for that special assignment. I doubt they'd take my resignation since dropping out would mean a delay. It's an important mission and I could be away for months. But it doesn't matter. We have Dad's ranch so we don't need the Soaring Hawk. Let the university get the Hawkins land."

"Except the Soaring Hawk meant a lot to Mom. God knows why after the way Saul treated her," Jordan said. He still remembered his mother talking about the history of the ranch and the pride she'd taken in how the Hawkins family had hung on through everything life could throw at them, even the infamous winters of the 1880s. "Look, I know you two can't accept, but I'm eligible for twenty-year retirement. I'll do it. Mom wouldn't want us to turn our backs on our family heritage altogether."

Concern deepened the exhaustion in Wyatt's face. "Jordan, it would be the most difficult for you. Grandfather Saul was always..."

Though his voice trailed off and he didn't complete the thought, Jordan understood. Saul Hawkins had been hardest on his eldest grandson. The only thing he'd ever done that Jordan felt grateful for was signing his underage enlistment papers the day after he graduated high school. And that was probably just to get rid of him.

"It's all right," Jordan said firmly. "I'm not a kid any longer."

"I'm sure he's still a tough old guy," Wyatt commented.

Jordan shrugged. "Saul can bluster all he wants, but I'm tougher than he ever thought of being."

Three weeks later

JORDAN STOOD FOR a long time focused on his mother's gravestone in the Shelton Community Cemetery. He'd thought that he no longer resented the past, yet renewed anger simmered in him.

It wasn't the original stone. Instead of the inscription *Beloved Wife and Mother* and being decorated with a carving of her favorite fancy irises, the new, smaller marker simply gave her name and the years of her birth and death.

He put the flowers he carried next to her name and walked back to his truck. Heavy fencing now surrounded the cemetery, but it was still on the edge of town and looked out over the vast, rolling grassland that was so much a part of this section of Montana. The hills to the west, layer after layer, rose into blue mountains beyond. This was the view he loved best. Those distant, snow-capped peaks had beckoned to him as a boy, suggesting unlimited possibilities.

And escape.

The last few weeks had been busy between paperwork with the navy and getting the details settled with the lawyers. Jordan hadn't stayed in contact with anyone from Shelton, but he'd remembered Liam Flannigan's reputation as a fair and honest man. So Liam would be the third party to say whether Jordan was making a good-faith effort to work and learn the business of ranching.

Jordan considered stopping at Kindred Ranch to speak with Liam, then decided to go directly to the Soaring Hawk. Delaying his reunion with Saul wouldn't change anything.

CHAPTER ONE

PAIGE BANNERMAN SAT on Saul Hawkins's porch, chatting with him as her four-year-old daughter ran around, chasing their border collie.

Mishka couldn't catch up to Finn, as the brace on her leg kept her from moving quickly enough. But it was wonderful to see her having fun. The most recent operation on her leg had gone well and the brace would only be needed for a little while longer.

Or that's what Paige hoped. It hurt when she thought about her little girl, still struggling to walk before this last surgery.

"It's past time that boy should be here," Saul grumbled, stirring restlessly. "I hoped the navy would teach him to be dependable, but maybe he has too much of his father left in him." The old complaint about his son-in-law lacked heat and seemed more habit than anything else.

"You aren't being fair," Paige chided

gently. "Besides, Jordan's letter said he'd be here on Friday afternoon. You told me that he didn't say what time. And Jordan is driving from Southern California, not Bozeman. That's a long way from Montana and things happen on the road beyond anyone's control."

"I suppose."

Saul settled back in his chair, still cranky. He was a character—rough-edged, but with a good heart. Age had caught up with him more than usual in the last year, or maybe he was finally acknowledging the advance of time and feeling it in a way he hadn't before.

Mishka came up the steps and planted herself in front of him, hands on her small hips. She'd learned the pose from her mother and grandmother, the same way she'd learned to scrunch her nose. "Be happy," she ordered.

He leaned forward, his frown disappearing. "You make me happy, Mishka."

She smiled brightly and hugged his knee.

The sound of a vehicle arriving turned their attention to the yard. It was a late-model pickup, with a California license plate, painted a deep metallic red that instantly made Saul scowl. He didn't believe in frivolity, and vehicles that weren't plain, practical colors were frivolous in his opinion.

The driver parked near the barn. The man who got out was tall and strongly built, and moved with easy confidence. Paige recognized him. *Barely.* He walked to the foot of the steps and fixed Saul with a cool gaze. If she'd hoped this would turn into a loving reunion, his rigid expression said it wasn't going to happen.

Obviously neither man was willing to speak first, so she got up and held out her hand. "Hi. I'm Paige Bannerman, one of Saul's neighbors. My folks own the Blue Banner Ranch across the way."

In Shelton County, "across the way" meant up the incoming ranch road, left or right on the public road and then down another private ranch road.

"Jordan Maxwell."

He briefly shook her hand without saying anything else. Paige sighed. Saul had asked her to be there when his grandson arrived, but she hadn't thought it would be this awkward.

"You may not remember, but we used to see each on the school bus when we were kids," she said. "This is my daughter, Mishka," she added.

Mishka had rushed over to hide behind her, but now she was peeking around and staring up at Jordan, eyes wide. Though she was comfortable with the adults in her world, new people remained a question mark.

His expression softened. “Hey, Miskha. How old are you?”

Mishka held up four fingers.

“Wow, four years old,” he said, sounding admiring. “Practically grown up.”

She giggled and hid her face again, more in play than fear this time.

Paige gave Saul a pointed look. Coaxing his grandsons back to Montana had been his idea, not hers.

He heaved himself to his feet. “I figured you’d use your old room,” he muttered, gesturing to the front door. “You know the way.”

“I’ll sleep in the bunkhouse. Or the ramrod’s quarters. I presume they’re unoccupied since you never wanted to hire someone for the job.”

Around Shelton it was more common to say *foreman* than *ramrod*, but not on the Soaring Hawk. Saul’s personality had fit the name—nothing subtle about him.

“Got no ramrod. That’s the job you’ll be doing once you hire some cowhands. But no sense in staying elsewhere when I have plenty of room.”

"No, I'll use the separate quarters," Jordan said firmly. "I'll drop my gear in there and then check the barns. I assume the evening chores need to be done. I've been in contact with Liam Flannigan several times and he said you were having trouble keeping hands on the payroll, so I'm sure there's plenty to catch up on doing."

Saul's mouth tightened. "I've asked Paige to reacquaint you with the Soaring Hawk over the next few months. She runs the business end of her parents' spread and does accounting for some of the ranchers around here, so she knows the local suppliers and other folks you'll need to deal with."

"I don't need to be reacquainted with the Soaring Hawk."

"It's part of my terms," Saul returned grumpily. "The agreement says there can be a periodic observer of you working. I choose Paige."

Paige suspected there was a whole lot of frustration behind Jordan's impassive face. The same for Saul, who sank into his chair as his grandson pivoted and marched back to his truck.

She rolled her eyes. "Stay with Saul,

Mishka," she told her daughter as she followed Jordan. She caught his arm and he spun with a precise speed that made her breath catch.

"What?"

"We can discuss the *observer* stuff later. This is the first I've heard about it," she said in a low voice. "All he mentioned was me riding with you part of the time. But I don't understand why you won't live in the house. It used to be your home."

She glimpsed a wintry chill in Jordan's gray eyes. "That place was never home," he responded in a clipped tone. "To me or either of my brothers."

"Oh." Paige remembered the talk when she was a kid, about Saul not being the most sympathetic guardian for three young boys still grieving for their mother, just better than a man who had lost himself in a whiskey bottle. "The truth is that Saul is getting older and doesn't move around as well as he used to. I bring him food, but it would be safest if someone was here at night in case he falls."

"I didn't return to be his caregiver. We have a legal contract about my responsibilities to the Soaring Hawk. And from the looks of things, it's in even worse condition than I expected. I can't prove myself as a rancher if I'm spending my time and energy taking care of him. Since he requires help, I'll hire somebody, along with the cowhands needed."

Paige couldn't deny the Soaring Hawk was in poor shape. Saul's peppery nature, combined with his failing physical strength and bad hip, had taken a toll on the ranch. The last few months had been particularly rough. Her father and brothers lent a hand whenever something urgent needed doing, but that meant taking time away from the Blue Banner. They could only do so much, and mostly did it out of concern for her and the animals that might be endangered.

Money wasn't Saul's problem. He had the resources to hire employees, but nobody wanted to work for him. His last two cowhands had retired a couple of weeks ago, privately telling Paige that they'd only stayed as long as they had because of the buffer she'd provided between them and Saul.

Luckily calving season was over, or the situation would have been even worse. But help or support wasn't what Saul wanted from his grandson; it was a chance to make up for the past.

"Why are you here, anyway, if not to observe me?" Jordan asked. "Are you a social worker or something?"

Her chin rose. "I started visiting as part of a community project that reaches out to older county residents who are alone. Now I come because we're friends."

"Then you must be the first friend he's ever made."

She shifted uncomfortably, knowing that might be true, at least since Saul's wife had gotten sick and died. He had an unparalleled reputation for orneriness. Nobody had wanted the task of checking on "Sourpuss Hawkins," so as his neighbor and founder of the Connections Project, she'd volunteered.

"Few people want to admit they aren't as independent as they used to be," Paige said, unwilling to say how challenging it had been to win Saul's trust. He'd done his best to chase her away from visiting, but by the time she'd adopted Mishka, they'd become firm friends.

"I can't imagine Saul ever admitting to a weakness."

"I didn't say it was a weakness," Paige said emphatically,

While she liked most people, she wasn't

sure how she was going to feel about Jordan. He seemed to be cut from the same cloth as his grandfather, though she didn't see any of Saul's finer qualities in him. Still, they'd just met, and it was a positive sign that her daughter had responded to Jordan's overtures. Mishka was nervous of newcomers. What Paige didn't know was if it stemmed from the traumas she'd experienced as an orphaned baby, halfway around the world, or the many medical procedures she'd needed since then.

"Regardless, I won't stay in the house," Jordan said with a note of finality. "That wasn't part of our agreement."

Paige glanced back at Saul, wishing he could have been a little less himself, and a little more like a conciliatory grandfather. Despite his best intentions, most of the time he was his own worst enemy. Too many years had gone by with him being lonely and angry at life to let go of it easily. On the other hand, a total about-face might seem suspicious to Jordan.

"Maybe you'll change your mind after you've been here a while," she murmured. "Saul wants you to succeed."

"TIME WILL TELL," Jordan said, assessing Paige the way he'd assess a new SEAL team member. She was slim and of medium height. There was a hint of stubbornness in her expressive face. And she had to be in her twenties, so if they'd ridden the school bus together, she would have been one of the really young kids who'd stayed near the driver.

She was also attractive, with long, golden-brown hair and creamy skin, something he wouldn't register in his assessment of a fellow SEAL. No wedding ring was in evidence. He knew little about women's clothes, but her snug black jeans and silky green shirt looked expensive, along with her shearling-lined suede jacket. And he'd bet she owned the silver Volvo SUV parked near the house; it wasn't the sort of vehicle that Saul Hawkins would purchase to haul hay or do other work around the ranch. He'd always bought cheap.

As for her daughter?

The small girl, with her dark, cautious gaze, reminded Jordan of the children in the turbulent regions where he'd been deployed so often. Seeing those kids and not being able to do more for them had been one of the hardest aspects of serving.

Paige tilted her head to a challenging angle.

"If you're so certain that Saul won't be fair, why are you here?"

"This land meant something to my mother. She—" Jordan stopped and cleared his throat. "Mom would have wanted me to give it a shot. Now, about Saul needing someone at the house to help out, I don't think he'll allow a visiting home health-care worker, if they even have any available in Shelton."

Surprise filled Paige's eyes. "A live-in housekeeper would be best, although he'll probably object to having anyone here unless he picks them personally. I made inquiries several months ago and no one seemed interested, but you could try advertising in Bozeman or Helena and offer to pay a relocation bonus."

Jordan let out a dry chuckle. "Meaning Saul's reputation precedes him. But I don't think advertising will be necessary. I have a retired pal from the marine corps who's tough enough to give Saul a run for his money. Sarge has been looking for a new challenge. My grandfather will surrender, long before it would ever cross her mind. She's a force to be reckoned with."

Dismay widened Paige's warm eyes. "Surely you don't want to see Saul defeated."

Jordan sighed. She seemed genuinely fond of his grandfather, however much it stretched credulity to believe. "He's the one who made this into a contest."

"I realize that, but…" She turned her head toward the porch, where Saul sat gazing at them with Mishka perched on his knee. A watchful black-and-white border collie was lying nearby. "Dignity is important. Getting old is hard, especially for someone who doesn't have much family. You start questioning everything, including yourself and what difference your life has made. Someday you may be in his shoes and wish you'd been more understanding."

With an effort, Jordan refrained from reminding her that Saul was the one who'd driven his family away, first when he disowned his daughter for marrying a man he didn't approve of, and then by the way he'd treated his son-in-law and grandchildren.

"I have no intention of taking his dignity away, and Sarge wouldn't dream of doing that, either," Jordan said. "But she also won't put up with any guff. Sort of like Saul, so maybe they'll get along great."

Although Paige obviously wasn't thrilled with the idea of a tough former US Marine being her friend's housekeeper, it wasn't her decision. Jordan had to deal with the situation as best he could. All of it. Including the idea that she'd be an "observer" to his ranching efforts, though he believed her claim that it wasn't something she'd known about beforehand.

There *had* been a clause in the contract about someone observing his efforts on Saul's behalf. But his own lawyer had said it shouldn't affect the outcome if Liam Flannigan—the third-party arbiter—was as honest as his reputation.

Jordan drew a deep breath. "Right now I suggest you collect your daughter and go home. I doubt my grandfather can be relied upon to keep a close enough watch on a child her age."

Paige's eyes narrowed. "Saul is careful with Mishka, but I don't ask him to take care of her because he worries too much. I'll be back tomorrow to start riding with you. We can discuss what I do at my family's ranch. Some supply companies are better than others. After all, when you need to buy something like protein cake or hay, it's helpful to know who provides the best quality for the price."

Her expression challenged him to reject the wisdom of obtaining genuinely useful information.

"Fine. How about 6:00 a.m.?"

"Sounds good." The early hour didn't appear to concern her, but being both a parent and daughter of a rancher, it wouldn't. From the little Jordan knew about raising kids, they could be early risers. The same with ranchers, whether or not they had children.

She turned on her heel and went to the porch, then lifted her daughter into her arms. The child peeked at him over her mother's shoulder before hiding her face again.

Jordan didn't linger. He grabbed his duffel bags from the truck and headed to the ramrod's quarters. Not surprisingly, the door wasn't locked; the ranch was fairly remote and crime had never been a big problem in Shelton County. Faint amusement lightened his mood as he remembered his middle brother *had* been responsible for a brief spree of pranks in town. Luckily Dakota had never gotten caught.

The musty odor inside the ramrod's quarters showed it hadn't been used in a long while, and there was a hole in the ancient mattress that looked as if a mouse had made a nest in there. But Jordan just opened the windows to freshen the air, rolled up his sleeves and changed into a pair of work boots. Cleaning would have to wait; the ranch was a higher priority.

When he stepped outside, the silver SUV was gone, though Saul was still sitting on the porch. Probably glaring in his direction.

It didn't matter.

Jordan dialed his retired marine friend as he began walking around the barns and other outbuildings to assess their condition. They weren't an encouraging sight.

"What's up, Jordan?" Sarge answered crisply after two rings.

Anna Beth Whitehall was a no-nonsense, retired master sergeant. They'd met soon after his navy boot-camp training ended and she had made a huge impact in his life, particularly by encouraging him to get his college education online while remaining on active duty. Becoming a commissioned officer wouldn't have been possible without the first degree Jordan had earned, and he hadn't lost time toward retirement by attending school full-time.

"Sarge, are you still looking for a challenge?" Jordan asked.

"What d'ya think?" she replied. "I take it this has something to do with your Montana venture."

"You're right. From what the daughter of a neighboring rancher has said, my grandfather needs an MP to keep him in line, but a housekeeper in disguise will do. You can set your own hours, run things the way you want, get the pleasure of arguing with my grandfather every day and be paid for it."

Anna Beth chuckled. "Sounds right up my alley. I've been thinking about a change of scenery. When do I start?"

"As soon as you can get here. Paige wanted me to stay in the house so he'll have someone there at night, but I'm not willing to do it. I'll be living in the ramrod's quarters, which are almost as bad as the worst barracks I've ever billeted in."

Another chuckle sounded over the speaker. "That's hard to believe. We've both had awful accommodations over the years."

Jordan thought about the hole he'd spotted in the thin, narrow mattress, which looked as if it could date back to being from World War II surplus supplies. The same with the metal bedstead and everything else in there. But mice living in his quarters were the least of his worries, and he'd definitely dealt with worse. "Yeah, you're right."

"By the way, who is Paige?" Sarge asked.

"The neighbor I mentioned. Young. In her twenties. She and her daughter seem to be good friends with my grandfather. Paige does charity work, so she's probably idealistic."

The last word hung in the air for a moment. *Idealism* was a touchy word, one they'd debated. They admired idealism and were wary of it as well. But no matter what, duty was important to them both. He looked at the whole of a task, and then took care of it step-by-step, day by day. That's how he would put the Soaring Hawk back together.

Sarge cleared her throat. "I'm packing as we speak. I can be there in two or three days. Possibly Monday. Just text me the address. My GPS will take care of the rest."

"Will do. Drive safe."

Jordan disconnected, sent a swift text and dropped the phone in his shirt pocket. Sarge didn't waste time. Maybe it had something to do with all those years in the marines. She was always ready for action and traveled light.

As he continued checking the ranch center, he made a mental list of the repairs needed.

It was a long one. The tractors and haying equipment were the same he'd used as a boy, so they would need work, along with everything else. Then he checked the paddock fence, where a group of horses was grazing. Spring had arrived early this year and the grass was coming in fast and furious, though last year's growth still stuck up in yellow clumps around the base of the buildings and fence posts.

Jordan grabbed the toolbox from his truck and hammered several boards more securely to their posts. It was a temporary fix. By the looks of things, the entire property was in a sorry state. Repairing fences would be a high priority over the coming weeks, along with hiring cowhands and driving the herds to summer pasture, assuming they hadn't already been moved. Then there was branding and vaccinating the calves and mowing for hay. If the bunkhouse was in as bad a shape as the ramrod's quarters, it would also have to be made livable for employees.

As for the horses?

Jordan paused briefly with the sheer pleasure of watching them. Riding was what he'd missed the most about Montana, and these were strong, clean-limbed and full of energy.

Clearly, Saul's appreciation of fine horseflesh hadn't diminished over the years; horses were the one thing where he'd eagerly acquired the best.

His investment might pay off now.

While Jordan hadn't communicated with anyone in Shelton during his absence, he *had* followed the local news, so he didn't think the Soaring Hawk had become known for breeding horses. Nonetheless, yearling and weanling sales were a potential second income for the ranch. They could be especially important, depending on how many cattle his grandfather still owned. Jordan had asked for copies of the account books and stock records, but Saul had refused, saying he could see them when he arrived. It was just like him, not wanting to reveal anything without getting something in return.

Determination charged through Jordan as he forked hay into the horse's feed trough and topped the water tank, which was badly in need of scrubbing. He'd succeeded at becoming a Navy SEAL, and he had every intention of succeeding as a rancher. He hadn't enlisted because he didn't like ranching; he'd done it to get away from Saul.

He ran a wheelbarrow into the paddock and

began removing manure. One of the horses, a chestnut stallion with a thick black mane and tail, watched and pawed the ground. Jordan ignored him. Curiosity slowly overcame the stallion's caution and he stepped closer, finally extending his neck to sniff Jordan's shoulder. That air was cold enough that his breath fogged as it streamed from his nostrils.

Jordan kept working until an equine nose nudged him harder, demanding attention.

"Hey, there, beautiful," he said, putting the shovel into the wheelbarrow. He patted the horse's shoulder, then put his hand on its halter. They shared a measuring sort of look that weighed and balanced and made decisions.

Gradually the tension in the stallion eased and he dipped his head for a nose rub.

"Good boy," Jordan murmured.

"That's Tornado," Saul announced from over by the paddock fence. "He's from a top bloodline. I got papers for him."

Jordan looked at Saul, thinking of what Paige Bannerman had said about old age. His grandfather, who'd once been so tall and imposing to him as a boy, seemed shrunken, his shoulders bowed by the years. His leathery skin was deeply lined, even more than most people his age, and his dark eyes appeared sad, rather than bitter. It would take a miracle to start trusting him, but she was right about dignity being important.

"He's a fine horse."

"Yeah, well, he's yers. The doc told me last year to stop riding unless I get a hip replacement. And even then I might not be able to. That's the new doc in town. Dr. Wycoff is sharing the clinic with his daughter, now that she's done with her training. Seems awful young to be telling folks my age what they can and can't do."

It was more information than Jordan had expected Saul to volunteer at one time.

"I'm sure she's qualified and has her patients' best interests at heart."

Saul shrugged and didn't argue. "Tornado is stubborn as a mule, the same as you. Maybe you'll suit each other."

Jordan kept rubbing Tornado's nose. If anything, he would have assumed his grandfather despised any reminders of his eldest grandson. Jordan had sometimes wondered why Saul had been hardest on him—he even suspected the reason, but it didn't matter. He would never have left Dakota and Wyatt alone with Saul if he hadn't believed their lives would improve without him there.

"There are more horses in the south paddock beyond the line of black cottonwoods," Saul added. "Mares, a stallion and a few geldings. They have a stream for water and what's left of the winter hay to eat if they can't find enough grass. They're quarter horses, too, mostly with papers."

"That's good to hear."

"Yeah, well, Paige brought food for dinner. Enough for two and then some," Saul told him. "Will you eat at the house?"

A refusal hovered at the tip of Jordan's tongue as he recalled the silent childhood meals around the ancient farm table, followed by them cleaning up while Saul went over the ranch accounts. Their homework had come last. At the same table. No one saying a word.

His gut churned with the memory.

Saul stiffened. "Come or not, it's up to you."

Jordan groaned. If it hadn't been for Paige Bannerman's comments about Saul and aging he wouldn't have thought twice about refusing. She was probably still young and naive enough to believe she could change the world. And maybe she *could* change part of it, but the best he'd learned to hope for was to save a few lives and relieve some suffering.

"Uh, sure. I'll come over after I've worked a while longer."

"That's fine. She put the food in one of those slow-cooker things, so it'll hold as long as needed."

Slow cooker?

Jordan suspected he was in for a bowl of chili. Homemade chili would be better than the military MREs he'd brought with him, but chili was the dish his grandfather had frequently prepared for those silent dinners.

"Then I'll be in around eight."

Saul nodded and limped back toward the house. A few feet away, he turned around again. "Nobody expects you to start working like this after such a long trip. You could stop now."

Jordan could almost swear the elderly rancher sounded wistful. "This is nothing compared to my days in the navy. I'll see you later."

He managed to remove most of the manure from the paddock and get cleaned up by the time he'd agreed upon, though it was with frigid water and a hose outside the barn, rather than a shower. As it turned out, the plumbing in the ramrod's quarters didn't seem to be functional. Repairs would have to wait.

Inside the ranch house, a beguiling scent wafted through the air. *Not chili*, Jordan thought, his mouth watering.

He found his grandfather in the kitchen, which was much brighter than he remembered. Saul was serving plates of pot roast and vegetables from a slow cooker. Butter and a basket of yeast rolls sat on the table, its scarred surface covered by a blue gingham tablecloth. There was even a brown bottle with a few wispy, early wildflowers in the center.

Jordan's eyebrows went up. "Flowers?"

"From Mishka."

Curiosity about the child and her mother swept through Jordan, but he didn't ask more. He had enough to handle over the next year without adding complications.

CHAPTER TWO

"HOW DID IT GO?" Paige's mother called, coming down the porch steps.

Paige made a face as she unfastened the strap holding Mishka in the child's car seat. "They're both stubborn beyond belief. *That's* how it went."

"You're the only one to get through Saul Hawkins's defenses in almost fifty years, so you have to be more stubborn than he is," Margaret Bannerman said with a wink. "But an iron will must be a prerequisite to becoming a Navy SEAL, which makes Jordan Maxwell your next challenge to overcome."

"I'm persistent. Persistence isn't being stubborn."

"You're forgetting I raised you. I know exactly how obstinate you are."

Paige grinned and helped Mishka to the ground. The little girl rushed over to hug her grandmother as if they'd been separated for months.

"How is my angel?" Margaret asked, smoothing her shiny hair.

"We saw a tall man. Bigger than Gampa or my uncas."

"Is that so? Was he nice?"

Mishka scrunched her nose. "I tink so. But he's sad, like Mr. Saul." She put her hands up and pulled her mouth downward as if rubbing away her smile. The expression held for a few seconds before another sunny smile broke out.

"I'm sure your being here will make him happy," Paige's mom said.

"Sweetheart, why don't you give Finn a dog treat?" Paige interrupted, not wanting her daughter to feel put on the spot. Despite being knee-high to a grasshopper, as her grandfather called it, Mishka had more love to give than anyone Paige had ever known. But it wasn't fair to place too much on her; she couldn't heal all the wounded hearts in the world.

Mishka went into the house, trying to skip, even with the brace on her leg. Giving treats to Finn was one of her favorite things to do. Paige had taken hundreds of pictures of them together since she'd brought Mishka back from India. Finn had gotten one look at the baby and become her faithful guardian. He'd be unhappy once Mishka was old enough for school and they'd have to be separated more often and for longer periods.

A hint of melancholy hit Paige.

It seemed impossible that Mishka would be going to kindergarten in a year. Paige worked from home and had her child with her most of the time, but now she understood why parents complained about their children growing up too quickly. Homeschooling was an option, except there weren't any other kids on the Blue Banner Ranch. Mishka had playdates and spent time with kids at various social gatherings, but kindergarten would be another place for her to make friends.

Mishka starting school was going to be hard on the entire family.

She was everyone's darling. She had three doting uncles, a devoted aunt who'd helped with her adoption and visited whenever she could, adoring grandparents and a great-grandmother, all of whom would walk through fire for her. As the eldest—and, to date, the *only*—next-generation grandchild, she occupied a special place with the Bannermans. There was always a lap for her to sit on, eager ears to listen to her stories and hugs galore.

"Is there anything you didn't want to say in front of a little pitcher's big ears?" Margaret asked softly.

Paige sighed. "Not really. It wasn't the reunion I'd hoped for. Saul couldn't resist being himself, and his grandson isn't any improvement as far as I can see. He's nearly impossible to read, but thinking about it, I'm pretty sure he was annoyed or downright angry about something."

"I'd be angry in his shoes," Margaret admitted.

"I could be wrong. Angry or not, he refused to stay in the house. He's going to use the foreman's quarters, or ramrod's quarters, as Saul calls them."

"Oh, dear. Mr. Hawkins doesn't get around well." Though Paige's mother had known Saul her entire life, she couldn't bring herself to call him by his first name—he'd scared her too much as a child. It was then, during his young wife's illness that he'd developed his stern, unapproachable demeanor. Later, after Celina Hawkins's death, he became even worse. Generations of Shelton children had told wild stories about what was "really" happening at the Soaring Hawk. Instead of ghosts or evil spirits, they'd had Saul Hawkins.

"I told Jordan that I was concerned about his grandfather being alone at night," Paige explained. "He says he'll get a housekeeper. Supposedly he knows a retired marine who might be interested."

Margaret pursed her lips. "It's hard to imagine Saul Hawkins and a marine in the same household."

"My exact thoughts. But whoever Jordan has in mind, they probably won't come," Paige said in a practical tone. "Why would someone move to a ranch in Montana to be a housekeeper for someone like Saul? Nobody from Shelton was willing to give it a shot. I know, because I advertised for months."

"Poor Mr. Hawkins has been alone for a long time."

And he has no one to blame but himself.

The unspoken comment hung in the air, and was all the more sad because it was true. He'd shut out the world a long time ago and was paying the price now.

Paige hooked elbows with her mother and they went up the porch steps. In contrast to the Soaring Hawk, there was fresh paint on the house and porch, and the barns and fences were in tip-top condition.

She and Mishka had also planted flowers all around the place. They would soon bloom, unless there was a late freeze. Paige's father had created minigreenhouse covers to protect the tomatoes, peppers and other plants in their garden, and something similar would go over Mishka's flowers as well, if frost was predicted. But it could still delay the blossoms.

Flowers weren't practical additions to ranch life, but Mishka had a passion for living things. Even in winter the house had numerous pots of something growing—geraniums, nasturtiums, herbs, or whatever took her fancy. Last year they'd tried carrots in a window box, but the plants had immediately gone to seed without making carrots.

Margaret opened the screen door. "What I don't understand is why you took Saul Hawkins to heart so much. You're fond of all the people you visit, but he seems extra special."

"Maybe we knew each other in another life," Paige returned lightly.

"You'll have to do better than that." Margaret kissed her and headed for the kitchen.

Paige sighed. She *was* fond of Saul and she wanted the best for him. She just wished that one of the other Maxwell brothers had accepted Saul's challenge, rather than Jordan.

In Saul's own words, Jordan was going to be the toughest grandson nut to crack.

JORDAN OPENED HIS eyes at 4:00 a.m. the next morning, the way he'd trained himself over twenty-one years in the navy, regardless of time zone. He immediately rolled out of bed, though he'd slept for less than three hours. He'd stayed up until after midnight, giving the horses in the paddock a long-overdue grooming, disinfecting his quarters with bleach, then trying to make sense of the ranch accounts and stock records. They were dismally depressing.

His first quick look at the messy ledgers and disorganized boxes of receipts and paperwork had made his blood pressure soar. "You said Paige Bannerman does accounting. Is she responsible for this?"

Saul had bristled. "Paige isn't my accountant. I do them myself. But the ranch is yours to run for the next year, just as we agreed. I've added your name to the accounts at the bank, so you can hire whoever you want and pay 'em. You can't prove yourself without enough freedom."

Jordan was surprised Saul had actually put his name on the ranch bank accounts, though it made sense. As for his remark that Jordan couldn't prove himself without enough freedom to do so? If anything, he would have expected Saul to declare his grandson would just hang himself if he had enough rope. Perhaps that wasn't fair, but life wasn't fair.

Oddly, Paige Bannerman seemed to believe Saul had good intentions, but Jordan thought this was just his grandfather's way of getting a year of free labor. Even if Saul had to put the land in a trust, it was no skin off his nose since it wouldn't belong to his grandson until after he was gone.

Jordan debated whether to continue sorting the records, then decided other tasks were more demanding. He dressed and headed outside to check the horses.

Unlike some SEALs, he was an experienced helicopter pilot, but one thing he agreed with his grandfather about was using traditional ranching methods; the idea of herding cattle by copter or ATV didn't appeal in the least.

He turned the lights on over the paddock

and Tornado trotted up, snorting and pawing the ground. Jordan stroked his neck. Last night his grandfather had mentioned the stallion was six years old and that he'd acquired him as a yearling. It must have been difficult for Saul to be told to stop riding.

Tornado blinked and shoved his head into Jordan's chest, making him smile. He'd almost forgotten how much he loved horses.

The brief, wordless communication with Tornado helped focus Jordan and he set to work. Paige would arrive soon enough.

The sun was nudging the horizon by the time he finished scrubbing the horse's water tank free of algae. Even before it had been thoroughly rinsed and refilled, the small equine herd crowded forward, eager for a drink of clear, fresh fluid.

Jordan hosed a stream of water into the tank, gazing at the eastern horizon. Pink-and-orange light was broken by thin bands of silver-gray clouds and the dark sky above was a deep blue. Most of the stars had already winked out of sight and he wondered why anyone would miss a sight like this for an extra hour or two of sleep.

"Kind of takes your breath away, doesn't it?" asked a feminine voice.

He turned his head and stared at Paige, wondering how he'd missed her arrival. Even her high-end SUV engine made *some* noise. And her dog was energetically scampering around as well. "You're early."

She shrugged. In contrast to the previous day, she was wearing worn jeans and a heavy denim jacket. "How about going around the south end of the ranch today? Saul usually has me ride Dolley Madison. She's the black mare with the white blaze on her forehead."

"What about your daughter?"

"My mom watches her whenever needed."

So Paige had a prearranged babysitter. Jordan had hoped her parental responsibilities would keep her away from the Soaring Hawk more often than not, though he wasn't sure why it mattered. In the navy, someone had always been evaluating him. How fast he could run or climb. How well he could solve problems. Superior officers did it officially. But most importantly, the men under his command had watched him, deciding if he'd be someone they'd follow into hell, if necessary.

That sort of approval meant everything.

"Anyhow," Paige said, "I brought breakfast burritos for you and Saul."

Jordan shook his head as he turned off the water. "Thanks, but it isn't necessary for me."

Paige made an exasperated sound and extended her hands. In one there was a foil-wrapped object, and the other offered a large insulated cup. "Coffee and hot food, ready to go. Don't be a grouch and make me throw it away. Saul should be so lucky. He's under a doctor's orders to drink herbal tea."

"I'm not a grouch, but I didn't ask to be fed."

"That's fine, because *I'm* not the one feeding you. My mother made breakfast and brewed the coffee. She knew I was coming over here and cooked extra."

"I only drink coffee black, with no fancy flavors or anything."

"Hardly a surprise." Paige pushed the cup and foil-wrapped burrito into his hands. "We don't do flavored coffee at the Blue Banner—my father and brothers would revolt. And I assumed you were a no-milk-or-cream kind of guy. It fits that warrior image you've got going. I'll check on Saul while you eat."

"I don't have a warrior image. I'm just a former Navy SEAL."

"Really? Couldn't tell from your short haircut, rigid posture, iron jaw and square shoulders. Or maybe it was the steely gaze that was the real giveaway." She turned and headed for the house, her border collie following close behind.

He opened his mouth, then closed it. Apparently Paige said whatever she thought, without filtering it first, which was disconcerting. He'd learned as a kid to guard his tongue, and his years in naval special operations had simply reinforced the habit.

The less said, the less you had to regret saying.

The scents of bacon and coffee reached Jordan's nose and his stomach rumbled. He should eat one of the military MREs he'd left in the truck, but the temptation was too great. He unwrapped the enormous burrito stuffed with meat, egg, potatoes and melted cheese. It was just as tasty as he'd thought it would be, enlivened with jalapeño peppers, and the coffee was the sort of strong, plain black brew he favored.

He gulped his first bites before slowing to enjoy the food. Jordan had certain rules he followed, and appreciating a good meal was one of them, because you never knew when the next was coming. There had been numerous times on missions when he would have traded a week's pay for a hot breakfast and cup of coffee.

As for Paige riding with him today?

A muscle twitched in his jaw. He wanted to head over and take a look at the old Circle M Ranch, where he had been born. Saul didn't know that his grandsons now owned it. That they'd acquired the land when it was about to be auctioned for back taxes. They'd hired a property agent in Bozeman to keep an eye on the buildings and arrange for any maintenance, though they hadn't been back themselves to see if the agent was doing an adequate job.

The Circle M was smaller than their grandfather's property, but adding a third of the Soaring Hawk acreage would make it viable for more than one family. And his deal with Saul had also included being left a third of the Soaring Hawk's cattle. All of which had made accepting the challenge even more important, because while Jordan didn't plan to have a family himself, there was Wyatt and Dakota to consider.

Paige came out of the house as Jordan was finishing the last of his coffee. "To be honest, I'd rather go alone today," he told her.

She didn't look perturbed. "Okay."

Okay?

Then she wasn't going to argue that he might get lost or something equally improbable? From the corner of his eye, Jordan saw Saul hobble outside and sit on a chair. Though there was a blanket folded over the arm, he didn't put it over his legs. Jordan set his jaw. The morning air was chilly enough that Saul must need the warmth, but maybe he was too obstinate to use it if someone was around to see.

"And I've hired a housekeeper," Jordan said in a low tone. "The retired marine I told you about. Her name is Anna Beth Whitehall, but everyone calls her Sarge. She should be here by Monday or Tuesday. So you can stop worrying about Saul, he'll be fine."

"That soon? He didn't mention it."

"Sarge doesn't believe in wasting time. As for my grandfather, I'll tell him when she gets here."

"I see." Paige's face was alight with sheepish humor. "You're planning an ambush, which might be your best move. To be honest, I didn't tell him when I advertised for a housekeeper. It was when his hip started getting worse. I never needed to talk him into agreeing, because no one applied. Are you sure you were honest with your friend about what they're taking on? I'm fond of Saul, but I know he isn't the easiest person to get along with."

Jordan shrugged. "I explained Saul is a challenge, not that it would have mattered. Sarge is bored with retirement and eager to start on a new project."

Curiosity replaced the humor in Paige's eyes. "How did you become friends with her?"

"It just happened." He handed Paige the insulated cup. "Thanks for the food. I presume I'll see you in a few days."

"Or hours," she returned in a dry tone. "But come to the house for a minute. There's something I need both you and Saul to hear," she added.

Jordan saw Saul giving Paige a wary look as they approached the porch. She set the empty coffee cup on the railing and planted her hands on her hips.

"We need to get something straight," she said. "I am neither a spy nor a babysitter. Saul, I'll work with Jordan when possible, but I'm not going to report his activities to you." She turned to Jordan. "With one exception. The *only* time I might say something to your grandfather is if I think any of the animals are at a serious risk."

"I want you to speak up," he returned promptly. "I'd just ask that you tell me, too, so I can address the situation. The cattle and horses come first."

PAIGE NODDED.

While trying to sleep the night before, she'd decided it was important to clear the air. She shouldn't get involved in the relationship between Saul and his grandson, and certainly not as some kind of spy. She also didn't intend to be a go-between. If something needed to be said, they'd have to say it to each other. Still, learning that Jordan had eaten dinner with his grandfather the night before was promising. She'd brought extra food, hoping it would be shared.

"That's fine by me," Saul agreed. "But maybe you could help my grandson sort out the ranch accounts. I got 'em all snarled up."

"Sure. If that's what he wants," Paige added hastily, sensing instant tension in Jordan.

She didn't know all the details of their agreement; mostly she knew Saul had used the land as an incentive to get his grandson to come home, and that Liam Flannigan was the third party who would decide if the terms of the agreement had been met. Liam and his family were good friends with the Bannermans. She'd had playdates with his granddaughter as a kid, and now *their* children had playdates. There was an age disparity between them, but they usually got along well.

"We can talk about it later," Jordan said. She tried not to roll her eyes as he headed back toward the barn.

"I shouldn't have suggested that," Saul murmured. "Jordan will think I'm interfering."

Paige also wished he hadn't suggested it, mostly because she suspected Jordan would seriously tax her patience. "There are going to be some ups and downs."

"I suppose." He plucked at the blanket over the arm of the chair. "That herbal stuff tastes like stewed grass. I shouldn't have told you what the doc said about coffee."

"I'm glad you did. And maybe you'll get used to herbal tea. There are a gazillion different kinds. Adding mint might help, or getting one of the stronger flavors, with roasted dandelion root or chicory."

Saul made a face. He hadn't liked the coffee she'd originally bought for him, either, preferring the brand he had used forever. Change wasn't something he embraced. Personally, she thought the coffee he favored tasted as if it had been brewed with potting soil.

Paige sorted through the yard equipment in one of the sheds while she waited for Jordan to leave. She was just as happy not to be going with him. There were a few tasks around the buildings she'd been meaning to take care of since spring had arrived and was sure he would object to her doing anything. Stiff-necked pride was something he had in common with his grandfather.

A few minutes later Jordan rode out on Tornado. She told Finn to stay on the porch with Saul and set to work.

First, the ramrod's quarters.

Jordan had mentioned to Saul that there was a problem with the plumbing, but she soon discovered it was just a winterization issue. She turned on the water from where the pipe branched from the main, along with the hot-water heater, then opened the faucets until they ran clear. Years of grime coated everything, undefeated by the fresh reek of bleach. Her sense of hospitality made her want to start scrubbing, but that might be considered an invasion of privacy. Besides, she was a guest herself on the Soaring Hawk, so she wasn't sure how the whole hospitality thing applied.

Her relationship with Saul had gone from a weekly visit to being more active in his life. Now it was hard leaving him to fend for himself. That might be why she'd felt defensive about Jordan asking a marine to be his grandfather's housekeeper. Still, his choice could turn out to be for the best.

"You shouldn't be doing all that," Saul protested as she stepped onto the porch after whacking down the weeds and grass and raking them into piles. "You don't work for me."

It was an old complaint, which she always ignored. Sometimes the best way to handle him was to simply do what was needed without arguing the point. That was what Jordan had done by hiring a housekeeper without consulting Saul first.

"Are you hungry?" she asked.

"Not after the breakfast you brought. At my age I don't eat as much as I used to."

The eldest member of the Bannerman family said the same thing, more or less, though Nana Harriet never called herself "old."

Experienced was the term Harriet Bannerman preferred. She'd weathered an amazing amount in her life, including wars, cancer twice, the loss of her two eldest children and saying goodbye to her husband after fifty-seven years of marriage. But she didn't talk about her hard times—she just talked about her blessings.

Paige wanted to be that resilient, if only because she hoped to pass the trait along to her daughter.

She'd put the garden tools in the shed when she saw a figure in the distance. It was Jordan on his grandfather's horse. The feminine half of her mind admired the way he rode, at one with Tornado; the more sensible half tried to ignore the sight.

Jordan didn't come to the house. He stopped at the main barn and unsaddled the stallion without looking around. His movements were strong and fluid. *Assured.* Paige had the feeling that the world could turn topsy-turvy and he would land on his feet. It reminded her of when she was little and saw him on the school bus. He was different now, and yet the same.

"Don't ask," Saul muttered.

She tore her attention from the man and horse. "Ask what?"

"How I could have driven him away. Any of the boys."

"That isn't my business."

"I didn't deprive 'em, but I didn't love 'em, either." Saul looked unutterably sad. "Not in a way folks could see, especially them. Now I look back and think—" His voice broke for a moment and he set his mouth. "Now I think of all that I missed. I figured I had to be hard on them, so they'd turn out okay."

"From what I've heard, your grandsons are fine men."

"They're strong, but there's more to being a man than strength. And I didn't teach 'em any of that. I can only hope they learned it anyhow."

Paige sighed. She ached for Saul, and she ached for the three little boys who'd come to live with him so many years ago. Childhood scars often ran the deepest of all.

Could people ever make up for their mistakes, or was it best to hope for forgiveness and healing?

"I guess you'll just have to wait and see what happens," she said finally, watching Jordan again. He hadn't looked in their direction; whether it was deliberate or from lack of interest was hard to say. And now he'd gone into the barn with Tornado.

She shook her head.

There was no reason for him to be interested in her or Saul. He had made his position clear; he'd returned to Montana to show his grandfather he could be a rancher, which took precedence over everything else. Succeeding meant he would eventually own a third of the Soaring Hawk. That was a lot of acreage.

But did he just want an inheritance, or did he also love the land? The best ranchers loved the land. It wasn't just an investment or inheritance, it ran in their veins, along with a true concern for animals.

Sighing, she got up. "I'll tell Jordan that I've sorted the plumbing issues in his quarters. Then I'll head home. Do you need anything before I leave?"

"Nah, you've done too much already."

Paige walked over to the barn and found Jordan inside, grooming Tornado. The horse was in sheer bliss. He loved being groomed, all except for the hoof pick. Though he'd never lashed out at her, she had seen more than one ranch hand use strong language after one of Tornado's well-aimed kicks.

She held her breath as Jordan grabbed a pick. Should she warn him?

"Uh, there's something you should know about Tornado."

Jordan glanced at her. "I groomed all of the horses in the paddock last night. So if you're talking about his feet, I already found out about his little quirk."

"But if you run your hands—"

"Down from his withers," Jordan said, finishing for her, "on his forelegs and hind, then he'll be fine. I figured that out pretty quick."

Paige walked over and gave Tornado a rub on his nose; he leaned into the caress like a contented dog. "I think it reassures him that you aren't going to do anything unexpected."

"Any other gems of wisdom you'd care to pass on?" Jordan's tone was wry.

"Not wisdom, but I fixed the plumbing in the ramrod's quarters. Not that it needed fixing. The water had been turned off and the pipes drained. The hot-water heater is on now, too. I ran the faucets, but more is probably needed. No one has lived there in ages, though the cowhands used it when one of them had a cold or the flu."

"I WOULD HAVE checked the water supply myself when I had time," Jordan said. He didn't like being in anyone's debt. While he believed Paige didn't plan to spy on his progress, he thought it was best all-around to keep a distance. "There's also a mouse infestation."

Paige didn't seem perturbed. "So I noticed. There may be more in the bunkhouse and outbuildings, too. Saul doesn't care for felines, which is why he doesn't have any barn cats."

"I don't feel the same. I called and ordered a load of clean hay for the horses. It'll be delivered later today, but I can't store it in one of the barns until the infestation is under control. Do you know anybody with kittens?" he asked.

"Possibly, if they haven't already found a home. I'll check around. The town veterinarian sometimes has rescues, too." She brushed bits of grass from her jeans. "I'd better get going. I'll see you tomorrow afternoon, since we go to church on Sunday mornings. Oh, I didn't mention it before, but you'll have to advertise for ranch hands. You probably won't get anyone coming by, looking for a job."

"I already contacted the newspaper to run an ad. It'll come out in a couple of days in the weekly print edition, and they'll post it on the website this afternoon."

"That's good, though you might look for other ways to spread the word. Or even expand your search to communities outside the county," Paige suggested.

Interesting.

"Any special reason?" he asked.

A guarded look crossed her face. "The employee pool is smaller than usual right now with branding and haying operations coming up. Let's go, Finn," she said to the black-and-white dog who'd followed her from the house.

Jordan kept his hand on Tornado's halter, watching as they walked to the SUV. Paige was unquestionably nice to look at. The sun glinted on her long, shimmering brown hair, catching gold and red highlights. She moved with an unconscious grace, and thinking about her expressive eyes, cornflower-blue shot with amber, could keep a man awake at night.

After the silver SUV disappeared up the ranch road, he looked around and scowled, noticing that the grass around the house had been cut into the semblance of a lawn, and the weeds at the base of the barns and paddock fence posts had been trimmed and raked. Nothing could conceal the peeling paint and generally shabby condition, but it was a facelift of sorts. Instead of resembling a ghost ranch, the place now had a more lived-in look.

All were jobs he would have gotten to sooner or later, but managing the horses and cattle came first. He hadn't even made it to the Circle M on his ride because he'd found too many fences needing repair. Finally he had turned back, knowing there was other urgent work demanding attention.

He shouldn't mind that Paige had taken care of the yard—no doubt she'd helped Saul in any number of ways since she began visiting—but he would have preferred doing it himself. He'd been a Navy SEAL; he relished monumental tasks.

Jordan set his jaw and went back to work.

From now on he would make it clear to her that he was in charge and he would handle anything that needed doing.

CHAPTER THREE

WHEN SAUL GOT out of bed the next morning, his left hip gave him a sharp twinge, worse than usual.

He groaned.

Getting old was tough. Sometimes he even wondered if he was being punished for his sins. Heaven knew he deserved it, but knowing that didn't help him get through the day. Life had hardly seemed worth living before Paige began coming to the Soaring Hawk, and now he was worse off physically than when she'd first come to visit.

A smile creased Saul's mouth as he remembered her quiet, insistent way of just *being* there. He'd bark at her to leave and she'd simply sit on the porch step and gaze out at the land, saying how beautiful it was.

She was unique, knowing when to be silent and just listen to the wind blow across the prairie grasses and through the black cottonwood trees. Somehow she'd realized how weary he was of being alone.

A heavy sigh came from his chest.

So much wasted time, and he was still stubbing his foot on his pride. Jordan had stayed in the barns yesterday afternoon working, not coming to the ranch house at all, and the light had remained on in the ramrod's quarters until well after midnight. Then this morning, he'd ridden out before dawn. Saul had heard him leave.

At least he was here. For a year. Surely a man could find an opportunity to prove his better intentions over twelve months. Even one who was prideful and set in his ways.

Saul dressed and went downstairs to drink one of the protein drinks Paige insisted he keep stocked. They were handy when he didn't feel up to warming a frozen meal in the kitchen. He liked it best when she visited with Mishka, but she had work and other responsibilities. Sometimes he felt guilty Paige spent so much time at the Soaring Hawk, yet his heart lifted whenever he saw them.

He sighed again as he settled into his chair on the porch. He'd never thought he would be one of those old men, sitting and watching the world go by. A Hawkins was supposed to die in the saddle, because that's what cowboys did. Maybe so, but being a rancher wasn't easy on the body. While his hearing was still excellent, arthritis, along with assorted injuries, had caught up with him. Even after the air warmed up during the day, a blanket felt good on his aching legs.

Saul's eyelids drooped as the early morning hours passed. Paige would bring him food from the Sunday church potluck as always, but until then, he didn't have anything to keep him occupied.

Suddenly the crunch of wheels on the gravel road leading to the house made him stir and he looked up to see a bright yellow Jeep parking alongside the house.

"Who are you?" he demanded when the driver got out and pulled a travel bag from the back. It was a woman with short, black-and-gray hair and a no-nonsense expression that belied her choice of a yellow vehicle.

Yellow.

He scowled. Yellow was a foolish color for a Jeep.

The woman looked him up and down. "I'm Master Sergeant Anna Beth Whitehall," she said crisply. "Retired marine. But you can call me Sarge."

"I'm not calling you nothing until I know why you're here."

She shrugged. "I arrived a day early, so I suppose Jordan isn't around. I also take it he didn't explain I was coming."

"You're one of my grandson's friends?"

"And your new housekeeper. Watch your step, I run a tight ship."

"I'm not having any housekeeper," he yelled, thumping his cane on the porch floor for emphasis.

"Judging by that stick you're using, you don't have much choice. I'm here to do the job, and since Jordan hired me, he's the only one who can fire me. Now, where do I put my gear? Jordan told me there are plenty of extra rooms in the house."

"You can't just come in here and—"

"Did you, or did you not, give your grandson permission to run the ranch as he saw fit?" Anna Beth Whitehall demanded.

Saul drew himself up in his chair. This was something he had not anticipated. "I didn't say he could run *me*."

"Same difference, since I'm betting this ranch is all you've thought about for at least—" she stopped and gave him another long visual examination "—ninety years?"

His chin jutted out so fast he practically dislocated his jaw. "I happen to be seventy-five."

She gave him a skeptical look.

"Very well, eighty-one."

Anna—he refused to call her Sarge—chuckled and lifted her bag over her shoulder. "I'm seventy-three. The marines retired me eleven years ago. Can you imagine? I have valuable experience and more get-up-and-go than the kids they're enlisting, but they decided I was too old for them. *Mandatory retirement*." Her tone was filled with disgust.

It was an injustice that Saul sympathized with, enough that he didn't instantly order her away when she opened the front door.

"Uh, wait." He pushed his blanket away, got up with difficulty and followed her inside. "This is my house."

"Nobody is arguing that. It fits you. Old and tired, with deferred maintenance. But still solid and respectable."

Saul blinked and looked around. *Really* looked. There were no pictures on the walls and the furniture was sparse. When something had broken, he'd just moved it up to the attic. The flowery paper his wife had chosen for the foyer was shredded and peeling. The carpet was threadbare on the broad mahogany staircase and the paint, particularly in the corners, was darkened by the smoke from a hundred pots of burned food.

All right, he might have failed to keep the place in good shape, but the building was sound and the roof didn't leak.

Yet, he added mentally. He'd been meaning to have it inspected for the last few years since it was no longer an option to do it himself. By the time the thought had registered, Anna Beth Whitehall had disappeared. He found her investigating the kitchen.

"It's better in here," she said, sounding pleased. "I cook, too. None of those trendy dishes, just good, rib-sticking meals."

"Paige painted a couple of years ago," Saul admitted. "Uh, Paige is a neighbor. She wanted to do the rest of the house, but I wouldn't let her. She's got too much else to manage, working and raising a little girl by herself."

"She sounds real fine." Anna looked curiously pleased. "What would you like for lunch? Or are you still in need of breakfast?"

"I had a protein drink. And Paige brings me lunch on Sundays."

Anna rolled up her sleeves. "In that case,

I'll choose my bedroom and start cleaning." She held up her hand when he opened his mouth. "No need to apologize. I figured the house would be rough when Jordan called and said you needed a housekeeper. Now go away. I have things to do."

Disconcerted, Saul turned and limped back to the porch, barely feeling the discomfort in his hip. He sat down and tapped his fingers on the arm of the chair, unsure of what had hit him.

How did you fire somebody who wouldn't go?

"TAKE MORE OF the chicken," Susannah Flannigan urged Paige as she filled two divided containers with food from the potluck. Other Connections Project volunteers were doing the same thing. Shelton didn't have a program to bring meals to people who were homebound, so the Connections Project helped out in that regard. But of the seniors Paige visited, Saul Hawkins was the only one who had difficulty preparing his own meals. And that was a relatively recent development.

"Won't your family eat it?"

Susannah shrugged. She was a bright, energetic lady in her seventies who could pass for someone much younger. And, since she was married to the rancher chosen to evaluate Jordan's performance on the Soaring Hawk, she was well aware of the situation with Saul and his grandson.

"A few pieces more or less won't get us anywhere," she said. "My great-grandkids gobble it like popcorn and my grandson-in-law is the same."

Paige smiled at Susannah's fond tone and added several pieces of chicken to one of the containers. She also carried a bag with corn bread and biscuits. Saul didn't consider it a proper meal without having some type of bread on the plate.

"Saul loves your chicken." She snapped the lids on the containers. "By the way, several weeks ago Kelly mentioned that Kindred Ranch has a number of barn cats looking for a home."

"We do, along with a whole bunch of other people. It was a bumper year for kittens throughout the county. In our case, a female showed up late last autumn, just as winter was starting. Heaven knows where she'd been living before and she was already pregnant—gave birth to five healthy kittens in the middle of a snowstorm. My great-grandchildren have tried taming them, but they're still skittish, so none of them would be good for Mishka. Anyhow, we're hoping all six can stay together. They're quite bonded as a family."

Barn cats could be found on most Shelton ranches. Though often too independent to become house pets, and in many cases too wild, they filled a need and received a home in the bargain. The town vet didn't entirely approve, yet he recognized being sheltered on a ranch was better than life as a homeless feral.

"I'm not asking for Mishka. She already has two cats, along with a rabbit, a goat and a guinea pig," Paige explained. "Not to mention the orphan calves we're feeding. But the Soaring Hawk ramrod quarters and barns are infested with mice. A colony of cats would fit in nicely."

"Excellent. They've had their shots and all, so just give us a call. We can deliver, or you can come pick them up." Susannah's expression revealed the usual eagerness of a cat lover who may have found a home for an excess of felines.

"I'll let Jordan know. It's his decision."

Since Paige always dropped by the Soaring Hawk after the potluck, she didn't drive into town with the rest of the family. Outside at the SUV, she found her mother had already buckled Mishka into her child's seat.

"Thanks, Mom. We'll see you later."

"She's my angel. Why don't you ask Jordan and Mr. Hawkins to dinner? Today would be fine, or another time if it's better for them."

Paige winced. "That could be tricky. I suspect they need more time adjusting to each other before going to a joint social gathering. Holding off might be wisest."

"Whatever you think is best, though there's something to be said for being on neutral territory. The Soaring Hawk is far from neutral."

"Maybe."

Paige put the food in a box, which also held the extra pie her mother had made for Saul and his grandson. She got into the SUV and saw her daughter was falling asleep, eyelids drooping as her cheek rested against the thick padded side of the protective seat. Paige would have asked her parents to take her instead, but they were already driving away. Well, if she kept the visit with Saul brief, Mishka might not wake up before they got home.

At the Soaring Hawk, Paige was surprised to see an unfamiliar vehicle by the side of the house. She waved at Saul and got out with the box of food.

"Where's Mishka?" he asked.

"Asleep in the car. She gets tired running around with the other children. It takes more effort with the leg brace, though I don't deny she has *ringleader* written all over her. Even the older kids do whatever she wants. They fall over themselves to do her bidding."

Saul grinned. "She's something. You watch, someday she'll be governor of Montana. And that'll just be the beginning."

"Of course, you're completely unbiased as her honorary grandpa."

"As if you don't think the same."

Paige chuckled. From the first moment she'd held her daughter at the orphanage in India, she'd been convinced Mishka was destined to do great things. Maybe all parents felt that way, but it had also become Saul's belief.

She held up the box. "Susannah Flannigan sent extra chicken and there's Sally Newsom's deluxe potato salad, Marge Benham's brown-sugar ham and several other dishes. Also corn bread and biscuits, and Mom made you one of her apple-crumb pies. It looks like you have company, but I brought plenty in case Jordan would be eating."

Saul's expression turned grim. "A woman arrived earlier and won't leave. Claims to be my new housekeeper."

Uh-oh.

"In that case, I'll introduce myself and serve you a plate."

He didn't object and Paige went into the house with the food. "Hello?" she called.

"Back here."

Paige followed the voice and found a surprisingly diminutive woman scrubbing the worn linoleum in a rear bathroom. Short, graying black hair framed a pleasantly determined face. She definitely didn't resemble the tall, tough warrior type Paige had envisioned from Jordan's brief description.

The woman gave her a cordial nod. "Hello, I'm Marine Master Sergeant Anna Beth Whitehall, retired."

"Paige Bannerman. It's nice to meet you. I didn't think you were expected for another day or two."

"I'm always impatient to start a new project and I figure Saul Hawkins will be a tough one. No offense intended. I understand he's your friend."

"No offense taken. Saul has been cultivating his reputation as a curmudgeon for a very long time. Besides, I may say something about Jordan that you don't like."

"I see him for what he is," Sarge said wryly. "The most common complaint is that he's tight-lipped and aloof, along with having the personality of an army mule. It's from all those years in Special Forces. Sometimes I want to give him a kick in the pants, except it wouldn't do any good and I'd just stub my toe."

Paige laughed and held up the box of food. "I have a meal from a church event. There's plenty for everyone. Is he around?"

"I haven't seen him. The chow sounds great. I'd offer you a cup of coffee, but I didn't find any beans or grounds in the kitchen. Not even instant."

Paige wrinkled her nose. "I got rid of it all when the doctor told Saul to stop drinking coffee. I understand Jordan calls you Sarge. Is that what you prefer, or would you rather be called Anna?"

Sarge cocked her head, looking thoughtful. "My dad called me Anna Beth. I've mostly associated with other marines and sailors and their families since I enlisted, but maybe it's time to be Anna Beth again."

"Then Anna Beth it is."

ANNA BETH NODDED her approval at Paige. She was a lovely young woman who seemed kind, concerned and definitely idealistic, just the way Jordan had described. And she'd obviously managed to get through to that old goat on the porch, which spoke well of her. She appeared to genuinely care about him, too.

Saul Hawkins reminded Anna Beth of a few commanding officers she'd served under. She learned to be tough from them and could handle a bad-tempered rancher now. Her primary concern was Jordan. Was returning to the scene of his childhood the best idea? People were the product of their past, for good or bad, but that didn't mean it was healthy to go back. The little she'd seen of Saul Hawkins explained a whole bunch about Jordan.

She pushed aside her musings and focused on Paige. "Let's go to the kitchen."

While Anna Beth washed her hands, Paige poured a glass of milk and took plates from the cupboard. "I'm sorry about the coffee," she said. "I've been bringing various herbal teas, hoping to find one that Saul likes.

Maybe the new ones I've ordered will suit him better. They're supposed to have a stronger flavor."

"No worries. I can set up a pot in my quarters." After investigating the house, Anna Beth had chosen to use a room and bath on the first floor, located directly beneath Saul Hawkins's bedroom. She was a light sleeper and if he needed her, he could rap his cane on the floor. "Can you tell me why he's still sleeping upstairs when he has trouble getting around?"

Paige began serving food onto a plate. "I've tried getting him to move to the ground level, but that's the room he shared with his wife. You wouldn't know it just talking to him, but he's very sentimental and doesn't embrace change well."

Anna Beth understood. She had a hidden core of sentimentality herself, though an armored tank couldn't drag the truth from her. When she'd enlisted as a young woman, she'd decided it would be best not to reveal her softer nature to her fellow marines. It was a hard habit to break.

She pointed to the pale yellow walls of the kitchen. "If he dislikes change so much, why did he let you paint? I couldn't help noticing the difference between this and the rest of the house."

"I told him it should look the way it did when his wife was cooking in here. That appealed to him. Here in Shelton County, a rancher's home life revolves around the kitchen, so this felt like the most important place to start doing anything." Paige seemed to be debating something to say, then looked Anna Beth square in the eye. "As Jordan's friend, you must have heard less-than-positive stories about Saul, but please give him a chance. He has a good heart beneath that crusty surface."

"Don't worry, I make up my own mind about folks."

"I'm glad to hear it." The younger woman put a biscuit and a corn muffin next to a slice of ham and picked up the plate she'd filled, along with a fork, a knife and the glass of milk. "I'll take his lunch to him. He prefers eating on the porch when the weather isn't too bad. I also need to check on my daughter. She's asleep in the car. Or was. Mishka is at the age when she takes short naps."

"Mishka? What a lovely name."

"It's her birth name. I wanted to honor her

heritage, so I kept the name when I adopted her."

Anna Beth followed Paige outside. The fact that Jordan had mentioned both Paige and her daughter was interesting. Equally interesting, she was a single mother who'd charmed his grandfather. She hadn't been exaggerating when saying that Jordan kept things pretty close to the chest. Over the years Anna Beth had gotten a fair picture of his grandfather and childhood in Shelton, but it was more from what he *hadn't* said, than from what he had.

So having Jordan volunteer information about Paige was decidedly unusual.

"THAT TOOK A WHILE," Saul grumbled when Paige put his plate and glass of milk on the small table next to his chair.

"I was introducing myself to Anna Beth."

"She isn't staying. You can tell her that for me."

"I'm standing right here," Anna Beth said in a dry tone from the door.

Paige let out a careful breath. "This is between you, Anna Beth and Jordan." She emphasized his grandson's name, hoping he'd be reminded of his primary goal. Besides,

Saul needed a housekeeper. She had only so many hours available and he'd already roped her into spending time with his grandson.

Her stomach did a strange loop at the thought of the hours ahead in Jordan Maxwell's company.

Romance wasn't an issue.

After two unhappy relationships in college, she wasn't looking. Men outnumbered women in Shelton, so if she wanted to get married, it wouldn't be too hard. Finding the *right* someone was a different matter. One of her brothers had gotten married soon after high-school graduation, but it had only lasted a few months. And her sister's marriage probably wasn't going to survive since Noelle's husband wanted her to give up the international relief work she loved.

The men Paige knew weren't mysteries, but Jordan was a complete unknown. That must be why the idea of dealing with him was so unsettling.

When she opened the SUV door she found Mishka yawning and sitting up in the car seat. "Hey, sweetie. Have a good nap?"

"Uh-huh. Can I see Mr. Saul now?"

"Sure."

Paige unbuckled the restraints and helped

her daughter to the ground. Mishka ran toward the house, only to freeze when she noticed Anna Beth in the doorway.

"*Mama*." She rushed back to hide behind her mother.

"I know, there's someone new. Her name is Anna Beth and she's going to help Mr. Saul take care of his house."

Mishka looked around cautiously. Her uncertainty with strangers was improving. The repeated trips to the children's hospital in Seattle were the biggest problem. There she was bombarded by encounters, usually associated with poking and prodding and uncomfortable medical treatments and tests. She maintained her composure, but at home she felt freer to express her discomfort with new people.

Saul beckoned to Mishka.

"Do you want to get back in the car?" Paige asked gently. "I'm sure Mr. Saul would understand."

All at once her daughter stuck out her chin and marched to the porch, resolve in every footstep. Paige didn't know if it was good or bad when the clopping of hooves sounded in the distance and she saw Jordan, riding in from the south.

She would hope for the best. Mishka had responded well to him at their first meeting.

By the time Jordan had dismounted and unsaddled Tornado, Mishka was sitting on Anna Beth's lap, chattering away as Saul ate his lunch. Jordan let the horse into the paddock and met Paige halfway across the yard.

He waved at Anna Beth, who waved back. "I see Sarge is here."

"Yes, and obviously she shares your preference for brightly colored vehicles. Bright yellow and intense red. Or did you pick a red truck, simply because you knew it would annoy your grandfather? It looks new."

"What? Oh." Jordan made a dismissive gesture. "I bought it from a friend before I heard from Saul about coming back to the Soaring Hawk. Braylon's wife had filed for a divorce and he couldn't afford the monthly payments. I don't know why he thought getting married would work out. Most Navy SEALs I've known are divorced."

Paige cocked her head. "You make marital disharmony sound inevitable for a SEAL."

"Maybe it is. My friends haven't managed, even after being discharged. The things we see change us."

The things we see change us.

His comment sounded like a warning, which was amusing since they barely knew each other. But maybe he'd gotten into the habit of being up front about his view of marriage and relationships to head off any misunderstandings. She'd just been thinking about the subject herself.

"That's too bad," she said. "I wanted to tell you that I spoke with Susannah Flannigan about a cat family they have, looking for a home—a mother cat and five kittens born late last fall. You can go get them, or they'll bring them over."

What appeared to be suspicion darkened Jordan's eyes. "I'd prefer going for them."

"I'm sure it's fine, either way. Just let Susannah know."

JORDAN DIDN'T KNOW what to think except it was interesting that Liam Flannigan's Kindred Ranch was where Paige had found extra kittens.

He didn't believe in coincidences.

Was this a subtle way for Liam Flannigan to check up on him? During their telephone discussions, Liam had adamantly declared he would only come over once every two or three weeks to take a look around. He might make suggestions and was available for questions, but that would be the extent of his involvement.

"Are you particularly acquainted with the Flannigans?" Jordan asked.

"This is Shelton, we know practically everyone. But Mishka also has playdates with Susannah's great-grandchildren, and their mother, Kelly McKeon, is a good friend. So I could pick up the cats for you the next time I'm over there."

Jordan tried to summon a memory of the extended Flannigan family, but drew a blank. Not surprising, considering he'd spent the past twenty-one years trying to think as little about his childhood as possible.

"I didn't know Liam had great-grandchildren."

Paige gave him a lopsided grin. "Why would you? They were born after you enlisted. Kelly is close to my age and has two sets of twins. Mishka is in the middle between them, age-wise. By the way, I brought food from a potluck. There should be enough for both you and Anna Beth. I've already given Saul a plate."

"Anna Beth?" Jordan shook his head. "She goes by Sarge."

"What *you* call her is between the two of you. She told me to use Anna Beth."

For some reason, it felt as if the ground had shifted beneath Jordan's feet.

Just enough to catch his attention.

He regarded Paige with a hint of wonder and wariness. A week ago he would have claimed that he was accustomed to adapting to new circumstances. Yet in a brief time, she had altered something he'd thought was immutable. Sarge was a tough, no-nonsense marine who'd refused to retire until she didn't have any choice. In all the time he'd known her, no one would have dared call her Anna Beth.

Maybe it was Paige's innocent idealism that cut through everything else. Idealism could be dangerous…and compelling. She was young and fresh and untouched by the horrors he'd seen around the world. But that was the biggest reason he should have little to do with her.

People like him weren't good for someone like Paige.

He was too cynical, too aware of the darkness that existed, and he knew his hard edges would just damage the idealism he found so intriguing.

CHAPTER FOUR

"I'VE BEEN THINKING about the ranch hands you need," Paige said. "I could talk to my father and see if he knows anyone looking for a position."

She wanted to help Jordan hire employees, if only because it meant things would be better for Saul. Shelton didn't have the same labor shortages often found in other parts of Montana, but there weren't many cowhands who would be willing to work for the Soaring Hawk, male or female.

"That's all right, I'll manage. Saul must have told you I'm supposed to do this myself. That's the agreement."

"I don't know much about your arrangement. What I do know is that no one can run this ranch alone. It's too big, no matter how hard or long you work. We help each other in Shelton. The Soaring Hawk is in poor shape, partly because Saul has pushed everyone away. Are you saying he thinks you should restore the ranch entirely by yourself? That can't be, because he tried to volunteer me to assist with the accounts and my father and brothers have come over from time to time when something urgent needed doing. Good commanders have to delegate, don't they?"

"Saul wants me to prove myself and I have every intention of doing so."

Paige didn't know what to say. She loved Saul, but she wasn't convinced this was the best way to mend fences with his grandson. On the other hand, Jordan was a former SEAL, so he was probably just as hardheaded as his grandfather. Who knew how much time it would take to demolish the barriers between them?

As for proving himself?

She thought a man who'd managed to get through SEAL training and spend all those years surviving such a dangerous occupation had already proven anything he needed to.

Maybe she should tell them both how she felt, she mused, but then decided it was best to keep quiet. Ranchers were a group of people unlike any other. Saul had taken care of the Soaring Hawk his entire adult life and felt a responsibility to it. So even if his true goal was reconciling with his grandson, he might also want to be certain that Jordan had the soul of a rancher before handing over a share of the property.

"Okay," she said finally. "Just don't forget I offered."

"Fair enough. I see Sarge and your daughter are getting along well. What's the story with the brace on Mishka's leg? Will it be permanent?" The blunt question seemed typical of Jordan.

"Mishka has had several surgeries and procedures, but her medical team thinks the most recent will be the last."

"Medical team? That sounds ominous."

Paige lifted her shoulders, then dropped them. "She was born with an issue and there were injuries soon after, during a flood. Even before the adoption went through, I contacted the children's hospital in Seattle because I wanted a place where they had all the specialists she would need. But Mishka is done with most of it. And once her leg is stronger, she shouldn't require the brace."

"Except you're still concerned."

There was a time when Paige would have said she wasn't a worrier, but that was before she'd become a parent. "Of course, I'm concerned—she's my daughter. Her biological parents are dead and her uncle had to leave her at an orphanage in Uttar Pradesh because he couldn't afford the medical care she needed. She's gone through enough."

"Mishka seems happy and well-adjusted. Isn't that the most important part?"

Paige blinked a tear away, wishing she didn't get so emotional when she thought about what might have happened to Mishka. "Thank you. She *is* happy. My dad calls her his ray of sunshine and she's been that way since the beginning. Even with her physical challenges, she was a bright, sweet baby."

Jordan hesitated, which didn't seem characteristic of him. "You, uh, seem young to have adopted a child."

"I had all the paperwork ready to go the day I turned twenty-five, which is the youngest someone can be when adopting a child from India. Noelle, my sister, had told me about the orphanages there, so I knew it was what I wanted to do. And, no, I don't expect to get married and have a baby of my own," she said, deciding to be blunt in return and answer the question people often asked, or hinted at asking.

The shift in his expression—a slight widening of the eyes—was barely perceptible, but she already knew she'd have to watch carefully to get any idea of his inner thoughts. If all Navy SEALs were like that, it wasn't any wonder so many of their marriages broke up. Communication was important.

"Are you coming to the house to eat?" she asked. "As I told you, I brought food from a potluck in town. Ham. Fried chicken. All sorts of goodies. My mom also sent a pie."

JORDAN HAD ALREADY taken one meal from Paige and eaten another she'd brought, and he didn't want to get into the habit. "Thanks, but I'll grab something in my quarters. I've got a busy afternoon ahead."

Amusement, rather than irritation, brightened her blue eyes. It seemed ridiculous to head for the ramrod's quarters when a meal was waiting at the main house, but he went, regardless.

Inside his quarters, he heard rustling and a low patter, as if dozens of tiny feet were scurrying away.

He stared at the kitchenette.

His boxes of MREs on the counter had been discovered and an army of mice must have thrown a rave in the hours since he'd left that morning. Bits of plastic and foil were scattered everywhere, along with crumbs of food. It was a mess. And entirely his own fault since he knew the lightweight packaging on MREs wasn't designed to repel rodents. He just hadn't thought the meals were this vulnerable, especially over such a short period.

His stomach rumbled, already dissatisfied after Paige had mentioned fried chicken and ham. He also hadn't confirmed a time to fetch the cat family from Kindred Ranch. Paige had offered to get them the next time Mishka had a playdate with Liam's great-grandchildren, but he hadn't agreed or disagreed to the proposal. Plainly, he needed those cats *now*.

Jordan turned on his heel and stomped up to the main ranch house. He nodded at his grandfather and Sarge. "Hey, Sarge. You arrived early."

She winked. "You know me, I don't dawdle around. Only stopped long enough for a little shut-eye. Are you going to eat with us, after all? Paige is inside, getting me some chow and Saul a piece of pie."

"I suppose." His pride wouldn't admit to what the mice had done to his MREs, even to Sarge. He walked back to the kitchen and found Paige heating something in the microwave. "I decided it's foolish to turn down good food," he explained.

"That's great. Do you prefer your chicken hot or cold?"

"I take my chicken any way I can get it."

The mix of scents from the food container brought back distant memories of Shelton Ranching Association potlucks from when Jordan's mother was still alive and healthy. They'd faithfully gone to all of the social gatherings with the association. He'd relished putting certain foods next to each other on the large paper plate so the flavors would merge at the edges, particularly sweet baked beans, ham and potato salad—staple dishes at the various gatherings.

Jordan hadn't thought about those potlucks in over twenty years, yet now his heart turned over in a way he'd no longer thought possible. His mother was gone. No one knew where his father might be, or even if he was still alive. His brothers were far away, living their lives, and he'd landed back on a dilapidated ranch in need of a miracle.

And just seeing Saul each day was testing his long-held resolve to leave the past in the past.

Paige took a glass bowl from the microwave. Baked beans bubbled in it and a tangy scent rose, a blend of molasses, hot mustard and bacon. The tightness in his throat and chest grew so intense that he clenched his teeth.

"You have the oddest expression," Paige murmured as she fetched another plate from the cupboard.

"Nothing odd about it. I was just reminded of the Shelton Ranching Association potlucks. The smell from the baked beans brought everything back."

"I'm not surprised. Scent is a powerful memory trigger. Mrs. Lansing has been taking her beans to every potluck for forty years, and also to families when there's an illness or death. They're the old-fashioned kind, slow-baked over a long period with farm-cured bacon. She keeps a freezer full to be ready at a moment's notice."

Jordan suddenly understood his reaction to the dish. As his mother's health deteriorated, folks had brought food to the Circle M. The offerings had included great quantities of those sweet, delicious beans.

"None for me," he said as Paige began spooning them out.

He kept his face neutral as she gave him a searching glance.

"Too bad, they're better than ever. Mrs. Lansing is a wonderful cook. She's never given out the recipe, but I think her secret ingredient is adding real maple syrup along with the molasses."

Jordan shrugged. "I just prefer something else. There's more than enough food. How many people did you expect to feed?"

"I didn't know how hungry you'd be. Why don't you choose whatever appeals?" Paige suggested, picking up the plate she'd filled, along with a dessert plate holding a slice of pie.

Left alone in the kitchen, Jordan swiped his finger over a drip from the beans and tasted it. The flavor was the same as he remembered and in an instant he was transported back to his parents' bedroom. His mother had become too weak to sit at the dinner table, so they'd eaten in there with her. She'd kept their spirits up, been cheerful even when she could barely lift her head, and had talked about the future as if they were all going to share it together.

But she must have known that future wasn't going to happen.

She couldn't survive without a heart transplant, and her rare blood type had made one improbable. In the end, she'd chosen to spend her last days with the family, rather than lie in a distant hospital, waiting for a donor heart that most likely wouldn't come.

Jordan shook his head to clear the thought. Refusing the beans had been a cowardly thing to do, so he filled his plate with a sampling of everything Paige had brought and put the remaining food in the refrigerator.

Outside, he sat on the porch step next to her. "I'll call Liam and let him know I'll come over tonight to collect the cat family," he said. "There's no need for you to do anything."

Saul harrumphed and sat forward. "I don't allow cats on the property. They're nothing but confounded little flea traps."

"I'm getting them, whether you like it or not," Jordan returned, fixing his grandfather with an unyielding gaze. "Rodents can't be allowed in the barns. The herds have grass to eat now, but at some point we'll need protein cake for winter, which the mice will invade. Contaminated feed is bad for the horses and the cattle probably won't even eat it."

"How would you know that?"

"Because I have two college degrees, one

in ranch management, and the other in animal sciences."

Saul thrust his chin out. "I see. Then you already figured on inheriting the Soaring Hawk when I was gone."

"*Saul*," Paige said sharply.

Jordan was rarely shocked, but he was startled by the embarrassed flush in his grandfather's cheeks.

"I apologize," Saul mumbled. "I didn't mean it like that. You were smart, studying those things. But we don't need cats. We can put down poison and traps."

"*No*," Paige and Sarge yelped, practically in unison.

Paige leaned toward him. "We've talked about this, Saul. Poison affects the wild food chain, not just mice and rats. I'd happily relocate the mice to another home using live traps, but that isn't possible, either. And snap traps alone would take a long time to get the infestation under control. Just the scent of a predator can discourage mice and rats. Cats are the best defense."

"I don't like 'em."

Mishka plopped onto her mother's lap and stuck out her bottom lip. "I love my kitties, Mr. Saul."

It was interesting to watch the emotions struggling for supremacy in Saul's eyes. His dislike for felines dated to before Jordan could remember—probably because his grandfather couldn't order a cat around. Yet there was no question he adored Mishka and hated to disappoint her.

"Uh, well, I suppose they have a place," Saul muttered. "I just don't want 'em in the house."

The four-year-old smiled happily. "Goody. 'Dopt lots of kitties, Mr. Jordan. You won't be sad with kitties."

Jordan suspected he might need an army of felines to get the rodent population under control. But he'd start with the ones from Kindred Ranch and go from there. Paige was right that the mere presence and scent of a predator could help drive his unwelcome visitors away. Fortunately grain for the horses was already stored in tight metal containers, which the mice couldn't get to.

"Shall I give Kindred Ranch a call?" Paige asked. She was either doing an excellent job of keeping a straight face, or didn't recognize the power struggle going on.

"Sure."

She took out her cell phone and dialed. "Hi,

Kelly, it's Paige," she said after a moment. "I talked to Susannah at the potluck today...yes, about the cats. Jordan wants to give the family a home and will pick them up tonight, if that's convenient." There was a long silence, with Paige nodding her head as if the person on the other end of the conversation could see her. "Okay, I understand. Is an hour and a half long enough?" Another pause. "Great, I'll let him know."

She disconnected and looked at Jordan.

"They'll round the family up and put them in carriers. Problem is, earlier is better than later, because Kelly's father-in-law is driving down from Canada for a visit. Mr. McKeon should arrive around 6:00 p.m. But not to worry, I'll fetch the cats for you and return the carriers at the kids' next playdate."

Jordan swallowed his bite of potato salad, thinking about the tasks he'd planned for the afternoon. It wouldn't make a huge difference if he was delayed a few hours. There was always too much to do on a ranch, no matter how many hands were on the payroll. Besides, nobody respected a ramrod who didn't work just as hard as everyone else; he wouldn't respect himself, either.

"Thanks, but I'll take care of it when I'm

finished eating," he said. "I haven't had a chance to see Liam yet, so this will take care of two tasks at once."

"You and Paige could go together," Saul suggested.

"Right," Sarge agreed. "Paige, if you're okay with it, I'd love to watch Mishka. Tell her I'm reliable, Jordan," she ordered.

"Er, very reliable," Jordan said, dismayed by the turn of events. "Sarge worked at various base day-care centers after she retired, including the one that took care of the commander's kids, so she's got all sorts of clearances. The captain wouldn't let anyone near his children without checking them out from top to bottom."

"Let me stay, Mama," Mishka pleaded. "Ple-e-eze? I'll be real good for Mr. Saul and Anna Beth."

"Don't you want to see your friends?"

"Nuh-uh." She swung her head in a definitive *no*. "Marc was a stinker at church."

"Why is that?" Paige asked.

"He says he's gonna marry me when I grow up. But I'm practically growed up now—Mr. Jordan said so. 'Sides, I'm gonna marry Casey. I told Marc and he got mad, then Casey said he was being a jughead." She frowned. "What's a jughead, Mama?"

"Uh, well, it isn't a nice thing to call people."

Mishka nodded like a wise little owl. "That's what his mama told him."

Paige looked torn about what else to say and Jordan had a similar response for different reasons. The expedient thing would be to accept her original offer to drive over to Kindred Ranch for him. On top of that, while Saul still didn't look happy about having felines on the property, there was a sly gleam in his eyes. Maybe by maneuvering the two them together, he still felt he had a measure of control over the situation.

Jordan put his fork down. "Don't worry about going with me, Paige. I'm sure you have other things to do."

"That's okay, I'm happy to lend a hand. We should take my SUV. Riding inside will be easier on the cats than being carried in the cargo area of your pickup."

She hadn't voiced it as a question and it seemed churlish to refuse, so he nodded and finished eating, mystified at how he'd ended up on his grandfather's porch in a convivial picnic gathering.

His plans for the day had been very simple: continue surveying the condition of the herds in the morning, along with repairing fences. Make plans for a belated move to summer grazing. Then come back and begin servicing the aging haying equipment and tractors, housed in a large barn on the perimeter of the main ranch area. If they were in as bad shape as the rest of the ranch, haying was going to be difficult. At this late date he wouldn't be able to rent equipment, and the possibility of purchasing some in time was slim.

Jordan wondered if he'd be forced to use the horse-drawn cutters and rakes his grandfather had kept for "just in case." They were museum pieces by now, though small ranches might still use similar equipment. The old-fashioned way would be a long, slow process.

The Soaring Hawk didn't have as many cattle as in earlier years so the herds needed to be rebuilt, but there were more than enough to cause a winter feeding issue. A ranch unable to cut enough hay could go bankrupt buying hay from someone else. Luckily his newspaper advertisement saying he was hiring cowhands would be published tomorrow, though it was worrisome that the online advertisement hadn't resulted in any inquiries.

Lost in thought, he was barely aware of Paige lifting Mishka off her lap, then getting up to take his empty plate. A couple of minutes later she returned with pie for both him and Sarge.

"Oh. Thanks."

The gesture was revealing. Paige's family was prosperous, but she didn't seem to have any pretensions. A few people might feel that since Sarge had been hired as a housekeeper, they didn't need to show her common courtesies. Sarge's appreciative smile suggested she was thinking the same thing.

Jordan dug in to the juicy dessert. The flavors of caramel, cinnamon and pecans perfectly complemented the tender apples.

"This is delicious," Sarge said. "Are you a baker, Paige?"

"I do a fair amount of baking, but caramel-apple pie is my mother's specialty. She's won several prizes at the annual Shelton Christmas Dessert Bake-Off."

"What about the county fair? No contests then?"

"Instead of a county fair, we have Shelton Rodeo Daze. That'll be next month. There's a chili cook-off and all sorts of other events. The rodeo raises money for our first-responder service. Especially emergency medical flights, which is important since we aren't near a hospital."

"I've never seen a rodeo. Jordan, did you ever compete?" Sarge asked.

"Only before my mother died. Kid stuff."

Jordan shot a glance at his grandfather, who was moving the last crumbs of pie around his plate without eating them. Saul hadn't allowed his eldest grandson to compete once they came to live on the Soaring Hawk, but he'd loosened up after Jordan enlisted, letting Dakota and Wyatt get involved in both the Shelton Junior Rodeo and Shelton Youth Ranching Association. Dakota had done well competing. He'd said little about it, but Jordan had discovered two saddles won by his middle brother in the tack room.

"The rodeo is a big deal in the county," Paige explained. "Even more since a famous rodeo champion bought a ranch here and started training professional rodeo contestants. That's Josh McKeon. Jordan, just so you know, Josh is Liam and Susannah Flannigan's grandson-in-law," she added. "Kelly McKeon's husband."

Jordon nodded.

He was starting to match some of the

names, piecing together information from both his childhood and what he'd read over the years in the Shelton newspaper. They posted about community events online and he'd checked regularly. Josh McKeon's move to Shelton had been big news, but Jordan didn't recall anything about him marrying Liam's granddaughter. Not surprising, since he'd usually been looking for information about his father. The hard part about the search was knowing it would most likely be an obituary, if anything.

"We should head out," Jordan said, getting up to return his plate to the kitchen.

He didn't have time for social gatherings, and hoped the visit to Kindred Ranch wouldn't turn into another one. At any rate, with Mishka remaining at the Soaring Hawk under Sarge's watchful eye, the trip to fetch the cats should be faster. The little girl was sweet, but having a kid along always meant the visit or errand would take longer.

ONCE JORDAN AND Paige had left for Kindred Ranch, Saul sat tapping his fingers on the arm of his chair. The wood was rough, needing to be sanded and covered with a coat of paint, but he paid no attention.

Sarge, or Anna Beth, or whatever her name might be went back and forth, with Mishka tagging along at her heels. Firing the woman was a problem, over and above the question of cats coming to live at the Soaring Hawk.

What if he offered her a month's pay, or something of the sort?

Of course, she was right that he'd told his grandson he could run the ranch. And he'd stuck his foot in it by saying such a stupid thing to Jordan about expecting to inherit.

Embarrassment crawled through Saul a second time. He was a fool. How could he make any progress if he kept putting the boy's back up?

Now he would also have to allow cats on the ranch. There was something about the way felines looked at a person that bothered him—almost as if they could see things he'd rather not have known.

Saul liked cows and horses. Period. He was getting accustomed to Paige's border collie, though he'd never seen much use for a dog, either. She claimed Finn was an expert at working cows and most ranchers around Shelton had a whole pack of one breed or another. But his wife had been allergic to dogs so he would never have them on the place. Then after she died…he just couldn't do it.

So much had changed when his parents died and Celina got ill. With her gone, it felt as if all the light in his life had vanished. He'd tried to find it again through raising their daughter, but when she was eighteen, Victoria had run off and married the most wild and rebellious boy in the county. It was only now, with Paige and Mishka, that he'd begun to feel alive again.

Saul changed position in his chair and sighed.

What kind of man disowned his child for following her heart?

So he hadn't approved of Evan Maxwell. The kid had spent most of his time racing around the county in his truck instead of tending to business on the Circle M, playing practical jokes and never taking anything seriously. He hadn't been the sort of husband Saul had wanted for his daughter, but Victoria had married him anyhow.

Saul knew if he'd been honest with himself, he would have admitted that Evan settled down afterward. It was Victoria's death that made him start drinking…something Saul had also done for a time after losing his wife, though only late at night in his room.

But another regret he couldn't escape was knowing that life on the Circle M must have been hard. He could have helped. At the time, the Soaring Hawk was in great condition, one of the most successful ranches in the area. Maybe if he had done more, Victoria would be here today, along with her boys and husband. Instead, he'd taken his grandsons away from Evan Maxwell, and then held it against the eldest for looking like his father, assuming he'd take after him in other ways.

Saul cleared his throat, wishing he didn't get so emotional. He loved Jordan. And the boy had turned into a fine man, no thanks to his grandfather.

"Do you have a bee in your bonnet?"

He looked up. Anna Beth, the name Paige was using for her, was standing on the porch, a broom in one hand. At least she hadn't asked if he was "all right," as if his health might be failing in front of her eyes.

He was old, not at death's door.

"I'm fine. Tend to your own affairs and stay out of mine."

She chuckled. "I'm your housekeeper. Tending to your affairs *is* my business."

Saul glowered. "Where's Mishka?"

"Drawing a picture. She showed me where her mother keeps art supplies for her in the kitchen. I doubt I've ever met such a sweet child."

Well, Mishka was one thing they could agree upon.

"Got some old toys in the attic," he said. "From way back. Don't know why I didn't think of it before, but they could come down for her. There's a sturdy rocking horse made by my great-great granddad. Also a doll cradle and other bits."

"I'll check it out."

Saul watched as Anna Beth swept the porch. It was easy to envision her barking orders at a group of marines. He sighed; he still didn't want a housekeeper, but he would have to put up with her for the present. At least doing that might show Jordan that he wasn't totally unreasonable.

CHAPTER FIVE

"WHY ARE YOU going into town, instead of Kindred Ranch?" Jordan asked, frowning as Paige turned her SUV off the rural country road toward Shelton. He'd checked the location of Liam's spread on a map and knew they were now heading away from it.

"Because you'll need supplies and it's best to get them beforehand," she said. "The cats won't be happy in the carriers, so the less time they're forced to be in there, in a vehicle, the better. Anyway, Kelly thought they'd need an hour at least to catch them. The farm store is open on Sunday afternoons. You should be able to purchase everything you need."

He hadn't thought about cat food or other feline necessities, just the problem in the barns and his quarters, which reminded him of the need to get *human* chow. He'd brought enough MREs to last a couple of months, but while some of them were likely salvageable, he'd be wise to buy groceries sooner rather than later.

Jordan remembered the Shelton farm store as tired and shabby, with half-dead plants in the garden section and broken crates in the warehouse. Now the place was large, covering the better part of a block on the far edge of town. It wasn't in perfect condition, but everything was clean and the extensive garden area contained healthy-looking, freshly watered plants and trees.

"Hi, Paige," called an older man as they went into the store.

"Afternoon, Chet. This is Jordan Maxwell, Saul Hawkins's grandson. He's the new ramrod for the Soaring Hawk. Jordan, meet Chet Dixon, the owner of Shelton Feed and Seed Farm Store," she said. "You'll probably be doing a lot of business together. You might remember Chet. He used to teach shop class at the junior high school, so he would have been one of your teachers. He bought the business from Ollie Collier fifteen years ago and built it up."

Jordan flicked a look in her direction, wondering if she'd deliberately planned the stop so he'd meet one of the leading suppliers in the area.

And someone from the past.

But the last thing he wanted was to discuss ancient history *or* answer questions about the present.

"Um, we're here for cat food," Paige explained when Jordan didn't say anything. "Also cat litter, litter boxes, scoops for the boxes and flea-and-tick-control products. Jordan, you should also get animal crates for any trips to the vet. The cats will need annual vaccinations and other care if they get sick or injured."

He frowned. "Litter boxes? Surely they'll just use the great outdoors for their business."

"You need to keep the family inside for a while to adjust to their new home," she explained. "Otherwise they could run away, trying to get back to Kindred Ranch. And you'll want an option for them in bad weather."

"Oh."

It hadn't occurred to him to keep the felines contained for an adjustment period, but he'd never lived with cats. Wyatt and his wife had rescued a couple, though. They were sleek mini panthers with purrs that could raise the roof. Whenever he visited his brother and sister-in-law, the one called Salem came in at night and curled up at his feet, his purr vibrating louder than a white-noise machine. Wyatt had sometimes joked that Salem would sneak home with Jordan if given a choice.

Jordan made a mental note to text Wyatt later to ask how Amy was doing. The doctors had stabilized his sister-in-law's pregnancy, but her condition remained serious.

As the various supplies were collected on a flatbed shopping cart, Jordan spotted a selection of convenience foods in a refrigerated display case. He added sandwich makings to the order, but when he took out his wallet to pay the total, Chet waved his hand.

"Not to worry, I'll put everything on the Soaring Hawk account. There's no extra charge and you can settle up once a month."

"I'd prefer to pay for everything now." Jordan took the invoice and checked it over. The prices were reasonable enough, though he didn't know how animal supplies should be priced. Nonetheless, it appeared the store wasn't taking undue advantage, despite their relative monopoly in such a small community.

Paige looked upset for some reason, and even more when Jordan refused to let Chet or the teenager working at the store help load everything into her SUV.

She was silent as she drove toward Kindred Ranch, then sighed. "Why were you so stiff back there?"

"I don't know what you mean."

"I suppose you don't," Paige muttered. "That was a chance to impress Chet, along with his son. For your information, I wouldn't shop there if I had any concerns about their honesty, so there wasn't any need to pour over the invoice as if it was riddled with secret charges and errors. Are all SEALs that awkward and suspicious of people, or is it just you?"

The question took him aback. "Both leadership and teamwork are required from SEALs. But I wasn't awkward or suspicious with Mr. Dixon, I was simply being careful. Regardless, I didn't see any point to heading down memory lane, which is clearly what you had in mind when making introductions."

Paige slowed and made a left turn down the Kindred Ranch gravel road. "It's important to get to know people around here. I thought you might remember him."

"Well, I don't. I'd rather discuss what you told me about labor shortages. How about the hands who used to work for the Soaring

Hawk? If they were any good, maybe I could talk to them about coming back."

She made a face. "Most were ready for retirement and left when they qualified for Social Security benefits. They loved the work, but ranching can be a hard life when you're older and working such long hours. Especially when it isn't your own ranch and you're wearing out your body for a few hundred dollars a week."

Jordan thought there was more to the story, and also that Paige was too loyal to reveal what she knew.

The gravel road opened onto a tidy ranch, with a sprawling two-story house and several outlying ranch buildings. Paige parked near the house and two youngsters raced over as they got out. Quite obviously, they were identical twins.

"Where's Mishka?" one asked excitedly.

"Sorry, Marc, she didn't come this time."

"Are you Mr. Maxwell?" asked the second boy. It had to be Casey, the one who'd called his brother a jughead.

"Yup, Jordan Maxwell."

His dark eyes widened in admiration. "Gosh. Grandpa Liam says you're a Navy SEAL. That's like—"

"It's almost as awesome as our Dad being a rodeo champ," his brother interrupted excitedly. "I'm going to tell everyone you're here." He dashed away.

Casey let out an exaggerated sigh. "Sorry, Mr. Maxwell. Marc didn't mean to be rude."

"Don't worry about it," Jordan said, amused by the kid's effort to sound mature. "Call me Jordan. I'm guessing you're Casey. Mishka mentioned you both."

A goofy grin filled the boy's face, which also turned red. "Yeah, she's cool."

Just then Liam Flannigan arrived with Marc and several other people. He was a tall, vigorous man, despite his years. Other than his hair turning white, he'd changed very little since they'd last met. "Jordan, I'd know you anywhere. You look just like your father."

"So I've been told, but I don't think it endeared me to my grandfather." The admission startled Jordan. While he and his brothers had debated the possible reasons for Saul's special animosity toward him, he'd never told anyone else.

Liam frowned. "I'm going to be frank, I think Saul Hawkins is absurd, requiring you to spend a year on the ranch this way. He's also a hypocrite, considering how badly the

Soaring Hawk has deteriorated. Nonetheless, I'm here to help and offer advice, though from what you've told me about your college studies, you could teach me a thing or two."

"I doubt that, sir."

"Please, it's Liam. Now, let's get you acquainted with the family. I know you've already been introduced to my great-grandsons, more or less. Navy SEALs are rare around Shelton, so they're very excited to have met you." Liam ruffled Casey's hair.

Jordan restrained his frustration. With the exception of Josh McKeon and Liam's four great-grandchildren, who'd been born after he enlisted, he vaguely recalled the others. The Shelton Ranching Association had been the biggest social outlet for his mother and father, and Liam's family had also been active in the group. They seemed like nice people, but he didn't expect to spend time with them. Too much was riding on the next year to waste energy on potlucks and meetings.

"Liam, I promised Jordan this trip wouldn't take too long since he needs to get back to the Soaring Hawk," Paige said after a polite interval. "Were you able to catch the cats?"

"Sure. We'll go get them."

The six felines were loaded in three animal

crates and they weren't happy. They took one look at Jordan and hissed, correctly identifying him as the reason they'd lost their freedom.

Temporarily, he wanted to assure them.

"The two brown tigers are Gus and Bo," Casey explained. "Gus has the white feet. The ginger is called Marmalade, and the black-and-white tuxedos are Frances and Oreo. Oreo has more black on him. The—"

"The mama is Lady G," Marc said, breaking in. "She's the big, fluffy one who kinda looks Siamese, 'cept she has some stripes. Mom says Siamese cats are supersmart. Lady G is in this box."

Aware of Liam's watchful eye, Jordan dutifully peered into the animal crate Marc had pointed out. The larger cat inside spat and let out a series of hot-tempered yowls that had to be a not-too-polite commentary on his manners, parentage and general failure to properly appreciate her rights as a superior being.

Jordan wondered if he should cover Marc's ears. Translated, her tirade would probably be much more rude than being called a "jughead." Then her offspring started offering equally discontented complaints, seeming to have inherited her raucous voice.

"We'd better get them back to the Soaring Hawk," Paige said over the racket. "Jordan, do you want to drive while I sit in the back and try to calm them down?"

"You can get us there faster," he told her. "I think they're too angry to listen to a reasonable voice."

She laughed. "Probably."

Goodbyes took another few minutes, but they were finally driving away, ears ringing with feline complaints. Once they reached the smoother paved road, the cats settled a little, though grumbles still came from the rear of the SUV.

He looked back and saw Lady G glaring at him through the air slots of her carrier. As soon as she caught his gaze, she spat again. Jordan chuckled. She looked too fancy to be a barn cat, but she had the soul of a tiger. She'd give the resident rodents a run for their money.

At the Soaring Hawk they began unloading supplies. Paige suggested keeping the cat family in the tack room for a few days, but Jordan had a different idea.

"I'll put them in my quarters," he said. "There's more space than in the tack room and I can keep a better eye on how they're adjusting."

They'd also rid the place of mice in nothing flat.

"In the meantime, you'd better take Mishka home," he added. "Your family must be wondering what's keeping you."

Paige smiled faintly. "I called them earlier to explain, but I need to help Mom with dinner and have other things to do."

She seemed ready to leave, which pleased Jordan and gave him a kick in the gut at the same moment. He didn't want to understand why.

"Then I'll see you when I see you. With Sarge here, you won't need to bring food or check on my grandfather."

Paige lifted an eyebrow. "Saul is my friend. I don't *just* come to bring food to him. And I'm also supposed to be an observer on the ranch. Remember? I've got appointments with clients and have other visits to do tomorrow and the next day, but I'll be back on Wednesday. I'll bring Finn in case you want to work some of the cattle."

Jordan watched her walk toward the house, unhappy about his reaction to her. Feature for feature, Paige wasn't as beautiful as Liam

Flannigan's granddaughter, but she possessed something special. It bothered him because being attracted to any woman was highly inconvenient.

With a sigh he got the cat's litter boxes ready in his quarters and put out food and water, then brought in the carriers. He opened the mama cat's kennel door first. She stayed inside for an instant, then shot like a speeding bullet toward one corner of the room. When she turned around, a mouse hung limply in her mouth.

"You just did that to impress me, right?"

She walked over and deposited the mouse next to his shoe. Payment or retribution?

The adolescent kittens in the other two carriers had become silent. He opened each crate in turn and they stepped out, stretching luxuriously, noses high in the air, joining the sibling who'd ridden with their mother. Suddenly they dropped their bellies to the floor, bottoms wiggling with excitement. Apparently their new digs had turned into a very intriguing place.

If they were as avid as they seemed, the rodent population was going to move out, or be quickly dispatched. However unhappy the felines had been about their relocation, they seemed pleased now.

Jordan looked at the ancient refrigerator and realized he hadn't checked whether it was still working after all this time. He examined the cord for frays and didn't find any, so plugged it into the wall. The machine shuddered and started. Hoping for the best, he put the groceries he'd purchased inside, dealt with Lady G's "gift," and cleared the mess the mice had made of the MREs. Luckily they'd only chewed into the top layer; there would be enough to last until he had time to shop for groceries again or order more. He stowed the intact packages in the fridge and freezer since the mice probably could get into either.

Jordan looked down to see Lady G drop another mouse at his feet with a smug expression on her face.

The next couple of days were going to be interesting.

AFTER PAIGE TALKED with Saul for a few minutes, she went into the main house to find Mishka. There was a scent of lemon oil in the air and she could tell the mirror in the foyer had already been cleaned. It would be a relief to see the old place properly maintained.

She'd tried, but there was only so much she could accomplish since Saul mostly wanted her and Mishka's company.

"Hi, Paige," Sarge said, coming out of the front parlor. "We found toys and an old rocking horse up in the attic. Saul said she could play with it, but I've only let her ride when I'm next to her. Right now she's having fun with a set of ancient paper dolls. I'm amazed at how careful she is with them."

"You should see her when she picks up baby chicks and rabbits. No one could be gentler. Thanks for being cautious about the rocking horse. Mishka is learning to ride real horses, but she isn't there yet, much to her displeasure."

"She seems young for riding lessons."

Paige grinned. "Not in Montana. I was riding solo a year younger than my daughter is now. But with her leg and other issues, I've dragged my feet."

"I don't blame you. Saul mentioned you'd be out working with Jordan part of the time. Will you let me take care of Mishka when you go? I can help with any exercises needed to strengthen her leg and I've already cleaned the sunroom to use as a play area. Come and see."

Off the parlor was a spacious room with wide windows facing three directions. Paige knew that Saul's wife had spent long hours here during her illness, looking out at the trees and rolling hills.

Mishka was playing with the paper dolls in front of a south-facing window, so engrossed she hadn't noticed her mother's arrival. A variety of other toys and books were scattered around—also antiques, by the look of them.

Paige had often wished she could explore Saul's attic. She'd heard it was jammed with furniture and trunks and every imaginable bit of trash and treasure, going back to when the Hawkinses had first settled in the Shelton area. Not that this was the original house, which was a hundred yards or so to the west. The current house had been built in the 1920s and was an interesting blend of multiple architectural styles.

Her family home was different. The Bannermans, already an experienced cattle-raising family from North Dakota, had bought the ranch in 1953 and renamed it the Blue Banner. Her great-grandparents had remodeled and added on, along with subsequent generations. Very little of the original structure remained, so there weren't any corners filled with forgotten family treasures.

Nana Harriet had saved a few sentimental items for her children and grandchildren, but now she lived in a retirement complex in town and kept things simple. She celebrated her memories with electronic picture frames in every room, displaying a constantly changing array of family photos and places she'd visited. It was Paige's parents who had accumulated little mementoes, such as their children's art projects and christening clothes.

"It's generous of you to offer to babysit, but you'll have your hands full with Saul," Paige said, turning and keeping her voice low.

Anna Beth winked. "Nah, I can handle him with one hand tied behind my back. It would be lovely to have your daughter here. Children keep us young, that's one of the reasons I volunteered at the day-care centers at the base."

"What were the other reasons?"

Anna Beth gave her a wry look. "Boredom and feeling useless. I hated being retired. Felt as if I'd been thrown away. However old-fashioned it may sound, I want to be useful, not sitting on my duff watching TV, or knocking a golf ball around. One day I stopped to help a young military wife whose car had broken down. She was frantic. Desperate to get to the base day-care center because they charged a late fee and she couldn't afford it."

"I mostly work from home, but I've been fortunate to have my mother to help with Mishka when I meet with clients," Paige explained. "Lots of families don't have that option."

"All too true. Anyway, I drove her to the day care to pick up her kid, and then I fixed up the car. Gave it a good tune-up and replaced the thermostat."

Paige smiled. "So you're also a mechanic."

"I know my way around an engine. My dad worked at a garage when I was growing up. He was a single father and I didn't have a place to go after school, so I learned how machinery worked. He was really proud when I joined the marines. Pop lived to see me become a sergeant. I made master sergeant after he died."

"Master sergeant is quite an accomplishment."

Anna Beth shrugged. "I did okay. The next day I went to the day-care center and said I'd help out for free, but if I did, they couldn't charge late fees. Guess it was an offer they couldn't refuse, though officially I was paid. The money just went to cover those fees. I realize they have to make a living, too, but some of those young families are barely getting by."

Paige glanced around the space that Anna Beth had cleaned to be a playroom for Mishka. The offer was generous, but should she agree? She gestured that they should step away, wanting to talk where they couldn't be overheard.

"I suspect there's more to your babysitting offer than what you're telling me," she said. It wasn't that she didn't trust Anna Beth; she just wanted to know the whole story and what she might be getting into.

A sheepish expression grew on Anna Beth's face. "Well, if Jordan gets used to having a child around, he might be more open to having a family of his own. I want what's best for him. I suppose you could say he's almost like a son to me, though don't you dare repeat that to him or Saul."

"You needn't worry about me saying something out of turn," Paige assured her. "But I don't think you're going to change Jordan's mind. He sounds determined to stay single. Quite up front with his opinions on marriage, even though I didn't ask. I'd be insulted, except I understand. Marriage isn't for everyone."

Anna Beth waved her hand. "That's just his defense mechanism. Did the same myself because I figured a husband would hold me back."

"Do you regret it?"

The older woman pursed her lips. "Sometimes. Especially since the marine corps made me retire." She made a disgusted sound. "I don't want that for Jordan."

Paige glanced around the foyer and wondered when children's laughter had last rung through the house. Aside from Mishka, who made everything bright. It seemed unlikely that Jordan and his brothers had laughed much here and she was sad to think about them growing up in such a solemn atmosphere.

As for Jordan's reasons for not wanting to get married? Being held back in his career didn't seem to be part of that decision. It was more likely to do with what he'd said about being a SEAL. *The things we see change us*, though she suspected those changes had begun when his mother died and he had to live with Saul.

“How about it?” Anna Beth urged. “You know Saul would love having Mishka here even more often. I just met the man and can already see how much he adores her.”

“That’s true. She loves everyone, but she has a special relationship with Saul. To be honest, my parents are jealous.”

Anna Beth chuckled. “First grandchild?”

“Their only grandchild so far. It’s nearly impossible to keep everyone from spoiling her. Me, included.”

“I’m no expert, but I think you’re doing a fine job. She’s sweet, polite and wants everyone to be happy. So let me watch Mishka when you’re out with Jordan on the Soaring Hawk. His stoic demeanor aside, he isn’t a bad guy. There’s nothing he wouldn’t do to help someone he cares about, or somebody who just needs help. Why, he paid way too much for the truck out there, just because a member of his SEAL team needed the cash.”

Paige was sure Jordan was a good friend to his navy buddies—men as tough and fearless as he was himself. She also didn’t question that he was a genuine hero, one of those people who quietly saved the day without looking for credit.

It was his tough outer shell that was hard to

take, which meant being around him would be annoying and exasperating and a few other things besides. Little emotion reached his eyes and he rarely smiled. That didn't mean a volcano wasn't simmering or that he wasn't passionate deep down—the temptation would be to push him to reveal those emotions.

She gritted her teeth, frustrated by her wayward thoughts.

She'd never been attracted to the classic strong, silent type, so she needed to spend less time thinking about Jordan as a man, and focus on getting through the next few weeks and months of observing him as a rancher. The job was ridiculous, but she would enjoy being even more active than usual. It wasn't that she didn't like the business end of ranching, but she loved hands-on tasks as well.

"I accept your kind offer," she said to Anna Beth. "At least for part of the time. But if taking care of Mishka gets to be more than you want to do, you'll have to let me know."

TWENTY MINUTES LATER Anna Beth watched Paige and her daughter drive away, happy with her first day as a housekeeper. It had been a long trip from San Diego, but she didn't have anything to keep her there besides working at the base day-care centers. She'd been taking a break from it, regardless. Life had gotten dull with no challenges to keep her blood stirring. Just as bad, the weather in Southern California was too bland for her taste, and the housing too expensive to stomach buying a place of her own. Instead she'd been living in the navy base housing.

Anna Beth looked around the large farm home with satisfaction. She wasn't fanciful as a rule, but she thought buildings had a soul, and the soul of this place had been neglected for too long. Elbow grease, paint and TLC were in order. Not that Paige hadn't done her best, but she had her own life to lead.

Through the window, Anna Beth saw Jordan walking toward an outbuilding, a heavy tool chest balanced on one shoulder. Saul Hawkins was still in his chair on the porch and his head turned slowly, as if he was tracking his grandson's progress across the main ranch.

She would take her time making up her mind about the old rancher. He seemed to think Jordan needed to prove something to him, but from the way she saw things, Saul was the one who had more to prove.

CHAPTER SIX

WHEN JORDAN WOKE on Wednesday morning, a warm weight rested on his chest and he saw the faint outline of Lady G. He was accustomed to her presence now, but their first night together had gotten tense.

His years of being alert to the slightest change in conditions while on assignment had made him overreact whenever she leaped on him. She liked to periodically settle for a catnap, and other times simply bounded around the room, using him as a launching pad. But he no longer jerked into alert mode when she landed; his subconscious now recognized she wasn't a threat.

The entire cat family had proven to be skilled hunters. The bountiful opportunities to stalk and pounce mice had taken the edge off their resentment at being confined. Before long he would introduce them to the barns. In the meantime he was storing the fresh hay for the horses on the far side of the paddock in an effort to keep the mice from invading it.

He reached out to switch on a lamp. “Get your mouse breath out of my face,” he told Lady G.

She yawned, her teeth gleaming in the low light.

“Yeah, you’re tired from chasing mice all night. Just don’t get bored, that’s your job. This is a working ranch, no loafing around allowed.”

She delicately licked her paw. As he moved to sit up, she jumped down and walked away, tail waving. She wasn’t a cat with an ego problem.

Jordan dealt with the “gifts” she and her half-grown kittens had left him before showering and getting dressed. When he grabbed his boots, he diligently shook them out to ensure there were no unwelcome visitors taking refuge inside.

He’d forgotten to do it the previous morning.

Outside the sun was far enough below the horizon that stars were still winking and sparking in the dark sky.

Paige would soon arrive and there was no point in putting her off again. The whole idea of an "observer" was irritating and he didn't need a privileged do-gooder getting in his way. For any questions, he would do research on the internet or speak with an experienced rancher like Liam Flannigan.

An hour later he'd taken care of the basic tasks around the barns and saddled both Tornado and the black mare, Dolley Madison, who was restless from not getting enough exercise. She was another fine animal, equal to Tornado. He rubbed the white blaze on her nose and she nickered at him, impatiently pawing her foreleg.

"Behave yourself," he admonished, wondering if she'd be too much for Paige to handle. If so, they could switch mounts. Jordan had worked Tornado the most, needing to learn his quirks and moods. It was only on the stallion's days off that he was riding the other horses in rotation.

He stretched. His fitness regimen in the navy had prepared him for a return to ranch life, though he'd still had a couple of mildly sore days. They hadn't been a problem—he had worked through worse on countless missions and training assignments.

Over by the house, Jordan saw Paige arrive. She got out of her silver SUV and he heard the happy chatter from Mishka as she greeted his grandfather and Sarge.

"Hi, Mr. Jordan," she called in turn, waving at him.

Resigned, he went over to say hello in response. He couldn't help himself, any more than he'd been able to resist giving his MREs to kids in the far-flung corners of the world, or buying an electronic savings bond for the new son or daughter of one of his team members. Children were innocents and they deserved a better life than many of them received.

"Hi, Mishka. Hey, Finn." He rubbed behind the border collie's ears. The white tip of his tail was a blur as he wagged furiously.

"I see you have the horses ready," Paige said. She appeared to be restraining a smile.

"Yeah, I need to get an early start."

"Then we should leave. Mishka, be good for Anna Beth and Mr. Saul. I'll be back later."

The four-year-old nodded and yawned. She wore a thick yellow sweatshirt and held a blanket to her chest. A child-size backpack adorned with a unicorn sat on the porch nearby. She didn't appear stressed about her mother going somewhere without her—no separation anxiety, or whatever it was called with children.

As they rode out, Paige turned in the saddle and blew a kiss to her daughter, then settled forward with a sigh of pleasure. "I haven't gone riding this early in ages. There's nothing like seeing morning arrive from the back of a horse."

Jordan nodded, aware that he was watching *Paige* more than the light growing in the sky. He told himself it was to be sure that Dolley wasn't too rambunctious, but that was a lie. Paige sat in the saddle as if she'd been born there. Her slim body moved easily with the mare, and the rising sun behind them made her golden-brown hair glint with a halo of red.

"You should fasten that jacket and put on your hat," he muttered, pressing his cowboy hat tighter to his head.

Paige shrugged. "You're just wearing a flannel overshirt. I'll button up if I get cold, and it isn't light enough yet to need a hat. What's your plan for today?"

"I've isolated a small section of the herd on the southwest edge of the ranch. They're closest to the summer grazing land. Getting there and moving them will take most of the morning and afternoon. You may want to consider going back."

She laughed. "You can't get rid of me that easily. Finn and I will help. Finn is an expert at moving cattle. My dad claims each of our dogs are worth three ranch hands on a horse because they can get into spaces a horse can't and change directions faster. I got him from a local breeder who's an expert at training herders. Not that herding dogs need much training. They're born with the instinct. Finn mostly keeps an eye on Mishka, but his abilities really kick in with cattle."

Finn was ahead of them, but both times he heard his name, he turned his head and yipped, quivering with excitement and delight.

Jordan knew that certain dog breeds were reputed to be good herders, he'd just never seen it in action. The times that neighbors helped with branding the Circle M's cows, their dogs had mostly seemed to be getting in the way.

Those happy, chaotic days felt as if they were from another life, one that didn't wholly belong to him.

Then something occurred to Jordan and he looked at Paige. "Some of the ranchers used to lend a hand when the Circle M was branding, and I remember my folks would help at other ranches. Was your family ever there?"

She shrugged. "Probably. I was pretty young at the time, but I'm sure our parents were acquainted. Maybe not well, but the Circle M isn't that far from the Blue Banner. Mom and Dad would have tried to participate, the same with my grandparents."

Jordan set his jaw, unsure of how to handle the information. In his head he knew that ranchers commonly joined forces to handle big tasks, but he'd spent the later part of his childhood watching his grandfather go it alone with his grandsons and hired hands.

He checked to be sure the satellite phone was securely fastened to his belt. So far he hadn't gotten any inquiries about the job advertisement, and nobody had come to the ranch looking for work, either, just the way Paige had predicted.

On Monday afternoon he'd phoned the grocery market in Shelton, and also spoken to Chet Dixon at the farm store. Both businesses kept community bulletin boards and said they would put up a notice announcing job openings at the Soaring Hawk. But the tone in Chet's voice had reminded him of Paige when she'd talked about the labor shortages around Shelton. Hesitancy, a shade of doubt and a sense of something not being said.

Saul must be the reason.

Jordan's hands tightened on the reins, making Tornado throw up his head. "Sorry, boy," he murmured, easing his grip.

Fingers of light were reaching up from the eastern horizon, painting the high cirrus clouds pink and burnishing the edges with silver. The hills and stands of pine trees ahead were also catching the early rays, along with the tops of the black cottonwoods that edged the waterways and filled the gullies. He'd seen dozens of beautiful places around the world, but couldn't think of any that could compete with the land around them.

"Look at the mare's tails," Paige said, gesturing to the cloud streaks overhead.

He frowned thoughtfully. "I'd forgotten that's what they were called."

"You've spent half your life away from Montana. Do sailors have a different nickname than mare's tails?"

Jordan searched his memory, and then shook his head. "Not that I'm aware of. But I'm in the habit of watching the weather because of the impact it could have on a mission."

Paige nodded. Beneath the lapels of her coat, he saw she wore a blue shirt that matched the shade of her eyes, and her form-fitting jeans were soft and faded with use. Nothing pretentious. The cowboy hat hanging from a strap down her back had seen long years of use, along with her riding boots. It would be easy to forget she belonged to such a well-off family.

"Things were chaotic at Kindred Ranch the other day," she said, "but you should know that Casey and Marc aren't the only children in the area who view Navy SEALs as superheroes. You may encounter a fair amount of awe from the local kids."

Jordan made a scoffing sound. "Being a SEAL doesn't make anyone a superhero. Or a hero, period. There were too many people I couldn't save. Besides, Casey and Marc already idolize their father." The twins' adoration for their rodeo-champ dad had reminded him of his own feelings for Evan Maxwell, who'd seemed invincible before his wife's death. He hoped nothing would disillusion the McKeon boys.

"Uh, yeah, that's a long story." Paige didn't

add anything, suggesting she wasn't planning to tell the tale, which suited Jordan. He avoided scuttlebutt whenever possible, something else he'd learned in the navy.

"It's too bad nothing has tempted anyone to apply for a job here," he said. "I haven't gotten a single inquiry about working for the Soaring Hawk. Has my grandfather totally antagonized every single potential ranch hand in the area?" he asked, trying to sound casual.

"I never said that."

"You didn't need to. I can read between the lines."

THOUGH PAIGE MADE a face, she kept her mouth shut. She was still trying to navigate between her loyalty to Saul and being up front with Jordan according to her instincts.

But was Saul's testy reputation the only reason Jordan hadn't gotten any calls from job seekers?

She wondered, especially recalling how awed the McKeon twins had been at meeting him. There could be concern about working for someone reputed to have superhuman abilities and superhuman expectations. Her ideas of what a SEAL did were vague, but supposedly they could operate in any environment and in the toughest circumstances. Hollywood certainly seemed to view Navy SEALs as an elite, practically invincible group.

She cleared her throat. "If you think Saul is the problem, there are ways to assure potential job seekers that you're the Soaring Hawk's ramrod, rather than your grandfather," she said at length. "One place to start could be calling yourself the foreman, instead."

"I prefer *foreman* over *ramrod* as a job title, but about the rest? Maybe I should take out a full-page ad in the newspaper saying 'Trust me, I'm in charge and I'm nothing like Saul Hawkins.'"

Paige rolled her eyes. She still thought the two men were remarkably similar, except Jordan was more annoying. "Where is the herd you want to move?"

"In the pasture ahead. It's small and we used it when I was a teenager as a holding pen. There isn't enough grass for more than a day or two, but the Soaring Hawk has a large amount of leased grazing land."

"I'm aware of that," Paige returned in a dry tone. She was a rancher's daughter, so she knew quite a bit about open range grazing. It was important to a successful beef ranch. "I helped Saul renew his federal grazing permits last year."

Based on how Jordan's face tightened, she suspected he had mixed feelings about her being involved in renewing the permits. Well, too bad. She was the one who'd been here, not him, and losing the permits could have affected the Soaring Hawk's value.

Spotting something worrisome, she drew Dolley to a stop.

"What's up?" Jordan asked.

She gestured to the plant growing in a low marshy area. "That's hound's-tongue. It's a nonnative species and toxic to foraging animals. We've just started seeing it in Shelton County. If you want to go ahead, that's fine, but I can't leave it here."

"Of course not."

Paige dismounted and removed the collapsible shovel she'd fastened to Dolley's saddle. Though she was officially the Blue Banner's business manager, she always rode with the tools to repair fences and deal with any number of problems, including toxic plants. Jordan dismounted as well and tried to take the shovel.

"Let me show you," she said. "The entire taproot has to be gotten, or it'll grow back."

She sensed his displeasure, but he didn't object.

Paige carefully dug out the plant, checking the root to be sure that the tip hadn't broken off and remained in the ground. She stuffed it in a trash bag that would be burned later as a precaution, then took out her phone and made a notation.

"What's that?" Jordan asked.

"An application to record the GPS coordinates with the location and type of invasive plants, so ranchers can check to verify they haven't grown back. A geologist friend from college created the program. He adapted it when I asked about the possibilities. I'm sure there's more than one app that can be used, but this is the one I prefer."

"May I?" Jordan took the cell and examined the screen. She showed him several of the features and he nodded. "Can it be loaded to my satellite phone?"

"I don't see why not. Just go to the website for the Shelton Ranching Association. There's a link. Also links to resources on identifying and controlling noxious plants."

"I'm not a member of the association."

Sheesh.

"You're a rancher in Shelton County, that's all the membership you need. We don't have a password to the site, just go and download the program. A few of the cowhands who worked for Saul used it, so you'll be able to see which toxic weeds they found on the Soaring Hawk, and where."

"How did you manage that? I can't see my grandfather giving his blessing to a computer program."

Paige glared, her temper getting the better of her. "For heaven's sake, this shouldn't be a contest between your methods and what Saul would or wouldn't do. Or trying to prove that he's wrong about everything. It should be about doing what's best for the herds and the land. I'm sure Saul had ways to track any concerns on the ranch. This is just a different one."

Jordan didn't say anything for a long moment, and then sighed. "You're right. I apologize."

She was so shocked, her jaw dropped. "I'm sorry, too. I shouldn't have popped off like that."

"You're being a good friend. Look, I know my grandfather was an expert cattleman back in the day. Even as a boy I could see he had a gift with both cattle and horses. He just couldn't translate any of that to family. From my point of view, he's basically a stranger. I don't hate him, but at the same time, I have no reason to trust him, either."

Though there was little expression on Jordan's face, Paige was sure he meant every word. She still wondered if he'd been upset about something when he arrived at the Soaring Hawk. On the other hand, he'd driven a long distance and must have been tired. She could also imagine how intense it would be to come back for the first time in over twenty years.

She wrinkled her nose. "I assume it's pointless to say you *can* trust Saul."

"Trust is earned. You're an idealist, Paige. That's nice. But you're a lot younger than me. More than that, you can't understand what I've seen, or the things people will do to each other. You don't even know what it was like to grow up with Saul. And now the Soaring Hawk is falling apart. It's more realistic to believe my grandfather just wants someone to put the ranch back together for him."

Paige could see how the situation must appear to Jordan, but even if she couldn't prove it, she knew Saul wanted to make amends with his grandsons. The ranch wasn't in desperate straits. Not yet, though it would be soon without cowhands. Saul could have hired a ranch manager a year ago and there would be less reluctance among potential employees to work for someone outside the Hawkins family. Jordan's last name might be Maxwell, but he was still Saul's grandson. It was one of the reasons she'd suggested advertising job openings beyond the county limits.

"Obviously we aren't going to agree about this," she said, "but that doesn't change the promise I made to help as much as possible. And by the way, being an idealist doesn't mean I don't see reality."

"I said idealism was nice."

"Right. The way you'd say a baby bunny is nice," Paige retorted, aggravated all over again.

An unexpected, warm humor filled Jordan's eyes. "I apologize. *Again.* Now, about the hound's-tongue. I'm not familiar enough with it for ready identification. And there may be other toxic plants that I've only seen in pictures or videos. I'd appreciate your pointing any out that you spot."

She blinked at the swift change of subject. But then, Jordan wasn't a touchy-feely, discuss-his-emotions kind of guy.

"Uh, sure. Hound's-tongue lives for two years. It starts as a rosette of lance-shaped leaves, like this one. A stalk would have shot up next spring and developed reddish to purple flowers. The seed burrs are awful. They catch on everything and stick with a mind of their own. And the taproot can go down three feet. It's strong, so it *can* be pulled, but if a little is left behind, the plant will grow back. That's why I prefer digging whenever possible."

Jordan nodded. "We should check around before we leave. This one spread from somewhere."

Together they combed the area for the pest, but didn't find any. The seed had likely been carried to the area in an animal's fur.

In the midst of searching they located a damaged fence and Paige found herself watching the muscles bunch and flex in Jordan's strong legs as he handled the repair. If she'd ever imagined what a Navy SEAL would be like, she would have imagined someone like Jordan.

Tough. Capable. Able to do anything.

Her train of thought was so ridiculous, she

pushed it out of her head and turned around to inspect more of the fence. She tightened a loose wire before Jordan had a chance to say he'd do it himself, and then checked the next section. Fences were important to ranchers. A good deal of Montana was open grazing, but fencing near the ranch center was used for various reasons, including keeping the bulls separate from the females until the right time, and to manage the herds for winter feeding. Temporary pens were also useful.

Page glanced back at Jordan and saw him remove his lined overshirt, slinging it over the horn on Tornado's saddle. He wiped his forehead and went back to work, muscles flexing against his tight, khaki T-shirt.

Her heart thudded and she shook herself.

She wasn't a young girl, easily impressed by a handsome man; she was a mother with a daughter to raise. It wasn't that she thought Jordan was a bad person, but he was remote and difficult. Definitely not the sort of guy she'd ever get involved with, even assuming she was looking for a relationship.

Having the word *relationship* enter her mind was doubly frustrating. When you were single, the whole world seemed to think you were anxious to change your status. Every week, at least one of the elderly members at church would ask if she'd met someone interesting. Her own parents had trouble accepting she didn't plan to emulate their happy marriage.

On the other hand, that was part of the problem.

She and her brothers had grown up with such good examples of what marriage *should* be, it was hard to contemplate accepting anything less.

"You have an interesting expression on your face," Jordan commented as they put the tools back in the saddlebags. "You aren't still upset about that *nice* comment, are you? I didn't mean to insult you, though how *nice* could be an insult is beyond me."

Drat.

She needed to remember that even if Jordan revealed little of his own inner thoughts, it didn't mean he wasn't observant. He'd been a Navy SEAL, where being observant could mean the difference between life and death.

"How would you feel if someone called you nice?" Paige countered.

Jordan didn't say anything until they were both back in the saddle, then he shrugged. "*Nice* might have bothered me when I was sixteen. But it wouldn't now. Mostly I'd be surprised."

"Surprised?" she repeated, her eyes widening. "Come on, Jordan, I haven't heard you use a single strong word, lose your temper, or show any impatience with animals. You're stiff when you're uptight and anxious to get back to work, but not outright rude. From what I've seen, you're the embodiment of an officer and a gentleman."

"I'm not an officer any longer."

"You know what I mean."

Yet Paige wasn't sure that Jordan *did* understand. In fact, she could have sworn he was embarrassed by the entire conversation. He didn't see himself as a hero. But Liam Flannigan had checked him out before getting involved in the agreement with Saul. What little information Liam had learned—most of Jordan's service record was classified—showed that he was highly decorated and had an exceptional reputation.

"The herd I want to move is up ahead," Jordan announced, his tone telling her that he'd closed any further discussion of his better qualities.

She liked that he didn't have an arrogant view of himself. If anything she would have assumed a SEAL would need an excess of confidence and ego for the job. Instead he was serious—a little too serious for her taste—and quietly assured. He had an absolute certainty he could do what was necessary to save the Soaring Hawk. Problem was, he might have to back down on his pride and accept a hand from his fellow ranchers in order to succeed.

"You should stay here," Jordan said. He got off Tornado and lifted a loop of wire from the hooking post, dragging the gate out of the way so the cattle wouldn't get tangled as they left the pasture. Once back in the saddle, he eyed the herd for a long minute, then urged the horse forward.

Plainly he'd singled out one of the animals and it was the one Paige would have also chosen as a potential lead cow. The others would likely follow her.

She shifted in Dolley's saddle and made a signal to Finn. The border collie darted into the pasture and began rounding the herd in from the edges. The lead cow mooed a protest, but headed for the opening in the fence. The others went along, with Jordan's and Finn's encouragement.

"Go, Finn," Paige called. Finn knew the

process of moving a herd better than both of them and he reveled in the activity.

When the lead cow turned east instead of west, Paige yelled, “Hey, hey, hey,” and swung a rope to discourage her. Dolley responded with little direction since she was an experienced cutting horse.

Finn darted out and around, yipping. The cow swung her head at him and he expertly evaded the intended blow. She reluctantly reversed course, her calf trotting after her. Orneriness was normal in range cattle. They had to survive winter and periods of independence on the open range and, most importantly, protect their babies during a rough and wild spring birthing season. But the same qualities made them a challenge to work.

A quick count showed there were eighty in the herd, with as many calves.

Paige spared a look at Jordan and admired his technique. He and Tornado were already a team, chivvying the herd along. He would have figured out how to drive them to summer grazing without Finn’s help or her own, but surely he’d see it was easier this way.

Of course, he’d probably say he didn’t want easy; he just wanted to show he could handle it because of that stupid so-called bargain with Saul. But even her father, one of the most skilled ranchers in the state, would have trouble moving a hundred and sixty head of cattle without at least another ranch hand and a few herding dogs. It was a dangerous job. When she was a kid, a rancher from the north end of the county had died while driving a herd to summer grazing. No matter how careful someone was, there was always a possibility that the whole operation could go south.

You had to live with the risk, or do something else.

Or in Nana Harriet's case, she'd had to live with the risk in order to stay married. She hadn't grown up on a ranch—she'd been born and raised in Denver, Colorado, and she sometimes talked about how hard it had been to deal with the risks her husband faced on the Blue Banner, each and every day. Ultimately she'd loved him enough to understand ranching was in his blood, as it would be in her one surviving child and grandchildren. Why else would someone keep at it, year after year, through all the ups and downs?

Paige didn't question that Jordan was a great horseman, but she still wasn't sure if ranching was in his blood.

JORDAN DISMOUNTED AGAIN to close the wire gate and keep the herd from rebelling and going back into the pasture, then got back in the saddle.

He was impressed with Finn. The dog seemed to know exactly where to go, reading the stubborn range cows, darting, pivoting and nipping at their heels. Some direction was based on hand signals and shouts from Paige, but not all.

He was also a happy animal, splashing through the small stream in the pasture, his legs and fur getting cold and muddy, but his spirit unbowed.

"Ch-ch-ch-ch," Paige called, riding to one side to bring back a straying group of cows.

Jordan didn't know how he could have questioned whether Dolley would be too much for her to handle. Paige had grown up around horses and cattle, something he needed to remember, but at least he hadn't said anything foolish.

Bad enough that he'd thought it.

He was gaining valuable insight from her and would be a fool to deny it. Despite his studies and growing up on the Circle M and Soaring Hawk, his instincts needed flexing. The reasons for riding fence lines weren't just to do repairs and check on the herds, but to deal with problems like invasive plants and predators.

He drew in a long, full breath of air. The clean, fresh scent was unlike anywhere he'd been in the world. A reminder of why people chose this life, despite the uncertainty of beef prices and everything that nature could throw at a rancher.

The morning was passing quickly and he took point, ahead of the lead cow, to set the pace. Satisfaction settled deep inside him. The drives to summer pastures had been one of the few bright spots of life on the Soaring Hawk. Saul had still yelled at everyone, but his real focus had been on the cattle.

As the day wore toward noon, Jordan was all too aware that his job was being made immensely easier by Paige and Finn. Rather than having to ride back and forth, filling all the positions needed when driving cattle, Finn handled the responsibilities of swing and flank riders. Paige backed him up, also ensuring the cows and calves in the rear didn't straggle.

An hour later she rode forward to hand Jordan an insulated sack, then returned to the rear of the herd without a word. Inside were thick roast beef and Swiss cheese sandwiches, which beat the trail mix he'd brought by a thousand miles. They'd been wrapped in a way that made them easy to consume on the go. He ate in the saddle, still leading the herd and enjoying every bite.

"We're almost there," he called later, glancing back.

Paige waved. She was too far away for him to see her expression, but her body posture was relaxed and she was moving comfortably with Dolley. She might spend her days tending ranch accounts and chasing after Mishka, but she knew how to ride a horse like a pro.

The lead cow mooed and abruptly rushed forward. The others followed almost as quickly. She was older and must have recognized they were almost to the summer rangeland.

He urged Tornado ahead and jumped down to pull the wire gate open. The cattle streamed through with loud moos and bellows. The corners of his mouth curved as the calves ran and kicked up their heels, sharing the pleasure of the adults.

The small herd spread out on the hill beyond, the first Soaring Hawk cows to get their annual taste of the open range. More would join them. Jordan didn't let himself think about how he would manage to ride the leased grazing land to check on the herds, while still getting the branding, haying and everything else done alone.

This was his life now, and like those exuberant calves, he was going to enjoy the moment.

CHAPTER SEVEN

"EAT THE REST of your salad so I can finish doing the dishes," Anna Beth ordered.

Saul scowled.

Some housekeeper. She was more like a jailor. Eat this. Do that. Offering her advice and opinions right and left and scrubbing the house down to its bare bones over the last several weeks. He wasn't one of those marines she used to order around.

"You can't feed me greens like a horse and ask me to thank you," he returned in a huff.

"Don't give me that. I put a small serving on the plate, with a good hunk of meat, potato and veggies on the side. Plus the biscuit with jam and butter. I ate healthier during my survival training."

His scowl deepened as he finished the salad in three defiant bites. As much as he disliked admitting it, Anna Beth was a decent cook. And her offer to watch after Mishka meant the child was around more often. But Paige didn't bring her every day. She said it wasn't fair to him or Anna Beth, though he figured it was also a case of Margaret Bannerman wanting time with her granddaughter.

A vision of what could have been returned to Saul—his grandsons staying on the ranch, perhaps living there with wives and children. The original homestead restored and pressed into service, or new homes built as families expanded. Maybe Paige would have been one of those wives. It could still happen. Wyatt was already married, but Dakota might be a good match for her.

Or Jordan, though he was a bigger question mark.

Of all the boys, Jordan deserved a woman like Paige, but would he ever consider it? Saul had known it wasn't likely to happen, but he'd still pushed them together, hopeful there might be a spark.

He rubbed the polished wood of his cane, the same cane his grandfather had used when he got older. A bear's head and body formed the crook. It was hand-carved, with other designs down the sides of buffalo, wolves and soaring eagles. Made to honor his great-grandmother's heritage.

In the 1800s his great-grandfather had

courted and married a woman from the Assiniboine people. Great-Grandma Ehawee had taught her children and grandchildren to respect all animals and the world around them. Saul had been young when she died, but he still remembered her quiet serenity, with a smile as fresh as spring. And he'd sometimes wondered if she regretted marrying a rancher. It couldn't have been an easy choice, however much she and her husband had loved each other.

"You have to build up your strength," Anna Beth said, breaking into his thoughts. "Paige tells me you need a hip-replacement operation."

Saul set his jaw as she collected his plate. "I'll have one when I'm good and ready. When are you gonna get on a horse?" Early on he'd figured out that however gutsy and forthright his jailor might be, she took a cautious view of the equine species.

"I've driven tanks, Humvees and every other type of overland vehicle. I don't need to ride a horse."

He harrumphed, but didn't push it further. His memories of Great-Grandmother Ehawee had reminded him of his own regrets—regrets that had haunted him for so long, he didn't know if he could ever escape them. He'd talked with Paige about it, more honestly than he could have imagined telling anyone except his wife. Paige hadn't judged. She'd listened and urged him to take action, rather than just sit on those bad feelings.

He couldn't care for her more if she'd been his own kin.

"You be sad, Mr. Saul?" Mishka asked, coming out of the house.

Saul summoned a smile. "Not with you here, sweetheart. Shall we read a book?"

"Uh-huh. The velvety rabbit."

She ran back inside and returned holding *The Velveteen Rabbit* in her small fingers. It was a first edition she'd found in the attic, worn and read countless times. He remembered his parents reading the story aloud, and then reading it to his own daughter in turn.

"All right."

He lifted her onto his better leg and she rested against his shoulder as he read to her about the little toy rabbit that was loved into being real. He just hoped the same thing could happen to him.

JORDAN DRAGGED THE wire gate back into place and pulled the loop over the hooking post.

He'd read about devices that could be adapted to make wire gates tighter. Maybe next year he could investigate the option, but for now the current system worked well enough and had been serving ranches for generations.

The last of the herd was *finally* in summer grazing, ready for the next step. He had to admit, if only to himself, that it would have taken him much longer to move them without Paige and the dogs she was bringing with her—Finn and two other border collies from the Blue Banner.

He looked at them with respect. The herders worked hard and played harder, seeming to enjoy both equally. Maybe they didn't see any difference between play and work. After realizing how much they could do, he was astonished his grandfather didn't have a whole pack running around the place.

The same with cats. Lady G and her children had been very busy dealing with the uninvited mice. The situation was at a much more manageable level now, but he'd learned to leave his window open so Lady G could come in during the few hours he slept at night. Otherwise she sat outside, wailing in that raucous voice of hers, complaining about being neglected. It was enough to wake the dead, and more than enough to rouse him.

"Is that the last of the herd?" Paige asked as she rode up.

"I still need to bring up the bulls to breed with the cows," he said, remounting Radagast, the stallion he was riding for the day. "But the main herd is where they need to be. Saul's stock ledgers were fairly accurate."

"That's good."

It seemed typical of Paige that she didn't gloat or point out that his grandfather had done something right. Not that she lacked a temper, and she was just as stubborn as his grandfather had accused Jordan of being. *More* stubborn, but usually in a quiet way that was difficult to fight.

She also clearly knew the business end of ranching inside and out. A prime example was the hay Jordan had purchased as emergency feed for the horses. The quality was okay, but as it turned out, he'd paid twice what he should have.

When Paige learned the name of his supplier, she'd scrunched her nose. It was a cute gesture, one her daughter had learned well, and an unconscious reflection of her inner thoughts.

"Um, right. Cunningham Feed Company is reliable about delivering quickly," Paige had said diplomatically. "But if you need to purchase winter feed later on, you may be able to get a lower price for the same or better quality."

In other words, he'd overpaid. She would have been justified in saying "I told you so," but she hadn't. Instead she'd brought him a list of businesses that the Blue Banner and her clients had dealt with for years. Upon checking them out, he'd realized the Cunningham Feed Company had reaped an exceptionally high profit from the hay he'd bought.

But it wasn't a case of dismissing Paige's knowledge. He'd simply needed to obtain uncontaminated feed for the horses as swiftly as possible. It was bad enough they'd already been eating hay that the mice had invaded.

He'd since discovered the Soaring Hawk had no hay reserves from previous years, with the exception of the stack in the south field that his grandfather had mentioned. Luckily, spring had come early and the grass was growing in fast and plentiful. But the lack of reserves put the ranch behind. Buying hay, even at a good price, was expensive, so cutting and baling hay had moved to an even higher priority than before.

"It's good that the Soaring Hawk doesn't have to drive cattle across any public roads," Paige said as they turned the horses toward the main ranch, the dogs scampering ahead of them. "Three years ago we were moving part of the Blue Banner herd and a truck driver roared through, honking his horn. They scattered and one cow was so upset she lay down and refused to go any further. Dad had to transport her and her calf back to the main ranch for treatment. We don't give up on any animals, but she was a real challenge."

Jordan frowned. "That reminds me, I haven't seen any orphan calves on the Soaring Hawk. It's hard to believe there weren't a few from spring calving, if only ones rejected by their mothers."

"That doesn't happen often, thank goodness. There weren't enough employees on the Soaring Hawk to handle the orphans, so Saul sent them over to the Blue Banner. We can bring them back now, or do it later, but it's no problem to take care of them with ours. Mishka adores babies and we have a good record keeping orphans healthy and kicking, though obviously they're better off in a field with a mother."

"Since the Blue Banner is doing the work, they're yours." It only seemed right to Jordan that the calves belong to whoever had put the effort into raising them.

He gave Paige an assessing glance. She'd been coming most days and he suspected she was working evenings to keep current with accounting tasks for her ranching clients. Was it catching up with her? Most of the time she was cheerful, but earlier she'd gotten emotional when they found a dead calf, his mother mooing mournfully.

"You have to stop coming so much. It won't be any problem to move the bulls myself," he said.

Paige yawned and rubbed the back of her neck, confirming his suspicions. "I'm fine," she assured him. "Though I can't come for the next few days, regardless. We're flying to Seattle tomorrow and won't get back until Tuesday afternoon. Mishka has a checkup with her surgeon and, uh…" Paige hesitated. "One of her other doctors."

Other doctors? She'd said little about her daughter's medical issues, but he knew they must have been serious.

"Are they going to make a decision about the leg brace?"

Paige nodded. "Yes. The orthopedist doesn't want her to wear it any longer than absolutely necessary. I want her to be free of the brace, but I know it also offers some protection. She still seems so fragile to me. And yet if he says she isn't ready..." Her voice trailed off and she shrugged.

That could explain part of Paige's fatigue; she was anticipating the upcoming appointment. At the same time, Jordan still thought she was working too hard.

"Feeling conflicted over something like this must sound trivial to a soldier," she muttered.

"Not at all. Who's traveling with you?"

"Mom planned to go, but my grandmother had a dizzy spell a few days ago and is staying at the Blue Banner until she's steadier on her feet. If my mother isn't there, Nana Harriet will try to do the cooking and cleaning herself, just like she used to." Paige's expression turned wry. "Nana Harriet is unhappy that I'm bringing Mishka to the Soaring Hawk so often, but it would be tiring to have a child around all day, every day. Anna

Beth's offer to babysit turned out to be an extra blessing."

Jordan had an irrational urge to offer his company in Seattle, which was utterly off base. For one, he couldn't afford any time away from the Soaring Hawk. And, more importantly, what sort of comfort could he be to a sensitive woman like Paige?

None.

He cleared his throat. "Surely someone else can go along with you. If only as moral support."

"Dad offered, but I won't let him. We'll be fine," Paige said confidently. "I always book the fastest flight, and I've taken Mishka to Seattle so often the flight attendants know her by name. She's a favorite with them. The same with the hotel staff. When we get there, they always have a new teddy bear or other stuffed animal for her to take home. She has quite a collection by now."

Jordan wasn't surprised. Mishka had a charm and resilience that would enchant most people she encountered. Her shy smile, combined with her mother's winsome friendliness, would have endeared them both.

"You should reconsider attending the Shelton Ranching Association meeting next week," Paige said, changing the subject. "You can explain that you're in charge and need employees. Get Saul to sign a statement saying he's no longer running the ranch, if that'll help. Maybe it would break the logjam in getting applicants. But please don't embarrass Saul when you ask. Maybe just say it's important to clarify the line of command for new employees. After all, he's never had a ramrod or foreman before, so they might wonder. It all means the same thing."

This wasn't the first time she'd made the suggestion about the ranching association. She could be right. Jordan had been working twenty hours a day, trying to make up for the labor shortage, but even if he never slept, the Soaring Hawk had too many cows and calves for one person to handle. Along with too much land. The dogs were a great help, but even if he had an entire pack of his own, they couldn't build fences, groom horses or do countless other things.

The situation was tricky, especially since he didn't want his grandfather to start hoping he and Paige would get together romantically. Saul adored Paige and would probably be delighted to have her as a granddaughter-in-law,

She was more than appealing. That wasn't the problem. But even if Jordan was interested in getting married, the disparity in their experiences made anything between them impossible. Paige was nine years younger and had led a sheltered life in a large, loving family. She couldn't possibly understand what he'd gone through as a child or the horrors he'd seen in the navy. He didn't *want* her to understand.

"Jordan?" Paige prompted. "The meeting only takes a couple of hours and would give people a better sense of you. Though it would be helpful if you could relax when you're there."

"Relax?" He hiked an eyebrow at her.

"You can be a little, um, *formal* at times. You aren't in the navy any longer, you can stop standing at attention. The only time you relax is on a horse."

He shrugged. "Old habit. I'll think about going."

"Okay."

Jordan gave her a sharp look, but didn't see a hint of triumph that he might be conceding. Attending the meeting probably wouldn't cause any harm, he just didn't see it doing any good. Why would the local ranchers do something for him or the Soaring Hawk?

Saul had poisoned those waters a long time ago.

For that matter, Jordan still didn't understand why Paige was helping so much. She was fond of Saul, but surely not enough to work this hard. It wasn't feminine interest, a realization that had swiftly whittled Jordan's ego down to size. Without being aware of it, he'd gotten accustomed to women on the navy base flirting with him, even after making his position on long-term relationships known.

He should have thought things out before being so up front with Paige. She'd been amused by his presumption; he'd seen it in her eyes. Men must be chasing her, not the other way around.

It was for the best.

Jordan liked Paige, but he'd left the better parts of himself on nameless battlefields around the world. He was still figuring out how much remained. Under the circumstances, getting seriously involved with a woman had never seemed fair. A soldier's life wasn't easy and it was just as hard on their families.

Paige hoped Jordan would attend the ranching association meeting, but she knew better than to push. And if he went, she also hoped he wouldn't be as awkward as when they'd gone into town for cat supplies, or when the pharmaceutical representative had stopped by the ranch.

Allen Beckham worked hard to make sure his clients were properly stocked with calf vaccines and other medicines when they needed them. It was a business relationship when it came to sales, but he was local and entwined with community affairs, so a certain cordiality was expected. Not that Saul had ever been friendly to him, but Allen had clearly been willing to give Jordan a chance. Instead, Jordan was almost as uptight as his grandfather during the late-afternoon encounter.

Honestly, most of the time he really *did* act as if he was standing at attention. The only person he seemed to genuinely relate to was Anna Beth, who didn't take any guff from either Saul *or* Jordan.

"Do you want me to ask Saul to sign a statement?" Paige asked, only to immediately regret the offer, particularly when she saw the strained look on Jordan's face.

"No, I'll take care of it. Assuming that's the direction I decide to take."

"Sure," she said, relieved. The two men might need a kick in the pants as motivation, but she didn't want to become their intermediary.

At the main ranch Mishka came running from the house as soon as she saw them, Anna Beth following. She was remarkably fit and seemed to have little trouble keeping up with an energetic four-year-old.

Paige dismounted from Cinnamon, the mare she was riding for the day, and hugged her daughter close. They hadn't spent as much time together as usual and while she enjoyed riding and working with cattle, she also missed her daughter. Perhaps this was good practice for when Mishka started school, but knowing that didn't make it easier.

"Mama, I help make cookies."

Paige smiled at Anna Beth over Mishka's head. "That sounds like fun."

Next, Mishka hugged Finn and the other dogs, whose tails whipped with furious pleasure, and then held her arms up to Jordan. It was a scene that had been repeated each time they returned to the ranch and he no longer hesitated; he gave her an embrace in return.

Paige knew her child's enthusiastic affection made him uncomfortable and wondered if he'd always been like that, or if growing up with Saul was responsible. Saul deeply regretted the way he'd raised his grandchildren. Children needed love, and though he'd loved his grandsons, he had been unable to show it. He still struggled to let out the emotions he'd kept buried for so long.

One thing was certain—Paige's acquaintance with Jordan Maxwell was making her appreciate her own parents even more. She'd grown up in a household where she was showered with unconditional affection and support. Her sister had wanted to become a doctor and they'd thought it was great. Paige had decided to adopt a child from India and they'd backed her, every step of the way. If her brothers had wanted to do something besides ranching, her mom and dad would have cheered them on.

Staying on the ranch, or leaving, had been a choice.

At least Jordan was getting unconditional love now. Mishka didn't hold back and she seemed particularly fascinated by him. She finally released her hold on his shoulders, but only after giving Jordan a smacking kiss on the cheek.

Paige watched closely and could swear a hint of red was creeping up his neck. She caught Anna Beth's pleased gaze and suppressed a smile of her own. It was unlikely he would change his mind about having a family, the way the retired marine wished, but Anna Beth hadn't given up.

"Mr. Jordan, can I ask you something?" Mishka said.

"Sure."

"My friends have daddies, but I don't. Will you be my papa?"

Paige's amusement faded as a bleak expression crossed his face.

"Mishka, anyone would be lucky to have you as their daughter. I'm just not well suited to be the best kind of daddy," he said carefully. "But you have your grandfather and uncles. I'm glad you have so many people to care about you."

"That's right," Anna Beth said in an encouraging tone.

"Jordan can be your honorary uncle, the way Saul is your honorary grandpa," Paige suggested, trying not to get teary-eyed. How could Jordan think he wouldn't be a good father? He was amazingly gentle and patient with Mishka. "Come on, sweetheart. Let's groom Cinnamon," she urged.

"Okay."

Mishka trotted into the barn for the pail of grooming tools. She was a true ranch kid, unafraid of horses despite her small size, asking daily when she would be allowed to ride without someone behind her, holding her in the saddle. That was something else the doctors in Seattle were supposed to evaluate. When the time came, her grandfather had an older, unflappable mare picked for her to use, along with the small saddle Paige had used when starting to ride.

Anna Beth stayed and watched as Paige cleaned Cinnamon's hooves, then curried the mare's reddish-brown coat. Mishka knew the process; she carefully selected the grooming tools from the bucket and handed each to her mother at the right moment. Paige glanced at Jordan and saw he'd paused work on Radagast and was watching them.

He did that at odd times and she tried not to pay attention. It would be too easy to start imagining a warmth that wasn't there. Most likely he was still pondering whether Mishka's question meant anything. Paige wanted to assure him it didn't, but that would just make things worse. She wasn't embarrassed. Children asked that kind of question out of innocence, they didn't understand the larger picture. The hard part had been the expression on his face—he cared about Mishka, even if he didn't want to.

"Do you think some of the mares are carrying foals?" she asked as a distraction.

"I'll have the veterinarian come out to check, but there's a good chance they are," Jordan said. "Tornado was in the paddock with a group of mares, and the same with Radagast when he was in the south field. You know, I've been wondering about Radagast's name. Do you know where it comes from?"

Paige smiled. "Radagast is a wizard from *The Hobbit* and *The Lord of the Rings* books. He was also known as the brown wizard, which may be why the breeder chose the name. Saul didn't care for it when he bought Raddy as a yearling, but didn't want to go to the trouble and expense of changing the paperwork."

Jordan focused again on brushing the stallion. "Saul doesn't spend a single extra buck when he doesn't have to. I'm just surprised he's never bred horses to sell. I've checked, and several ranchers in the area do yearling and weanling sales on the side."

"He's traded colts and fillies for stock, but I don't know if he's ever considered breeding them for sale. Is that what you have in mind?"

Jordan shrugged, his face impassive. For all she knew, he planned to turn the Soaring Hawk into a horse ranch, or at the least the part he hoped to receive through a trust. It was an interesting idea since horse breeding could be supported with less land than a cattle ranch. Genetic tests were inexpensive now and could verify a foal's sire, so he could easily capitalize on any the mares might be carrying.

She lifted Mishka to let her daughter run a soft cloth over Cinnamon's coat. Teaching proper horse care was part of teaching her to ride. "Don't neglect your horse or the herd" was a cardinal rule that Paige had grown up learning. She was glad Jordan shared the same philosophy.

As a last grooming step, they let Cinnamon into the paddock so the mare could rest and graze. Dolley immediately trotted to the fence, demanding her share of attention; she didn't appreciate being left behind when Paige rode one of the other horses.

"Hey, girl." Paige fed her an apple.

"Hey, girl," Mishka echoed, reaching up a hand. Dolley dipped her head lower to receive a pat on the nose.

"That child is remarkable," Anna Beth murmured.

Her wariness toward horses had not been lost on Paige and she gave her a sympathetic look. To someone who'd never been around them, horses and cattle would seem large and unpredictable. Caution was important, no matter what your level of experience, but dealing with them was second nature to someone who'd been raised on a ranch.

"One of the first things I did when I returned from India with Mishka was introduce her to horses," Paige explained.

"Mama 'dopt me," Mishka said, picking up on the exchange. "I got picked special."

"You sure did," Anna Beth agreed. "Jordan, would you like to come in for cookies and milk with the rest of us?"

He hiked an eyebrow. "You have to be kidding."

"No back talk to me, young man. I happen to believe cookies and milk are a very good thing. You can't live on coffee alone, though heaven knows you've tried over the years."

Jordan laughed. "Yes, ma'am, but I have work to do."

Whoa.

Paige nearly fanned herself. He was attractive as a surly, unsmiling cowboy. Laughing, he took her breath away.

They left him to whatever tasks he had in mind and went to the house. Saul was watching them and disappointment crept into his face when his grandson stayed behind.

Paige gave water to the three dogs and washed her hands, then sat on the porch steps while her daughter and Anna Beth went inside to get the promised snack. Luna and Philby, the border collies Paige had been bringing from the Blue Banner, flopped down on the grass, while Finn came over to lean against her leg, tongue lolling happily. She scratched under his ears and he made a low, snuffling sound of pleasure.

"I've been thinking about something," Saul said slowly. "Do you think my grandson would like a dog to help on the Soaring Hawk?"

The question took her by surprise. "I'm sure Jordan has recognized how much they can do. He works well with Finn and the others. What made you think about it?"

Saul worked his mouth. "My jailor. She's got a head full of ideas and loves to share them. Not that I ask, she just volunteers. But this one might not be so bad. I never had dogs on the place because they made Celina sneeze. I don't know, I'm still making up my mind."

"From what you've said, I'm sure your wife would have loved having both cats and dogs if her allergies hadn't been such a problem."

He sighed. "Yeah. Guess I'll look into it. You got Finn from Claire Carmichael at the Carmichael Ranch, right?"

Paige nodded. Her parents always had a few young dogs coming along for the future, but she'd wanted one that was specially trained since she hadn't known when she'd be traveling to India as part of the adoption process. She'd gone twice, falling more in love with the country during each visit, with each of those visits lasting longer than the adoption process required. Leaving Mishka behind the first time had torn her apart, so she'd returned early, determined to stay until she could take her daughter home.

"Claire is an expert with border collies," Paige said. "She also started working with Australian shepherds a few years ago. Her dogs are in high demand, but you could call and see if she has any available. I'm sure either breed would be good."

"I'll do that." Saul sat back, his expression thoughtful. "Has Jordan said anything about me or the past?"

"I'm not here to report what he says," Paige reminded him. "And I'm careful of what I say about you, too. You're my friend. I don't want to break a confidence."

"Don't worry about that," Saul told her brusquely. "Tell him whatever you think would be right for him to know."

Before he could say anything else, Anna Beth and Mishka returned. Anna Beth carried a tray with glasses of milk, while Mishka balanced a plate filled with enormous chocolate chip cookies in her hands.

"They look delicious, darling," Paige said, taking one of the saucer-size treats.

Mishka sat next to her as they drank milk and munched on the cookies. Paige brushed a lock of hair from her daughter's cheek and kissed the top of her head. She might miss Mishka being a baby, but she also loved seeing her grow and learn.

The afternoon air was warm, but a cooling breeze blew in from the surrounding grasslands, filled with the scent of growth. It would soon be summer, with all the activity associated with the season. Life rarely slowed down on a cattle ranch, but that just meant they enjoyed the moments of peace even more.

Her gaze wandered toward the far barn, where Jordan had gone. It was on the edge of the main ranch and contained tractors and other haying tools. The green hills and blue mountains beyond made the aging building appear picturesque in the distance, rather than tired.

Anna Beth had mentioned hoping to help service the various pieces of haying equipment. "A machine is a machine," she'd said when Paige asked if she was familiar with the tools for haying. It was funny that horses bothered her, but not the mowers with their cutting knives, or the wicked-looking tines on the hay rakes.

Paige wrinkled her nose, knowing Anna Beth's offer to watch Mishka meant she was more limited in using her mechanical skills for Jordan's sake.

Life was complicated.

"We're going to Seattle tomorrow," she said casually. She usually didn't tell Saul sooner than the day before to make things easier on him. "We'll fly back on Tuesday."

Saul sighed and his face went glum, but he didn't ask about the doctors Mishka would be seeing. They tried not to talk about it in front of her, because anticipation made the visit worse.

Paige had caught herself with Jordan, too. She knew his mother died from heart failure, and had suddenly realized it could be disturbing to learn Mishka would be visiting a cardiologist.

He was a big, tough Navy SEAL, but Paige had wanted to protect him from a sad memory.

She didn't want to know what that meant.

CHAPTER EIGHT

"MAMA, MAY I have tapoca for dinner?" Mishka asked at the hotel restaurant on Monday night.

"Tapoca?" Paige asked. Usually she could figure out what her daughter meant, but this was new to her.

"Tapoca pudding. Anna Beth says it's yummy."

"Oh, tapioca pudding. We can check the menu, but they're more likely to have chocolate and vanilla. You have to eat a meal first, and then you may have dessert. I'll make tapioca for you at home."

"Okay." Mishka kicked her feet; she was still getting used to no longer having the brace on her leg.

Normally quiet with medical personnel, she had giggled and hugged the surgeon when he'd declared she could stop wearing the thing. He'd also okayed her riding a horse, which probably explained the hug.

Then Mishka had seen the cardiologist, more as a precaution than anything. Her congenital heart problem had been corrected soon after the adoption.

From now on, she mostly needed checkups, which wasn't too different than other children her age. This was the news expected and confirmed by each prior visit, but it was still good to hear the doctor's positive report. As usual, he'd warned her in private that a future procedure was always a possibility, but he didn't think it would be needed. Mishka had rebounded beyond all expectations.

For some reason Paige's thoughts drifted to Jordan. It was endearing the way he'd fussed about them traveling to Seattle alone. Well, *fussed* was too strong a word. She hadn't seen his concern in a bad way—as if he didn't think she was able to handle the situation by herself—but it was curious that he'd recognized her mixed emotions about the trip.

If there was anyone who wasn't in touch with his own feelings, it was Jordan Maxwell. Even her parents had seen the medical appointments as merely an affirmation of Mishka's steady progress, while Paige had gotten stressed about the outcome, either way. She always did.

That was parenthood.

She'd adopted Mishka with her eyes wide open, knowing how serious her medical condition was from the very beginning. It hadn't mattered. Paige had seen Mishka's picture and known she was her daughter.

The server came over and smiled. "Hello, Mishka. How is my favorite customer doing?"

"Hi, Taffy. We went to the science center after my 'pointments. I don't hafta wear a brace anymore."

"That's wonderful!" Taffy worked for the restaurant attached to the hotel and had helped them the evening before and on other trips. "Do you want the cheesy spaghetti again tonight?"

Mishka nodded. "And chocolate pudding, cuz Mama says you prolly don't have tapoca. Um, ta-pee-oh-ca," she corrected herself.

"Your mama is right. How about you, Paige?"

If Paige could have gotten away with it, she would have said she wasn't hungry, but that wouldn't set a good example for her daughter. "The portabella-mushroom burger and a side salad with vinaigrette. Also a glass of milk for Mishka."

"We'll get that served right away. You look done in."

"Thanks, Taffy. It was a busy day."

Soon they were back in their room and curled up in bed. Mishka's even breaths told Paige she'd immediately fallen asleep, but it didn't come as quickly to her.

Why had she thought of Jordan?

Much to her annoyance, he'd popped into her mind over and over during the trip, at the most inconvenient moments. She wanted to believe it was because they'd spent so much time together during the last few weeks, but she wasn't sure. She kept remembering his face when Mishka asked him to be her papa.

Her daughter's innocent question had bothered Jordan. He'd looked empty, as if it was impossible for him to consider being a father. She knew it was difficult for soldiers when they returned to civilian life, but she didn't believe Jordan was incapable of giving or receiving love. In his own way, he'd even shown understanding for Saul. While Paige had worried about a retired marine becoming Saul's housekeeper, Anna Beth had turned out to be an inspired choice. Now Saul was too busy sparring with her to think as much about his aches and pains, or fuss about the Soaring Hawk.

Watching Saul and Anna Beth together was interesting. It was almost as if they were starting to have feelings for one another, or at least becoming friends. Paige thought it was a great idea.

As for Jordan? When it came down to it, she thought he had as much love to give as Mishka.

“Ugh.” She rolled over to lie on her back. Seattle was a wonderful place with museums, professional sports and other things to see and do. But even with the hotel curtains drawn after nightfall, artificial light seeped in, along with the inevitable city noises. On the ranch, just moonlight crept under the curtains, and any sounds were from crickets and cattle and horses in the distance, or the wind sweeping across the grass and through the cottonwood trees.

Home.

And now Montana was also the home to an obstinate former SEAL who aggravated her beyond belief. She didn't know if he was going to show up at the ranching association meeting on Wednesday, or how he would act if he did. He could even make the employee situation worse, if that was possible.

She'd almost suggested trying to hire some high-school students, but the ones with any experience were likely already employed, or had the promise of employment.

Paige thought about Chet Dixon's son at the feed-and-seed store, along with Jordan's brisk refusal to let him help load the supplies purchased for the cats. Her hometown might be remote, but that didn't mean social media hadn't found them, particularly with kids. A Navy SEAL was practically a rock star in a place like Shelton, so an online description of the encounter would have been shared immediately.

Chet's son was a popular teen. By evening, every kid in the county must have read the story, along with their parents. It would have raised questions in their minds about whether he was too much like Saul to be a good ranch manager.

She sighed and turned over again, wishing she could clear her mind for a few hours. It had been a lot easier to sleep before meeting Jordan Maxwell.

Anna Beth hummed as she rolled paint over the walls in her bedroom. Already Montana felt more like home than any of the places she'd lived as an adult.

Next she was going to do Saul's bedroom and the hallway upstairs, no matter how much he objected. With the exception of the kitchen, the walls were darkened throughout the house, making the atmosphere gloomy. It had to depress him. Notions about proper decorating and feng shui-ing a space were a mystery to her, but she was confident that light was important in any setting.

She had already discovered the most tedious part of painting was covering the mahogany crown molding and baseboards to keep them from getting splattered. And, while she wasn't as worried about protecting the threadbare carpets, she'd have to be careful wherever the hardwood flooring was exposed.

After that she'd tackle the foyer. The yellowed, peeling wallpaper adorning the lower level might have been pretty once; now it was dreadful.

"Nobody gave you permission to paint in here," Saul barked from the door.

Anna Beth kept working. "Jordan told me

to put the paint and other supplies on the ranch account at the hardware store." Glancing over, she caught a pained expression on Saul's face.

She'd seen the way he watched his grandson when he thought no one would notice, revealing a longing that had nothing to do with being unable to ride and rope and be the cowboy he'd once been. He wanted something, but Anna Beth wasn't sure Jordan could give him whatever it was.

Saul's matchmaking hopes, if any, were another question.

Paige was a fine young woman with more backbone than Jordan probably gave her credit for having. It took courage to adopt a child with serious health problems. But even if Saul hoped they'd get together, Anna Beth was less certain. It would be great for Jordan, maybe not so much for Paige. Some men were hard on the women who loved them.

"And Paige picked the color with her daughter," Anna Beth added. She'd brought home paint samples for Paige and Mishka to choose from, knowing it would smooth the way with the old rancher. "It's called butter ash, which must mean somewhere between pale off-white and gray. Actually, Mishka wanted a brilliant raspberry, but her mother talked her around."

"Oh."

"Tell me about your wife," Anna Beth said, partly as a diversion, and partly because she was curious about the woman who still seemed to haunt the old house.

For a moment she thought Saul would stomp away. Instead he sat on a chair near the door and laid his cane across his lap. "You're only the second person to ask me that in over forty years." He pressed his lips together for a long instant. "Celina was kind and gentle. Too gentle, maybe. She didn't belong on a rough-and-tumble ranch, but she loved me."

"I've seen her picture in your room when I clean. She was beautiful."

Saul waved a hand. "Celina never wanted to be called beautiful. 'Beauty is, as beauty does,' she used to say." His face fell. "She'd be ashamed of me."

"It's never too late to change."

Saul's fingers traced the finely carved end of his cane. He did that often, as if finding some comfort from it. "Old men get set in their ways."

"That's just an excuse."

He snorted. "You got an answer for everything."

"I'm a marine. I'm supposed to solve problems."

"You said they retired you."

Anna Beth ran the roller through the paint in the pan. "Marines never stop being marines. 'Semper fi. Always loyal.'"

"Even if they weren't loyal to you?"

It was a valid question after the way she'd grumbled about retirement. She still thought experience should count, but she supposed young people needed a chance and older folks couldn't compete with their fearless youth. Kids rarely had a sense of their own mortality. Regardless, now she'd found a new adventure to keep her going.

"The military has rules," she said with a shrug. "I knew the score going in and figured on retiring at twenty years, but serving gets in your blood. They gave me a generous pension, though. Can't complain about that part."

"There's no retiring as a rancher until your body does it for you. Leastways, not for me."

"Might be different if you'd had family to take over."

Saul gave her a shrewd look. "I thought you wanted to know about my wife."

"It's all connected. I enlisted at eighteen. After Pop was gone, the marines were all I had, but I made friends who became my family. Like Jordan."

"Then you must already know he was seventeen when he enlisted. He'd graduated high school a year early and was still valedictorian. Smart, just like his mother."

SAUL DIDN'T MEET Anna Beth's perceptive gaze. She couldn't know the nights he hadn't slept, all too aware he'd be responsible if his grandson got killed in a war before he even came of age.

"What else do you want to know about Celina?" he asked, hoping Anna Beth wouldn't ask about Jordan. She'd come to her own conclusions, no matter what he said, and his grandson must have given her an earful. But the truth was, he hadn't been able to handle knowing he'd failed Jordan and had hoped the navy would give him something better.

"What do you want to tell me?"

Saul thought about it. "After our daughter started school, Celina wanted to learn how to pull a calf. I was teaching her when she got sick."

"You mean helping a cow deliver her baby. Do you need to do that very often?"

"Often enough, and more with heifers. That's a first-time mother. Longhorns don't have much trouble calving, but I can't see having them on the Soaring Hawk. Let 'em stay in Texas."

He went on reminiscing about his wife, saying things he'd kept in his heart since she was first diagnosed with leukemia. Things he hadn't even told Paige. How good Celina had been, how patient and brave, how he'd started missing her before she was gone and wished he had made the days they'd had together count for more.

Anna Beth kept working, nodding periodically and throwing out an occasional question. She'd already painted the high ceiling and two of the walls with impressive efficiency. He mused that a woman like her would have been a good partner on the ranch, a thought that seemed disloyal. Not that Celina had wanted him to remain alone; she'd urged him to remarry so their little girl would have a mother.

Celina would have liked his jailor and laughed at the way she kept putting him in his place.

"You haven't said anything for over five minutes," Anna Beth commented, breaking into his thoughts. "You can't have run out of things to talk about."

"I told you the most important parts." Saul felt at peace for the first time in a long while. Anna Beth was a good listener. "I've signed a paper for Jordan to show employees, saying he's in charge. Maybe you could take it to him when he gets back."

"You need to take it to him yourself."

Saul sighed. "My grandson doesn't want to see me."

"He would if you tell him about Paige's phone call yesterday."

That was true. Jordan's feelings toward Paige were a mystery, but he seemed fond of Mishka. He might want to hear how the little one's medical appointments had gone.

Saul got up. "I'm going to sit on the porch. You have paint on your nose."

Anna Beth's chuckle followed him through most of the house.

She had a good sense of humor for a jailor.

JORDAN WAS FRUSTRATED that he couldn't get Paige out of his mind, and equally frustrated to discover he missed her company while he was working on the Soaring Hawk.

He didn't need people. He was as close to being a loner as anyone he'd ever known. The navy could have stationed him in the Antarctic to count penguins and he would have been fine.

Friendship with Paige would be akin to walking in a minefield. His instinct was to protect her and Mishka, but how could he protect someone from getting a broken heart? Not to mention, Paige didn't seem to *want* protection. Clearly she wouldn't have minded having company in Seattle, but her family's needs and those of the Blue Banner had been more important.

Jordan hated that he found her so intriguing. She was skilled on horseback, active in community affairs and familiar with ranching—from the price of hay to the business end of a cow. She worked hard and didn't mind getting her hands or jeans dirty with a mucky task.

People adored Paige.

Next to her he felt like an ill-tempered clod. All of which made Jordan wonder if he actually *was* an ill-tempered clod. He didn't enjoy thinking he took after his grandfather, yet it seemed to be a distinct possibility.

A crow flew close overhead, cawing loudly, but Tornado didn't break step. Whatever Saul had paid for the stallion, he was worth every penny.

He kept wondering if his grandfather was trying to matchmake between him and Paige. The old man was crafty. But Paige had unequivocally said she wasn't interested in getting married and Jordan believed her. Somebody must have hurt her in the past, enough that she'd put aside the idea of a lifelong partner.

Jordan's stab of anger at the unknown man troubled him, though of all people, he knew how deep the unseen wounds could run. The astonishing part was that Paige was still open and caring. *Vulnerable* was the word that came first to mind. He just hoped she had learned to be more cautious.

As for Mishka asking if he could be her father?

His stomach swooped at the memory. It had reminded him that he wasn't daddy material. Yet for a brief moment, he'd wanted to be her father and Paige's husband more than anything he'd ever wanted in the world. But wanting something and knowing what was right were two different things.

"Home, Tornado," he said.

The stallion understood what "home" meant and his pace quickened. They'd just driven the last of the bulls up to summer pasture for mating. Jordan would give them a couple of months with the general herd before separating them again, which should make for a manageable calving season in the spring.

Cocky and anxious to answer the call of nature, the normally rambunctious bulls had proven little trouble to move. Maybe they'd understood what was ahead if they cooperated, most of them having gone through this process before.

Back at the main ranch, Jordan had put Tornado's saddle on the paddock fence when he saw his grandfather limping in his direction.

He gritted his teeth. While he didn't actively avoid Saul, he didn't make any effort to speak with him, either.

"Paige called yesterday," Saul said when he got close. "I thought you'd want to know that Mishka's appointments went well. She won't need the brace any longer."

"Is Paige concerned about the decision?" Jordan asked before he could restrain the question.

"Why should she be concerned?"

"I just wondered. It's a big step." Jordan didn't know if she'd been confiding a deep fear, or had merely felt a random stab of misgiving when she spoke about Mishka still seeming fragile. Most likely it was just a momentary thing since he couldn't see Paige sharing something deeply personal with him.

"It's an *important* step," Saul insisted. "We've been waiting for this after all those surgeries to her leg and the one on her heart. I would have danced a jig if my hip would have let me."

"What's wrong with Mishka's heart?" Jordan's own pulse surged as he remembered his mother. He hadn't known the little girl suffered from a cardiac issue and the knowledge was a cold slap in the face.

"She's fine now, except for keeping an eye on her," his grandfather said. "Paige explained how they fixed it. I just didn't understand the technical jargon. The important thing is that the doc says she isn't likely have more problems in the future." Saul held out an envelope. "I, uh, signed that paper for you.

You're right, new employees should be sure of who's boss. Makes things easier for everyone."

"Thanks."

Jordan put the envelope in his shirt pocket, deciding to read the document later. He'd cautiously worded his request to Saul, mindful of what Paige had asked about not embarrassing him. At first it had felt like he was prevaricating, but she was right. All he needed was something to assure employees that they wouldn't have to deal with his grandfather. Everything else was semantics.

"Is Paige coming over in the morning?" he asked, trying to sound offhand. He didn't think he'd succeeded.

"She'll try to drop by, but she has to meet with clients and see a few other folks. She's also taking Harriet Bannerman home and getting her settled."

"Then Mrs. Bannerman is feeling better," Jordan said, recalling what Paige had said about her grandmother's health.

"Sounds like it. Paige told me to remind you she'll be at the ranching association meeting tomorrow evening."

Jordan tried not to be disappointed that she wouldn't be coming in the morning. She didn't owe anything to him or the Soaring Hawk. As for the association meeting, his urgent need for ranch hands had overcome his reluctance about attending. He was also giving thought to Paige's comments about his demeanor.

Feeling foolish, he'd even spent a few minutes in front of a mirror, trying to relax his shoulders and practice smiling. Except he'd looked more like a wolf baring its teeth. Somehow, he didn't think having people see him as a wolf *or* a fool would help him get job applicants.

Life had been easier in the navy. Recruits got assigned to his team. They learned to work together. Orders were obeyed. Training was conducted. Missions were planned and executed. The work itself was complex, but the human dynamics within the navy were different from civilian life.

"Uh, yeah, I'm going to the meeting, too," Jordan said. "Paige thinks it would be helpful to meet some of the other ranchers in the county."

As soon as he'd asked his grandfather to sign a statement clarifying the Soaring Hawk's chain of command, Jordan had accepted he would be attending the ranching association meeting. So tomorrow he'd sort out the supplies for branding and vaccinating the calves, then he'd go into town and try not to act as if he had his hat in hand, asking for people to come work for him.

"Paige believes the association is important," Saul muttered. "She tried getting me to go. Almost talked me into it, then my hip got worse and I couldn't sit in those folding chairs they use while nattering on about stuff. Odds are the coffee isn't any better, either. Weak and watery."

For the first time that Jordan could remember, he and his grandfather shared a look of understanding. Paige had a way about her, a quiet obstinacy that was more effective than if she was loud and demanding.

"So I can look forward to uncomfortable chairs, endless talk and a bad cup of coffee," Jordan said lightly.

"That's the shape of things. My folks used to go, but I haven't been to a meeting since before I was married. Don't figure I missed much. Mark my words, they'll be talking about the annual rodeo and calf diseases, the same as they were sixty years ago."

Jordan grinned. "I'll let you know."

"Do that. Except for Paige being there, I

wouldn't have considered attending. She's a good kid."

Kid was almost right. Jordan's humor faded a little. He didn't remember Paige from the school bus, but he could imagine her there—ponytail, happy, giggling with her friends, totally unaware of the darker side of life. He *did* recall her brothers and older sister. The Bannermans were a close family. Even then he'd envied what they had together—everything he'd lost.

Now?

He sighed. Paige mentioned her family often, sometimes with exasperation and always with affection. He suspected big brothers could get on a sister's nerves, but they sounded happy. And though her grandfather was gone, her grandmother remained very much a part of her life.

Those kinds of ties still appealed, but Jordan was realistic. His brothers were in different parts of the world. They talked periodically and emailed or texted back and forth, but it wasn't as if they had what Paige and her family shared. Maybe he was to blame, as the eldest. Despite his grandfather, he could have done more to keep them closer, both as children and in the years since.

"Is something wrong?" Saul asked.

Curiously, Jordan didn't want to explain and sound as if he was putting blame on Saul. It was Paige's influence; she made him want to be a better man, and a better man wouldn't pile guilt on a grandfather who couldn't change the past.

"Nah. For future reference, I've moved the last of the bulls in with the cows up in summer grazing. I'll leave them there a couple of months."

"Good, good," Saul said. "I…" He cleared his throat. "I'm sorry things are in a bad state here on the ranch, they just got ahead of me. You're doing a fine job."

Jordan stared as his grandfather turned and walked back to the house. Praise? The old man had never offered a word of approval to him in his entire life, *or* admitted a weakness. It was like having his universe upended.

PAIGE ARRIVED EARLY at the Shelton Ranching Association meeting. She chatted with the different members, talking about Jordan and how hard he was working. She explained that she'd gone riding with him a number of times while he moved the herds to summer pasture and seen both his horse and cattle sense.

It was true, but he needed to be there himself to convince people he wanted to be part of the ranch community.

The meeting started without Jordan and she ground her teeth in disappointment. Just when she was giving up hope, the side door opened and he walked inside.

Some of the air whooshed from her lungs. Each time she saw him, he was more attractive. His hair had grown in the weeks since arriving and he no longer looked quite as military, but he still moved with a fluid confidence that was sexy and reassuring at the same time.

Several other women in the room had their gazes on him as well. At least one single woman looked starstruck. And others, if they weren't single, were probably calculating his potential for an unmarried family member or friend. Matchmaking was a popular local sport.

Don't get your hopes up, she wanted to tell them.

Fingers grasped her elbow and tugged.

"You didn't say he was an Adonis," whispered Suzie Anderson. "I am *so-o-o-o* asking him to dinner. I'll make my beef bourguignon and raspberry chocolate mousse cake. Guys are always impressed."

Suzie had moved to Shelton the previous summer when her sister married a rancher in the area. She taught at the grammar school, but came to the ranching association meetings in order to meet men. Blonde, curvy, with a bubbly personality, she was already popular, and Paige felt a flash of irritation that she'd set her sights on Jordan. It was silly and she immediately squashed the feeling.

"I hadn't thought of him as an Adonis, but he's good-looking," she agreed. "Very serious, of course."

"Yeah, and kind of old."

Paige felt her eyes widen. Jordan wasn't old. But Suzie was twenty-three and young for her age.

"Um, he's thirty-eight, I believe."

Suzie chewed the inside of her lip, still looking with longing at Jordan. "Does he like to party?"

"I'm afraid not." It was something Paige could answer with confidence. Jordan Maxwell wasn't a partier; he could barely manage a short conversation.

"Oh, well." Suzie looked around and saw

another cowboy winking at her. She winked back and seemed to forget Jordan.

Paige slid off her chair and walked around to the back of the hall. "Hey," she murmured to Jordan, who was looking as if he might turn and leave.

"Hi. I understand you got a positive report in Seattle."

She smiled brightly. "Yes. It's all good."

"I also heard your grandmother has improved."

"The doctor decided it was her blood-pressure medication making her dizzy. He adjusted the dose and she's doing much better."

"That's good news." Jordan gestured toward the crowded room and the speaker at the front. "How am I supposed to do this?"

"They're covering agenda items right now, but after that, the president will ask if there's any new business. I'll introduce you then. Explain Saul has given you full management of the ranch and you're looking for employees. Say if they know anyone available, you'd appreciate a referral to the Soaring Hawk."

Jordan frowned. "I'm not going to beg."

"Nobody said you were. Just try not to look as if you're preparing to attack a terrorist camp when you get up there. You know, grim and forbidding."

He made a disgusted sound. "Very amusing."

"Yeah, I can tell you're rolling with laughter. Come on, think about Mishka when I introduce you."

His expression softened. "All right."

Paige stayed next to him as the president explained they'd received the "All-Around Best Cowboy" and "All-Around Best Cowgirl" saddles for the rodeo. She whispered that each year the association donated the saddles to be awarded in both the adult and junior divisions of the upcoming rodeo. The president went on to explain the saddles were in the storage area if anyone wanted to inspect them. He then asked if anyone had encountered calf scours since the last meeting, and if so, what treatment had proven most successful.

Scours was a dreaded calf disease, normally seen in calves under a month old. It killed quickly and was hard to cure. Luckily none of the ranches had been badly affected this year, just a few calves born unusually late in the season, from one of the spreads on the eastern edge of the county.

Jordan seemed to be shaking next to her and she looked up to see suppressed amusement on his face.

There was absolutely *nothing* amusing about scours.

"Hey, what's up?" she asked softly, but he just shrugged.

"Private joke. Ask my grandfather."

Interesting. But at least he didn't look quite as intimidating when she introduced him a few minutes later.

In fact, he looked downright pleasant.

CHAPTER NINE

JORDAN DIDN'T KNOW if his efforts at the ranching association meeting had done any good, but he didn't have time to sit around, waiting to find out. The next morning he put a note on the main barn door in case anyone stopped by, saying to call his cell number if applying for employment, and kept working.

Saturday was the day he'd picked to start branding calves and he made his plans as if he wouldn't have any ranch hands by then. Doing it alone would be challenging, to say the least. One man setting up temporary pens in the summer grazing area, and then separating the calves from their mothers, followed by branding and vaccinating? With enough ranch hands they could do the job in a few days, but alone he might have to stretch branding over the summer to also allow mowing for hay.

He couldn't expect Paige to keep working with him. Saul might be a friend and honorary grandfather to Mishka, but that didn't give Paige more hours in the day. Despite his thoughts, Jordan stayed at the main ranch doing tasks, rather than leaving at first light.

An hour later than usual, Paige arrived.

He hated that it mattered to him.

Mother and daughter greeted Saul and Anna Beth on the porch, then Mishka spotted Jordan by the barn.

"See, Mr. Jordan?" she cried, running to him without a hint of the hesitation her leg brace had caused. "I'm all okay."

"You sure are." Jordan swung her into his arms, warmth crowding his chest. "Did you have a good time on your trip?"

"Uh-huh. Mama and me went to…" She scrunched up her face and looked at Paige, who'd followed close behind.

"The Pacific Science Center," she said.

"That sounds like fun," Jordan told Mishka. "But are you happy to be home?"

"Yes, cuz I get to ride my horse now."

Paige's face was wry as her daughter chattered about her plans for the summer, which included lots of horseback riding, then gently reminded her that she still needed more lessons.

"Gampa is going to teach me."

"Grandpa is really busy right now, but we're all going to give you lessons and help you practice. Me, your uncles, Grandma and Grandpa."

"I know." Mishka wiggled and Jordan put her down. She ran back to the porch and climbed up on Saul's knee, giving him another kiss on his cheek.

"My grandfather is crazy about that child," Jordan murmured.

"I can't blame him, but I'm biased. What are we doing today?" Paige asked.

He looked at her. She was dressed for work as usual, yet he hesitated. "Don't you need to rest after your trip?"

"It was hardly a marathon voyage. Besides, I had a light day yesterday and must have slept for twelve hours on Monday night at the hotel. You're still getting ready for branding, right? Before I left, you mentioned Saturday was your target date."

Jordan nodded. "That's right. I've already delivered a load of fence panels to the summer grazing area. I'll bring more up there today. I'm hoping to make a couple more trips and get the temporary pens set up in the afternoon."

"Great, I just want to be sure Anna Beth

didn't have other plans. If she does, I'll run Mishka back to the Blue Banner first."

She went over to the house and talked again with Anna Beth and Saul before bending to hug her daughter.

Jordan's throat tightened at the sight. He was growing a little too fond of the mother and child.

"So what did the doctors say?" he asked when they were in the truck. He had to drive slowly; the dirt track wasn't too rough, but there were gopher holes.

"Mostly checkups from now on," Paige explained. "With a few trips in between to the local clinic. I'll keep bringing her to Seattle annually because they know her history inside and out, but it's the best news I could have gotten."

"What about the cardiologist?"

From the corner of his eye, he saw Paige jump. "Who told you about that?"

"Saul. He mentioned it was a routine appointment."

"It was. Mishka had a congenital heart defect they corrected when she was a baby. They're careful monitoring her, especially because of the surgeries on her leg, and she'll have to be aware of it as she grows up. But I don't want it defining her life."

Jordan waited a long minute. "Why didn't you mention the cardiologist when you told me about the trip to Seattle?"

"I'm not sure." Paige sighed. "No, that isn't true. I'm used to all of this—if you can ever get used to your child going through surgery and having that kind of problem—but I thought it might be upsetting because of your mother. A reminder of a sad time you didn't need. You're already dealing with a lot, coming back after so long."

Jordan wasn't accustomed to people trying to protect him and it gave him an odd sensation. "That was thoughtful, but I'm fine. And I'm glad Mishka is all right."

The truck jounced and Paige braced herself with the grip handle above the door. "Me, too. Now tell me what was so funny last night. I asked Saul and he said he couldn't explain."

"It's just something he told me before I went to the meeting, that the agenda used to be mostly about the rodeo and calf diseases. Turns out, that's *still* the agenda."

Jordan looked at Paige long enough to see the cute way she always scrunched her nose.

"They're important topics."

"I'm not saying they aren't, but apparently nothing has changed in sixty years."

PAIGE DIDN'T MIND the teasing note in Jordan's voice. "Ranching hasn't changed that much, either," she said mildly. "The rodeo is a big deal, bigger now than ever, and we're still fighting scours and other problems."

"I studied calf diseases as part of my college studies and have tried to keep up with the current information, but I'm not looking forward to an outbreak."

"My dad thinks thoroughly cleaning the calving barn helps. After we had a particularly bad season, he even built a second barn, so we could alternate between using one and sterilizing the other during calving season."

"That won't be possible on the Soaring Hawk. At least not for a while."

"He admits that two calving barns are excessive, but he was upset about the outbreak. We lost a large number of calves. Ranchers are well-acquainted with death, but that doesn't mean we like it." Paige pursed her lips, suddenly curious. "Why did you study animal sciences and ranch management? I can't imagine they're subjects that benefit the navy, even if some of those ships are large enough to carry a herd of dairy cows."

Jordan shrugged. "My commanding officer told me he cared less about what I studied than proving I was willing and able to learn. I always planned to come back to Montana eventually, though it had nothing to do with the Soaring Hawk. My brothers and I own our dad's spread, basically getting it for the unpaid taxes. Dad tried to sell the Circle M, but he'd let it get too rundown. That's why my lawyer specified the northern third of the ranch to be the land Saul puts in a trust. The property adjoins there."

The revelation made Paige's jaw drop and she tried to recover her aplomb. "I don't think I'll share that piece of information with him."

"Thanks. I'm not sure how he'll react if he learns my dad's ranch will be connected to the Soaring Hawk in common ownership. Basically, they were sworn enemies."

Paige focused forward, trying not to wonder if it meant anything that Jordan had confided in her. The beginnings of trust, maybe? Anna Beth had mentioned he was accustomed to keeping most things to himself, partly because of his years in Special Forces.

As for Saul, she didn't think he held any

lingering resentment toward his former son-in-law, but he might be discouraged if he thought Jordan wasn't entirely relying on the deal they'd struck. The Circle M wasn't a bad ranch and while it had been neglected for a long time, it had a fair amount of quality pasture. The leases to any rangeland must have expired, but Jordan might be able to do something about that.

One plus was that the Soaring Hawk had more leased rangeland than it needed and the permits would likely convey to a new owner when the time came. If Jordan's lawyer was any good, he or she would have nailed that down before the contract was signed, including whether any stock was part of the deal.

"Do you mind me asking how detailed your agreement is with Saul?" she asked. "I understand if you'd prefer not answering, but what affects one ranch has a tendency to affect all of us."

Jordan dropped the truck to an even slower pace as the rough track rose higher into the hills.

"The paperwork was comprehensive. I hired a lawyer in Bozeman who deals with cattle ranches to go over it and handle the negotiations. While she asked for minor changes, there weren't any obscure legal backdoors Saul could use to wiggle out of what we'd agreed."

"I don't think he was interested in back-doors."

"Maybe, but I couldn't take the chance."

They got to the boundary fence and Paige promptly got out to open the wire gate. After Jordan had driven through, she pulled it into place and hopped back in the truck. It was the best way to speed things up, but he didn't seem to appreciate the effort.

"Are you sexist, or still clinging to your rugged individualism?" she asked at his tight-lipped expression.

"I'm not a sexist," he returned, looking offended. "Ask Sarge. I'm all for letting women serve as SEALs or doing whatever they're capable of doing."

"Then rugged individualist it is. Sooner or later you'll have to accept that we're in this together. I mean, all of the ranchers in the area, not you and me," she clarified hastily. "All of Montana, for that matter."

"I've taken your help, haven't I?"

"You were unhappy about Saul making me his observer and you still get touchy about me doing stuff."

Jordan rolled his eyes. "Because it's my responsibility and you can't work as a ranch hand at the same time you're taking care of your clients and daughter and everything else. It isn't fair to you."

Hmm.

"That's sweet, but I'm fine."

Paige debated whether she should tell him about the community work day she was arranging, but maybe she should leave it as a surprise. Attendees at the ranching association meeting had been impressed with Jordan, so she'd started a phone chain this morning, asking everyone to gather at the Soaring Hawk on Saturday to help with branding and vaccinating calves. Because it was traditional for the host ranch to feed the crowd, she and her mother were cooking the food, along with Anna Beth if she wanted to be involved.

If Paige hadn't immediately started the ball rolling, a work day would have had to wait. Shelton Rodeo Daze was next week and it wouldn't be right to ask ranchers to come during the huge event. The rodeo was one of the few times in the busy spring and summer months that they relaxed from the pressures of ranching. Not that they wouldn't enjoy getting together with neighbors to accomplish a task, all the while visiting and eating volumes of food. And it would be a good beginning to the rodeo festivities.

Paige glanced at Jordan, remembering something else she needed to know before Saturday. "I've been wondering if you've ever heard of freeze branding."

"Sure. Research suggests it could be easier on the calves than hot branding, if slightly more expensive. But I'll need to have special branding irons made. I plan to check in to it for next year, provided I'm still here. Liam will make that decision."

"I'm sure Liam thinks you're doing a good job. He was pleased with your progress when he came over last week, right?" she asked in a rush. "Anyway, I've checked the Soaring Hawk branding irons. They aren't ideal for freeze branding, but usable."

Jordan gave her a narrow look. "You've checked our branding irons?"

"Two or three years ago. I was trying to talk Saul into switching. We used freeze branding on the Blue Banner. My dad is a firm believer. We were the first ranch in the county to start."

"Then I'll consult with him once the pressure is over. Right now I have to just focus on getting the branding done. I can't afford any delays."

"I understand," she said, knowing Scott Bannerman would bring supplies for freeze branding to the work day. Her family and every employee on the Blue Banner were experienced with the process, along with a few other ranchers in the area. Now she'd just have to come up with a way to convince Jordan to accept everything from the supplies to his neighbors' participation.

But since Liam Flannigan had enthusiastically agreed to be there with his granddaughter and grandson-in-law, the day should be a success. Surely he'd tell Jordan that he approved of cooperation between ranchers. Mutual help and support was how Shelton had survived through all the good times and the bad.

Besides, Jordan would get an earful from her if he didn't behave himself.

"WHAT ARE YOU DOING?" Saul demanded on Friday evening.

Anna Beth kept working. "Cooking."

"For the entire US Marine Corps? You've

chopped so many onions, my eyes are burning from the porch."

"Don't exaggerate. Did you take the calcium and vitamin D that I put on your tray? Because I know you've been hiding your vitamins in the chair. You wouldn't want Paige to find out."

"You'd tell her? What am I saying—of course you would."

Anna Beth gave him a stern look. "No, I wouldn't, but I'd tell the doctor. You don't want your old bones crumbling into dust."

She chuckled as he stomped away. Saul's bark was decidedly worse than his bite, and beneath that crusty exterior was a decent human being. It didn't excuse the way he'd treated his grandsons, but forgiveness on that score wasn't up to her.

As for the way he talked about his wife?

She sighed, undeniably wistful. If a man had ever loved her half as much, she would have married him in a cold minute, no matter what it did to her future in the military.

Well, that was life.

She'd had a successful career and was on a new venture, one where she could focus on helping Jordan. She'd been reading about ranching every night on her phone when she went to bed and knew there was plenty she could do, even if she didn't know how to ride horses and rope cattle.

Anna Beth looked out the kitchen windows. Open land stretched as far as she could see to the east, the grass rippling in the wind. It reminded her of the ocean, with its restless waves. After enlisting she'd rarely lived away from the sea, but she felt the appeal of this place. Montana's open skies and wide prairies could reach into your soul, the same as the ocean.

She could even see growing fond of Saul, though it was less easy to see the old codger returning the emotion. The yearning in his voice when he talked about Celina was palpable; as if his heart had been buried with his young wife.

Or was it?

He genuinely cared about Paige and Mishka, and Anna Beth thought he might have affection for Jordan, too. If Saul could open his heart it would be best for him and all of his grandsons. Though, admittedly, it was Jordan's future Anna Beth was most concerned about.

"What are you making anyhow?" Saul

asked, reappearing at the kitchen door. "You've been cooking all day."

"Right now I'm doing chili and corn bread. A group of ranchers are coming to help with the branding tomorrow. Paige and her family set everything up. It's a surprise, so don't tell Jordan," she added when a frown grew on Saul's face.

"Then nobody has applied for a job."

"Not that I know of, but Paige says most of the ranchers get together and help each other with branding. Why don't you help me finish cooking for the big do?"

Saul blinked at her. "Can't make chili worth a darn, though I fed the boys plenty of the canned stuff when they were kids. Later Dakota and Wyatt started cooking and the chow got better. I'm lousy in the kitchen."

"I happen to be a great chili chef. You can sit at the table and finish the chopping. That doesn't take any skill."

Anna Beth mixed the last batch of corn bread and put it in the oven. The Bannermans were bringing beverages and side dishes, along with ribs, hamburgers and chicken to barbecue, but she'd insisted on doing the chili, corn bread, snacks and breakfast burritos. It was no big deal. There couldn't be a marine alive, woman *or* man, who hadn't gotten used to peeling spuds and washing dishes at some point in their career.

"A big chili cook-off takes place during the Shelton Rodeo Daze," Saul said as he cut green peppers. "That'll be on Tuesday. You have to make enough for visitors to each have a sample."

"I'll keep it in mind for next year." Entering the contest might be fun, but Anna Beth wouldn't have participated, even if there was enough time to prepare. She'd want to learn more about the area first; it would be easy to step on someone's toes in a small town.

She washed dry pinto beans and put them into two covered roasters with a good amount of onions, peppers and tomatoes. Once the other baking was done, the beans would cook overnight at a low temperature in the oven. In the morning she'd combine them with thirty pounds of seasoned diced steak and more vegetables. The amount was more chili than Paige had suggested making, but Anna Beth figured leftovers could be frozen or sent home with people. Better than running short.

Over at the table, Saul mumbled something about his arthritis.

"You don't have to help," she told him.

"Nah, I'll manage. I just have to make my fingers do what I tell 'em."

Making the effort was important and he wasn't doing a terrible job, arthritis or not.

"When you're done, I have molasses cookie dough you can roll into balls for baking."

"That's fine, but don't you think Jordan will wonder what all this cooking is for?"

"Jordan won't know, he's out on his horse," Anna Beth said, annoyed. Paige had worked with Jordan most of the day rounding up the first batch of cows for branding, but after she'd left with Mishka, he had immediately ridden out again. He hadn't even stopped long enough for a meal, which was exasperating. Anna Beth knew he didn't want to sit down with his grandfather, but she'd put food in his quarters. The least he could do was eat it.

"*Ma-r-rr-o-ow*?" said an inquiring feline voice.

"Get that creature out of here," Saul ordered, glaring at the ginger tabby who'd gotten into the habit of sneaking a snuggle with Anna Beth after she'd gone to bed.

"I will not." She scooped the cat into her arms and Marmalade began purring like a perfectly tuned motor.

"I said I won't have cats in the house."

"Stop being difficult. They're just too self-sufficient for your tastes because they don't take orders and can't be herded like cows."

"They aren't the only one who won't take orders," he said pointedly.

Anna Beth grinned. She'd given her share of commands as a master sergeant, but she didn't have a huge need for control.

"Give Marmalade a chance. Charming fellows such as yourself need all the friends they can get."

Saul gave her a dour look and bent his head again over the peppers.

Anna Beth sent the ginger tabby on its way, washed her hands and donned a fresh apron before blending a third batch of dough for buttermilk donut bars. The house was fragrant with all the baking she'd finished in the last two days. Though large quantities of cookies sat on the old farm sideboard, she'd decided buttermilk donut bars would be a good thing to offer the volunteer crews midmorning. She wouldn't fry them until tomorrow to ensure they were extra fresh.

From what Paige had said, there would be groups working on branding, while others rounded up the cattle scattered across summer grazing. Families would be coming as well. The work day should help Jordan catch up, and he might gain a few employees if he impressed them sufficiently with his leadership.

Anna Beth stopped stirring as she contemplated whether it was a good idea to surprise Jordan with the neighborly work day. He could handle an emergency in the blink of an eye, but this was different. On the other hand, he was so stubborn, he might refuse to let anyone come if he found out ahead of time. Surely once they were there, his command instincts would kick into gear. Besides, she had faith that Paige could bring him in line.

THE NEXT MORNING Jordan was in the barn when he heard vehicles arriving. He knew Paige had already gotten there and went out to see what was going on.

Trucks were parking around the barn and more were coming down the ranch road, their headlights bright in the early dawn. Most seemed to be hauling horse trailers.

Paige came racing over to him, at the same time waving at the newcomers.

"What's going on?" Jordan demanded in a low voice.

"Your neighbors are here to help with the Soaring Hawk branding and vaccinating. We've arranged food and everything else that's needed."

He stared. "How? I didn't ask them to come."

"*I* asked and they were delighted to participate. Hey, Bill," she called to a man walking toward them. "Jordan, you remember Bill Gorson from the Shelton Ranching Association meeting the other night. He's our president this year."

Jordan stiffened. "I'm sorry, Mr. Gorson, but I really don't think—" He stopped when Paige dug an elbow into his side. He glared at her.

"Stop shooting yourself in the foot," she hissed softly, "and start deciding where you want the crews to work. This is your chance to show what kind of foreman you can be."

"Paige, I can't—"

"Yes, you *can*." She stepped forward, smiling at Bill Gorson with the full force of her personality. "It's great you could come on short notice, especially with the rodeo festivities starting next week."

"Our pleasure. Jordan. Paige and Liam

Flannigan have been telling us good things about your work here on the Soaring Hawk."

"Er, thanks."

"Jordan is doing a terrific job," Paige said easily.

She went on, charming the gathering crowd, explaining a five-gallon dispenser for coffee was on the porch, along with breakfast burritos and other goodies. Everybody was urged to eat and drink their fill and take whatever appealed for later munching, though more treats would be coming throughout the day. She then shooed them toward the food and beverages, saying they couldn't work on empty stomachs.

When they were alone, she grabbed Jordan by the arm. "Listen to me, Liam is here with his granddaughter and grandson-in-law," she said in a low, urgent voice. "We attend work days at his ranch and he reciprocates. This is something neighbors do. Your grandfather even helped Anna Beth with the food."

Saul?

Jordan frowned.

"Nobody can do this entirely alone," Paige continued without giving him a chance to speak. "We all know it, so get off your high horse. Overinflated pride is a stupid thing to choke on."

"But it isn't practical. We only moved a small herd to the branding area yesterday. The rest are scattered across the ranch's summer grazing."

"That's all right. At least fifty adults are coming with their horses and dogs. Some of them can work on rounding up the cows and their calves. They're also bringing more fence panels to set up pens for a second branding team. And my father has his freeze branding supplies, so you'll be able to see how the process works."

Jordan shook his head. "No."

"*Yes*. This is another chance for Dad to demonstrate how freeze branding works," she argued. "He'll be able to show it off to a variety of ranchers, from traditional to modern. You'll be doing him a favor."

Jordan wasn't sure if he wanted to yell or kiss Paige. She made everything sound so reasonable. Fifty or more? How could there be that many neighbors willing to come help the Soaring Hawk after Saul's behavior over the last five decades?

"These people don't know me," he said. "They didn't care about us before, why do something for me and the Soaring Hawk now?"

Paige pulled him back into the barn. "Jordan, I get you're angry that nobody stopped Saul from taking you away from your father, but it's hard knowing the right thing to do in child-custody situations. Stop blaming people for something they didn't understand, or else felt they shouldn't interfere with. You don't have all the facts and it was a long time ago."

His breath hissed out. He wanted to deny the accusation, but she might be right. There was still a part of him, deep inside, that felt if the community hadn't stopped Saul from taking them away from their father, he couldn't trust them now.

But the truth was, Evan Maxwell *had* been drinking heavily, though he hadn't been abusive otherwise. Maybe he would have straightened himself out if he'd had his kids there, and maybe not. Dakota and Wyatt didn't know about their dad's arrests for drunk driving and bar fights, but Jordan did. Compared to Saul's respectability, Evan's record would have looked pretty damning in family court. It might explain why he hadn't shown up for the hearing, because he'd known there wasn't much point.

Jordan closed his eyes briefly and Paige put a hand on his arm.

"Can't you see everyone is rooting for you to succeed, including Saul?" she whispered. "Fifty people working together can get much more done in one day than you could do alone in a hundred. The whole is greater than the parts, isn't that what they taught us in school?"

The sound of additional vehicles arriving forced Jordan to focus on the present, rather than the past. Refusing help from his fellow ranchers would be petty and rude at this point.

"All right. I have to get out there and establish a plan of action. You can explain later why you didn't tell me ahead of time about inviting half the county to the Soaring Hawk."

He hesitated, then gave in to temptation and cupped Paige's jaw with his hand, dropping a swift, thorough kiss on her mouth. She looked shocked when he lifted his head, but at least she didn't slap his face.

"Uh, okay. These are your neighbors, be nice to them," she ordered.

Jordan was tempted to ask when he hadn't been nice, but he was afraid she might tell him.

PAIGE'S ENTIRE BODY TINGLED.

She'd never experienced so much electricity from a single kiss and was disconcerted at feeling that way now.

Get a grip, she told herself.

It didn't mean anything. Jordan had been clear about his vision for the future and it didn't include the kind of relationship she would want.

Maybe she was just unsettled because of the email she'd gotten a few days ago from the adoption agency. Mishka's uncle had written, asking how she was doing. Paige had heard stories of children being returned to their biological family and it was impossible not to wonder if she might be facing a legal challenge to the adoption. But how could she have ignored the request? A man was suffering, unsure if his niece was all right after having so many health issues. He knew she'd been adopted, but wouldn't have heard anything since then.

Outside Paige heard Jordan's voice, clear and authoritative above the chatter, and the sound of horses being saddled. Collecting her composure, she went to the barn door and looked out. He was forming crews for the various tasks and some of the ranchers were already on horseback or preparing to drive their horses to the summer grazing area.

To an outsider, branding after moving the herds might not make sense, except the cattle *had* to reach summer pastures as quickly as possible. Otherwise you could end up having to feed them valuable hay or graze them on the grass you needed to mow for winter. Besides, generally calves weren't old enough for branding until after they were moved.

Ranching was a balancing act and there was always so much to do. Paying too many cowhands—though usually a shortage of labor was the problem—ate in to profits. "We get one big payday a year," her father liked to remind everyone on the Blue Banner. So it was a sensible choice for ranchers to band together on certain tasks.

Jordan glanced back at her in a quieter moment and lifted an eyebrow.

Was he already regretting his kiss?

Paige tried not to reveal what she was feeling on her face, but how could she be sorry about a kiss that put all other kisses in the dark? Jordan probably had more experience in that area, so it wasn't a big deal to him. Or he could be thinking he had to "warn" her again that he wasn't interested in marriage.

Problem was, she might be changing her own mind on the subject.

CHAPTER TEN

SINCE PAIGE WAS the one who'd invited the ranchers to the Soaring Hawk, she felt as if basic hostess duties rested on her. So she tried to put Jordan's kiss and other concerns from her mind.

Luckily the Blue Banner had been involved in countless work days over the years. They had stacks of ice chests for food and beverages, five-gallon insulated coffee dispensers and a massive barbecue unit they could tow behind a truck, large enough to create a feast.

She loved every minute of community gatherings, whether it was haying or branding, or just to socialize.

But branding was a particularly chaotic time with calves squalling and mama cows bellowing displeasure at the temporary separation. To reduce stress on the calves, teams coordinated to brand and vaccinate in the shortest time possible. There was plenty of action to go around.

It was also a family affair and Paige hoped Jordan would be able to deal with kids running about, asking questions and offering to help. This was partly how they learned to be ranchers. She'd begun roping and dragging calves to the branding teams before she was ten. Mishka was already practicing with a lightweight rope on the kitchen chairs, determined to become part of the operation as soon as possible.

"I'll make the first run up to the temporary pens area with the coffee, sodas and donuts," she told her mother and Anna Beth, who were chatting and cooking together as if they'd been friends for life. Mishka had wanted to help fry the donut bars, but she was too young to be around hot oil, so she and Saul had been assigned to glazing them when cool enough.

"I wanna go, too," Mishka cried.

"So do I," Saul said, getting up.

Oh, dear.

Paige had an immediate vision of Saul at the branding pens, barking orders and countermanding his grandson. He was much better off staying at the house with Anna Beth.

They were a good pair, though Paige wasn't

sure they'd recognized the affection growing between them.

She cleared her throat. "Saul, I thought you weren't going to get involved in Soaring Hawk management in order to give Jordan a clear field to operate. Today of all days, everybody needs to see he's in charge, with no challenges to his authority."

"I'm not going to challenge him, I just want to watch what's going on. And this way I can prove I won't be sticking my nose in where it isn't needed. I won't even get out of the car."

She couldn't refuse. The longing in Saul's face was palpable. He'd lived his whole life to the rhythm of ranching, and now age and infirmity were keeping him on the sidelines.

Paige loaded coffee, food and an ice chest into the SUV before buckling Mishka into her car seat, warning her that she'd have to stay in the car with Saul. There was no way Paige would allow her daughter to run around while branding was going on, not yet. Saul got into the Volvo with difficulty, but she didn't offer her assistance, knowing he'd be offended. When she took him to medical appointments at the clinic, she borrowed her mom's car because it had a lower seat.

The makeshift dirt track to the branding

area was heavily marked now with the number of vehicles and horse trailers driven up it that morning. She would be going back and forth all day, bringing fresh coffee, sodas and snacks. Saul grunted a couple of times when a wheel hit a deeper rut and the vehicle jounced, but he set his jaw and didn't complain. Mishka just giggled. She was eager to visit one of the permanent theme parks in California and never failed to remind her "uncas" of their promise to take her on a big roller coaster someday. In the meantime, she would have to be content with the kiddie rides at the Shelton Rodeo Daze carnival each year.

Paige loved the way her brothers fought over who got to take Mishka on the Ferris wheel or buy her ice-cream cones and other treats. They'd be doting fathers. Her middle brother had come close. The family had adored his wife, but everything fell apart a few months after the wedding; Zack and Carla were the only ones who knew the reason. Maybe they'd just been too young.

Ugh.

Paige tried to think of something else. Today of all days she couldn't afford to dwell on a sad memory.

"I almost forgot how far it was to summer grazing," Saul commented.

"For some reason it seems longer in the truck, but we're almost there."

Paige parked at a good vantage point for Saul to watch.

First, she exchanged the five-gallon container of coffee on the tailgate of Jordan's truck with one filled with fresh brew, then brought the ice chest and donuts over, along with more cups and other supplies. One advantage of Jordan's red truck was that it stood out against the other more soberly colored vehicles. Everyone would know where to find refreshments.

Her tasks done, she went over to the temporary corral to watch her father demonstrate freeze branding. The old-timers were pooh-poohing it as usual, but Jordan discussed the process with him for a few minutes and agreed to use the Blue Banner's supplies, provided the Soaring Hawk repaid the cost. Paige was thrilled and could see her father and brothers were also pleased. They'd embraced the method with a passion.

At a good point in the proceedings she called out there was coffee, soda and freshly made buttermilk donut bars in the back of

Jordan's red truck, then returned to her SUV to sit and watch with Saul and Mishka. The group of calves that she and Jordan had moved the previous day were swiftly separated from their mothers, given their shots, branded and released again.

Saul watched thoughtfully. And, more important, he didn't try to get out of the SUV. He simply watched and nodded at his fellow ranchers when they tipped their hats in his direction. Some looked surprised, but she didn't know if it was because Saul had acknowledged them in return, or because he wasn't trying to take over or ordering them away from the Soaring Hawk.

Shelton ranchers were a strong bunch, but there was a certain amount of caution in how they regarded Saul Hawkins, and Jordan by extension. Still, attendees at the ranching association meeting had liked Jordan and she hoped today would reinforce it. So far everything looked promising. A surprise work day might not have been the best idea to spring on him, but she'd been certain he would take command and delegate. He inspired confidence.

In her, at least.

During the lull of waiting for the next

group of calves to arrive, the volunteers and their kids went over to get beverages and snacks. Later Paige would bring up a load of sandwiches. With so many people working on different tasks, there'd be a steady flow of takers.

Just then she saw a notorious local layabout, Norm Landers, talking to Jordan. She jumped out again and hurried over to hear Norm asking about the possibility of employment on the Soaring Hawk. Jordan caught her gaze and she gave him a small shake of the head.

"I appreciate the inquiry," he told Norm. "I have job applications back at the main ranch and you're welcome to complete one after the branding is done."

Jordan walked over to Paige.

"I take it Norm is a problem," he said in a quiet tone.

"Only if you want him to work. If you want to pay him for lying under a tree all day, then he's your guy."

Jordan chuckled, making her tingle through every inch of her body. What would he do if she invited another kiss? The one this morning had been a great distraction to other concerns But it was more than that. Jordan had made her feel something she'd have a hard time forgetting.

"I appreciate the warning," he murmured. "I'll talk to you before making any job offers. Do you have a recommendation on Melody James?"

"You'd be lucky to get her. Melody has competed in both the junior and adult rodeos. She's never won top honors, but she has all the skills you need and is very responsible. Right now she's a cowhand on her uncle's ranch. The Big Jumbo is located on the southern tip of the county, closest to Bozeman."

"Why doesn't she keep working for her uncle?"

Paige made a face. "Because he sold the Big Jumbo to an out-of-state corporation that's turning it into a hobby ranch for executive vacations. They're even putting in a small airfield. Basically, there will be horses to ride and enough cattle to make the place picturesque. Most of the cowhands are remaining as general employees of the corporation, but Melody would rather be on a working ranch. I should have thought of her as a potential employee when I heard about the sale going through."

"SHE SOUNDS LIKE a winner." Jordan's opinion of Norm Landers hadn't been good, but he urgently needed cowhands and might have taken a chance on hiring him without Paige's warning. "I don't think Saul has ever employed women, so I'll have to figure out housing. Pretty sure the bunkhouse can be divided into two sections, one for men and the other for women. There are doors and a bathroom on both ends of the building, so major remodeling shouldn't be required."

The bathrooms were utilitarian but functional as far as he knew, the same as the one in the foreman's quarters. They dated back to his great-grandfather's day, which meant the plumbing and fixtures would have to be upgraded at some point. Another item for the to-do list, which was growing longer every minute.

"That's a good idea," Paige agreed. "Maybe the dining hall could be used as an employee relaxation and lounge area. You might also consider buying food supplies to stock the dining-hall kitchen. Incentives are a big help in keeping employees. We get weekly deliveries from a grocery supplier at the Blue Banner and you're welcome to piggyback on our order. You'll get a bigger discount."

He nodded.

She seemed to squirm a little. "And, um, I want to apologize for putting you on the spot about today. I shouldn't have presumed. I get excited and jump right in. The ranching association liked how you presented yourself at the meeting and I was trying to build on that. With the rodeo coming, it had to be done right away, or be put off for at least two weeks."

Jordan wanted to laugh. The day was turning into a huge success and Paige was apologizing? "Don't worry about it. If I can't handle an unexpected crew, I would have been a lousy SEAL."

It was true. After spending over half his life in the navy, Jordan was accustomed to challenges. Also to having his performance evaluated. It didn't bother him. He was tougher on himself than anyone else could be, which was why he hadn't been overly concerned about his agreement with Saul, other than ensuring it was aboveboard.

Today he knew the ranchers and cowhands were evaluating his performance as a potential boss, which was appropriate. Respect went two ways. This was his opportunity to show he could be a decent foreman on the

Soaring Hawk. Jordan didn't think Saul had wanted to be a bad boss, but he'd tried to run the Soaring Hawk with an iron fist, the way ranches were run in early days of the west. Ranching still required tough-minded people, but times had changed when it came to what employees had a right to expect.

"I'll need to reciprocate," he said. "Hopefully it won't be until next year when things are sorted out more on the Soaring Hawk."

"Don't worry, they know what you're up against. You'll lend a hand when you're able to afford the time."

A "ch-ch-ch," sounded in the distance along with the rumble of hooves and assorted other shouts. Memories stirred in Jordan of past gatherings and his mother's humor at the mixed cries of *heys*, *hiyas*, moos, yodels and the other ways ranchers called to cattle and moved them along.

Usually when he thought about his mom, he remembered her being sick, but that wasn't right. Victoria Maxwell had been a happy woman. Though she'd missed her father after he cut her out of his life, she hadn't dwelled on it.

A herd came over the hill, driven forward by the volunteers on horseback and their dogs. It would be the first of many groups they brought in.

"I'd better go," Paige said. "Mom and Anna Beth will want to start refilling the coffee dispenser, and you have calves to take care of."

"Er, yeah. Thanks for bringing the food and stuff."

"No problem. I'll be back before long. These folks have big appetites." She gave him a smile and returned to her SUV.

Jordan didn't understand how amid all the noise and bustle of people and animals, she suddenly felt like an oasis of calm.

His oasis.

No matter what was going on, there was a core of peace inside of Paige that seemed to reach out and envelop him.

He growled at himself and tried to dismiss the thought. A man with his history didn't have any business seeing a woman that way. Paige was too special; the possibility of hurting her was too great.

And he most definitely shouldn't have kissed her. It was frustrating that such an innocent embrace was sticking with him, yet he couldn't stop remembering how soft her lips had been, or how much he'd wanted to hold her even closer.

Jordan rubbed the back of his neck as he watched Paige maneuver the SUV around. Mishka and his grandfather both waved. It was remarkable that Saul hadn't gotten out to shout orders and confuse everything. Could he actually be mellowing in his old age?

Jordan would have said it was impossible, but if any mellowing was taking place, it must be Paige's doing. He was starting to think she could work miracles—and it was even more tempting to wish she'd work a few inside him.

THE BARBECUE THAT evening brought more memories back to Jordan, things he hadn't thought about in so long, it was as if they'd happened to another person. He'd let life on the Soaring Hawk overshadow the good times with his parents, but now they kept flooding his mind. Yet he also felt guilty, knowing that he should have helped his younger brothers remember their mother and father better, rather than always dwelling on the bad.

The ranchers and cowhands who'd come to help with branding weren't all strangers. He recalled a few of them from his childhood, like Paige's three brothers. The Bannerman sons took after Scott Bannerman, who was tall, lean and capable. The four men rotated working the grill, putting out burgers, chicken and ribs, while Margaret Bannerman and Sarge kept the food tables otherwise supplied.

Paige never appeared to rush, but she seemed to be everywhere at once, chatting with guests, helping with the food, or smoothing an awkward moment when Jordan wasn't sure what to say to the gregarious ranchers and their families. Some of them took the opportunity to consult her on business matters and it was clear how much she was respected.

She also managed to be close by when five more potential cowhands asked about job openings on the Soaring Hawk. Four received a discreet nod of approval from her; another got a subtle thumbs-down.

It made sense. Paige did ranch accounting and was active in the ranching association. She'd know who had a good reputation and who didn't.

Perhaps she wasn't as naive as Jordan had originally thought; he'd certainly enjoyed her wry humor when talking about Norm Landers. *If you want to pay him for lying under a tree all day, then he's your guy.* She loved

Shelton and its residents, but she was aware of her neighbors' faults.

"Hey, Paige, why'd you only get light beer?" one of the young men called as he filled his cup from a keg.

"Because you can't handle the fully loaded stuff," she retorted.

"She just doesn't want you getting tipsy and proposing again," someone else chimed in. "Jordan, maybe you'll have more luck at wooing Paige than the rest of us. We don't want her to meet someone from outside of the county and leave. That would be a disaster."

It was just good-natured teasing, but Jordan was interested to see the pink deepen in Paige's cheeks.

"Enough, or you won't get any more light beer, either. I'll break the tap on the keg if I have to," she threatened.

Chuckles rippled through the relaxed crowd. Someone was playing a guitar and a group was tossing horseshoes in an impromptu horseshoe pit. Over on the porch, Sarge had convinced Saul to play checkers. A hot competition had ensued, with one cowboy after another queuing up to play. So far Saul had beaten all challengers. He had also gotten into a long discussion about freeze branding with Scott Bannerman—not a debate, a real conversation.

Jordan wondered if it was really that easy. All those years of keeping everyone at a distance, and in a day the barriers were gone?

The men who'd teased Paige were drifting away, presumably to get more beer or food. He stepped closer to her. "Where's Mishka? I saw her eating earlier and thought she was going to fall asleep over her ice cream."

"Over ice cream? Not a chance," Paige scoffed. "She stayed awake long enough to finish two bowls and a slice of chocolate cake. But it's been a long, exciting day and she's asleep in the SUV. I made a nest of pillows and blankets in the back since it's easier to keep an eye on her there. Anna Beth and my family keep going to check, too."

"Mishka sure wants to get involved in everything."

"Yeah." Paige hesitated. "I'm sorry you had to hear those jokes about marriage and wooing. They kid around about all sorts of things. Nothing is meant by it."

"That's okay. I didn't see a single shotgun, so I wasn't worried."

"Shotgun?"

"Yeah, shotgun weddings." He was surprised she didn't catch the reference, but it had been a long day for her, too. Looking more closely, he thought there might be strain around her mouth. She had to be exhausted from all the cooking and organizing in such a short time. She'd also helped at the Soaring Hawk, building the temporary pens and rounding up cattle.

Paige rolled her eyes. "We don't do shotgun weddings any longer in Shelton. Anyhow, I'm glad you have some potential employees."

"I'll do the necessary checks and then start making job offers. Everyone has said they can begin in a few days, though two of them mentioned they'd appreciate time to be in the rodeo next weekend since they've already entered. Is anyone in your family competing?"

She shook her head. "Not any longer. We aren't even attending the events that often. It's huge now, with visitors coming from states all around and from Canada. Wildly busy. But we usually visit the carnival at least once during the week. My brothers show off at the game booths, winning toys for Mishka. We go first thing in the morning because it's quieter than during the afternoons or evenings.

You're welcome to join us. Even Navy SEALs get shore leave from their duties, right?"

"I'll think about it."

She looked startled by his answer, probably because she'd expected him to refuse outright. But a few hours with Paige and Mishka at the carnival could be fun, if foreign to his nature.

Still, Paige was making him want things that weren't realistic, which was risky. He also didn't like the visual of employees seeing their new boss go off for a morning of carnival festivities before their living arrangements had been settled.

"Stop thinking so much," Paige said, breaking into his thoughts. "It was a friendly invitation. No strings attached."

"I didn't think there were. I was simply considering the bunkhouse question. Cleaning won't be too time-consuming, but it may take a couple days to get the lumber and other supplies for the dividing wall, then I'll have to build it. Lodging is an incentive, so I don't want to say the bunkhouse isn't available right away. And it wouldn't be right to just hire men in the interim. Or just women. I can hang plastic sheeting in the bunkhouse to protect the half being used while I build the wall, but that only takes care of one group."

"Maybe you could…" Paige's voice trailed off.

"Yes?" Jordan prompted.

She gave him a wary look. "You could stay in the main house and let the women use your quarters while getting everything together. It's big enough in there for two bunk beds."

A few weeks ago Jordan would have refused to consider living in the house, however temporarily, but it was a workable solution. His target was hiring seven cowhands. The two women who'd inquired were strong candidates, along with three of the men. While that wasn't as many as he needed, five was a whole lot better than none. He had to find a way to equitably employ both men and women.

"I'll think about it," he said.

"Or you could sleep in the barn with Lady G," Paige suggested, humor dancing in her eyes.

He looked at her sharply. Did she know Lady G was bunking with him in the early a.m. hours? Surely not.

"Lady G and her family will get by without me," he said in a noncommittal tone, "though I happen to know one of them is visiting Sarge every night."

"So I've heard. Anna Beth calls Marigold a job perk."

He cleared his throat. "I should, uh, thank you for arranging the work day. Liam tells me that he wanted to suggest one himself, but it was tricky because of the situation with Saul. He thinks you're the only one who could have gotten away with it."

"There's no need to thank me. I love when everyone gets together this way."

"That doesn't mean you and your mom didn't work too hard."

"I told you, both Saul and Anna Beth helped."

Anna Beth.

Jordan was still nonplussed that his old friend was letting Paige and Saul use her given name. In all the years he'd known her, he had never called her anything but Sarge or Sergeant or Master Sergeant Whitehall.

He gazed around the ranch center, teeming with dozens of ranchers and their families. A few curious looks were being sent in their direction, but he wasn't bothered by speculation from people he didn't know. They had to be curious since Paige was responsible for organizing the work day. It would be natural to wonder if something was going on romantically between them.

There was no need to set them straight—they'd figure everything out sooner or later.

And so would he.

SAUL SHOOK HANDS with his latest checkers challenger. "You nearly won that last round."

"Nah, you wiped the floor with me," said the young man, a cowhand on the Blue Banner. He didn't seem to mind his defeat. "It's an honor to be beaten by the best."

"We still had a good game."

Saul was impressed. The kid didn't lack confidence, but he wasn't so competitive that he took his loss poorly.

The checkers challengers had petered out and Saul stirred restlessly. He wanted to give Jordan the herding dogs he'd purchased from Claire Carmichael; he just wasn't sure what to say. The three Australian shepherds were obediently sitting on the porch, where Claire had told them to remain, but they radiated suppressed energy. Something was up and they knew it. Saul reached down and stroked one of them on the head. The animal's unusual pale eyes turned upward and his tongue hung from the side of his mouth.

"Beau," he said, trying out his name.

Beau's entire body seemed to wriggle with pleasure. All three dogs had what Claire described as a blue merle coat, and they'd been born with naturally bobbed tails. Blue merles were the most expensive of the Australian shepherds Claire raised, but Saul had wanted to show Jordan that he didn't always scrimp. If he'd learned anything over the years, it was that money was a poor substitute for people.

Funny, he'd saved and invested, watched his pennies and never used credit, striking it lucky several times on some cautious investments, and yet would trade everything now to know his grandsons were happy.

"Good boy," he said, petting the dog again.

"You going soft on that mutt?" Anna Beth asked, a smug grin on her face.

Saul bristled. "You're soft on a cat."

"Apples and oranges. Can't compare them."

He snorted. Anna Beth was tough as nails. It wasn't always comfortable to have her around, the way she prodded and annoyed him, but he liked her. He *really* liked her. She didn't take back talk from anyone, including

Jordan. And she wasn't half-bad-looking, either. Not that looks were everything, but a pleasant face during the day was nice.

"The dogs were your idea," Saul reminded her.

"Getting one dog was my idea. You're the one who decided on three."

He considered making a huffy retort, except his great-grandmother used to say that pride went before a fall, and this was probably one of those times he would go *plop* on his face. Come to think of it, maybe having too much pride was the one thing he *had* taught his grandsons. He didn't need to be told Jordan had almost refused help from the other ranchers today—the boy might look like his father, but he took after the Hawkins side of the family.

Thinking about Great-Grandmother Ehawee reminded Saul that he'd never told the boys about her. He set his jaw unhappily. The memory of Ehawee shouldn't be lost and he hoped their mother had told them the stories she'd known. In the early days, before Celina's death, he'd often spoken of his great-grandmother; what Victoria had remembered after losing her mom was the question.

"What are you thinking, old man?" Anna Beth asked.

"That you should stop calling me *old man*. I still got some miles left in me."

"No one is saying you don't, but you'll have more miles if you get that hip replaced. Should I ask Jordan to come over?" she asked before he could tell her to stop pestering him about the operation. "He'll wonder if people leave and three dogs are left behind. I've been here long enough to know these folks are devoted to their animals. He must realize it, too."

"Go ahead."

Saul was tense as he watched Anna Beth talk with his grandson. He'd bought the dogs to show that he supported Jordan's work on the Soaring Hawk. He more than supported it—unknown to Jordan, a third of the ranch was already in an irrevocable trust for him. Saul had arranged for it as soon as the papers were signed. He would have done it when the lawyer said a trust was the best way to pass the Soaring Hawk on to family, but offering a challenge was the only way Saul could think of to get Jordan and the other boys back to Montana.

Each one of them would put their heart and soul into running the Soaring Hawk; they just had to be given an incentive to return. And he needed to live long enough for that to happen, because expecting them to leave the navy before earning their pensions wasn't right, either.

Paige was filling bowls at the food tables and he gestured to her.

"Hey, Saul," she said, coming over. "Something up?"

He put his hand on Beau's neck. "I got these Australian shepherds for Jordan. I'm gonna tell him now and want you to be here."

"They're gorgeous. I love the marbling in their coats."

"It's called blue merle. Leastways, that's what Claire Carmichael told me. I barely knew what an Australian shepherd looked like before we began talking, but litters of her border collies are reserved for years ahead of time. She brought these to the ranch a few days ago so I could pick out the one I wanted, and I decided to take all three."

He straightened as Jordan arrived with Anna Beth.

"Is something up, Saul?" Jordan asked.

"I bought these dogs for you, to help out on

the ranch. This one is Beau, and that's Dixie, and the other is Koda," he explained, pointing to each animal. "They'll obey the same commands as Paige's border collie, because they came from the same trainer."

Saul saw little change in his grandson's expression, except his eyes widened.

"You *bought* them?"

"You seemed to be getting on well with Finn and I hoped they would be helpful." He cleared his throat. "The dogs are also friendly to cats. I figured you'd want that."

DESPITE BEING SHOCKED by his grandfather's gift, Jordan leaned over and patted his thigh. "Come, Dixie," he called.

Dixie dashed to him. She was a beautiful animal. Her long mottled fur had more black than the other two dogs, but each of them had white chests and crooked white blazes on their faces. They also wore the same cheerful expression of the other working dogs he'd seen.

"Hey, girl," he murmured, rubbing behind her ears. She was bright-eyed and excited, apparently recognizing they were pals now and loving the idea.

Koda let out a yip. He'd obediently stayed

on the porch, but was looking at Jordan with a hopeful expression, practically dancing on his feet.

"Koda, here," he said.

Koda cleared the porch in a single bound. He crowded next to Dixie, gazing up eagerly. Jordan gave him attention and then looked over at Beau, who was sitting next to Saul. Beau's gaze was on Saul and Jordan suspected the two had bonded.

That was okay.

From what Paige had told him about herding dogs, they needed activity. Beau could work during the day and stay with Saul the rest of the time.

He went over to give Beau a pet, rather than calling to him. "Thanks, Saul, I appreciate the gesture." He looked at Paige and she raised her eyebrows. "I, uh, also need to talk about moving into the house for a while, if that's okay. Maybe starting Monday night. This way we could all get to know the dogs."

His grandfather's face brightened. "It's fine with me. What changed your mind?"

"I have to split the bunkhouse in order to hire both men and women. In the meanwhile, female employees can stay in my quarters, which need to be cleaned ahead of time. Oh, and you should know that I'm using *foreman* as my title now, rather than *ramrod.* It's more in line with local custom."

Saul looked alarmed. Lady cowhands on the Soaring Hawk *and* a job-title change? Neither was likely to win his approval, but which one would he protest about first? And would this be the end of his promise to stay out of ranch management?

A few of the ranchers were drifting over, aware that something was happening on the porch. As Saul opened his mouth, both Sarge and Paige pointedly cleared their throats.

"Letting female employees bunk in the foreman's quarters was my idea," Paige said quickly. "Just on a short-term basis. I'm sure Jordan will want to move back once he gets the bunkhouse divided and everything into shape. Good solution, right? Of course, Jordan was already figuring it out, so I can't take any credit."

Jordan was impressed. Paige had both offered a warning she approved, with the suggestion that he either had, or would have, come to the same conclusion. She was right; it just would have taken him longer to accept he needed to stay in the main house for a week or more.

No question of it, she was talented at human relations in a way he couldn't begin to emulate.

Not to mention so beautiful and desirable, his breath was catching whenever he looked at her.

CHAPTER ELEVEN

"THANKS, DAD," PAIGE whispered as her father carried his granddaughter to her bed later that evening.

Mishka was sound asleep and didn't stir, probably dreaming sweet dreams of fun and laughter. She found so much joy in life, she made everyone else enjoy it more, too.

Paige got a damp washcloth and wiped a smear of chocolate from Mishka's cheek, then kissed her forehead and tucked the blankets around her.

Scott Bannerman was waiting outside in the hallway and he put an arm around Paige's shoulders.

"You okay, sweetheart?"

"I'm fine, but will you and Mom take Mishka to church for me tomorrow? I want to go over and clean the Soaring Hawk bunkhouse."

Scott nodded. "Sure. The sooner Jordan

has employees on board, the sooner you can stop spending so much time over there."

"I haven't neglected the Blue Banner," Paige said firmly. "Or Mishka and my clients. Or the people I visit for the Connections Project. I'm having fun. Besides, Mom does just as much or more on the Blue Banner."

It was an argument she'd thrown out many times over the years. Ranching families worked hard together.

Instead of smiling sheepishly, her father frowned. "You're doing more than usual. The past few days you've been burning your candle at both ends and also in the middle. Is there any chance you're falling in love with Jordan Maxwell?"

The speculation made Paige's stomach drop, but she rose on her toes to hug him.

"Burning my candle at both ends?" she teased. "You realize a lot of people wouldn't understand such an old-fashioned turn of phrase, right? I mean, who burns candles any longer except scented ones for atmosphere?"

"No response about falling in love, huh? Go to bed before I fire a few more questions you don't want to answer."

Paige chuckled and went into her bathroom. She tossed her clothes in the hamper and stepped into the shower to let the warm needles of water soothe her fatigue. The family didn't need to be concerned, at least not about her being active and involved. She loved feeling as if she was contributing something to the world. Yet a yawn caught her and she rested against the shower-wall tiles.

All right, she couldn't deny the last three days had been more hectic than usual. It would have been easier to focus on getting ready for the work day and do nothing else, but she enjoyed hands-on ranch tasks.

And being with Jordan.

Paige uttered a wordless huff of exasperation and straightened. She scrubbed shampoo into her long hair and tried not to think she was washing away the last trace of his kiss on her lips or the touch of his fingers on her cheek.

"Totally ridiculous," she muttered to herself.

I'll never wash my face again.

That's what she'd decided after her first kiss with a boy. It hadn't lasted. She'd recovered from her initial brush with love, and would surely recover this time. But it was maddening that Jordan was making her question every single adult decision she'd made about the opposite sex. He had made his position perfectly clear and a single kiss didn't mean he'd changed his mind.

Still, sometimes the way he looked at her was spine-tingling; he was the most compelling man she'd ever met. It was terrible to contemplate him growing old and alone like Saul, but that wasn't up to her. Jordan's heart needed to heal and learn to trust, and that might never happen.

How could he think the terrible things he'd seen could make him a bad father? He cared. He was strong and gentle and fiercely protective. He'd even proven to have a sense of humor when he allowed himself to show it.

If only he could see himself the way she saw him.

Paige got out and towel-dried her hair before combing it out. She stared at her reflection in the mirror.

Once upon a time she'd wished she was a blonde or a redhead, or dark and mysterious. But now she wondered what would it be like to be a woman Jordan Maxwell wanted, to be the focus of all of his intensity and passion...

It hurt to realize she might never know.

THE NEXT MORNING Paige woke after dawn to find Mishka cuddled next to her in the bed, watching her face.

"I wait for you," she said. "Gampa said not to wake you up. Are you okay, Mama?"

"I'm fine. Thank you for letting me sleep. Did you have a good time yesterday?"

"The best."

"Good." Paige brushed the hair back from her daughter's forehead. "Grandma and Grandpa are taking you to church this morning while I clean the Soaring Hawk bunkhouse."

Mishka stuck out her lip. She was a good child, but could be obstinate. "I help, too. Please?"

"Another day, dear." She didn't want her daughter around mouse droppings and the work needed to be done as quickly as possible so Jordan could get his employees on the payroll. Anna Beth would likely want to help as well, so Mishka would need to stay home for a while. "Besides, you'll see your friends at church. You were disappointed that some of them didn't come yesterday."

"I sup*pose*."

Paige bit her lip to keep from smiling and getting emotional all at once. The day would come, not so long from now, when Mishka would be more interested in spending time with her friends than her mother.

"Shall we get dressed and eat take-homes for breakfast?" she asked. Years ago Nana Harriet had started called food left from barbecues "take-homes" rather than leftovers, and the name was still being used by the family. "I happen to know there's a piece of Grandma's chocolate cake left. That is, if your uncles and grandpa haven't gotten to it by now."

"Yummy!" her daughter cried and rolled out of the bed.

They found Margaret in the kitchen. "Don't tell me—you want grilled pineapple and barbecued chicken for breakfast," she joked, automatically handing Paige a large cup of coffee.

"And cake, please," Mishka said hopefully.

Margaret gave Paige an inquiring look and she nodded her permission. They didn't have dessert every day and nobody needed to encourage Mishka to eat fruits and vegetables since she liked them almost as much as she liked sweets. Either way, Paige couldn't see the difference between pancakes dripping with butter and maple syrup, and a modest piece of cake, except that one was labeled breakfast food and the other dessert.

Margaret took food from the refrigerator and served her granddaughter, while Paige chose deviled eggs and take-homes from the vegetable trays for munching.

"Thanks for everything you did yesterday," she told her mother. "The work day was a major success and Jordan has several good prospects for ranch hands."

"I had a great time. Anna Beth is delightful and I guess Saul isn't so bad."

"That must be the first time you've ever called him Saul."

"He seems to have mellowed."

"I love Mr. Saul," Mishka announced, reminding them both that she understood most of what was said around her, even if she couldn't always articulate it back.

"So do I, sweetie," Paige assured her, ruefully meeting her mother's gaze. She popped a last bite of deviled egg into her mouth and got up. "Mom, Dad said you could take Mishka to church for me, so I'm heading over to the Soaring Hawk. I'll see you later. We're going to eat take-homes tonight, right? Or do you want me to make dinner?"

"We'll be eating take-homes for a couple of

days, even with your brothers' appetites and filling up the freezer. I also sent stacks over to the bunkhouse dining hall for the cow-hands."

Paige kissed her mother and daughter, told Finn to stay and went out to her SUV.

They typically had loads of food remaining from a work day because they wanted to be sure everyone had plenty to eat and could never be certain of how many people would be able to come. Sometimes it was a larger group than originally planned. Anna Beth must have thought the same thing, because she had prepared a huge volume as well.

Thinking about Anna Beth made Paige smile. More than ever she was convinced a romance might be blossoming between Saul and the retired marine. The hint of a romance blossoming between Saul and the retired marine was a helpful distraction from other thoughts…like the letter she'd sent to Mishka's uncle. No matter how many times she told herself that she'd done the right thing, having absolute confidence it would turn out all right was more difficult.

She hadn't found the way to tell anyone else. Her parents and the rest of the family would only end up sharing her concern about the implications. They were *already* concerned, simply because Mr. Gupta had reached out in the first place.

The thought kept Paige preoccupied as she unloaded cleaning supplies from her SUV and brought them into the Soaring Hawk bunkhouse. She looked around and made a face. It was a traditional, old-time bunkhouse, more suited to the 1800s than the 21st century.

"You should be at home, relaxing," Jordan said from across the room.

She jumped. "Don't sneak up on people."

"I didn't sneak. I was measuring to see how much lumber and drywall is needed, and then went to check the plumbing."

"Are the bathrooms working?"

"More or less. Honestly, you need to take some time off. It isn't that I don't appreciate what you've been doing, but as I've pointed out, the Soaring Hawk is my challenge, not yours."

She grinned at him. "Am I complaining? People pay good money to dude ranches just to ride horses, work cattle and spend time with dogs. I'm getting to do it here for free."

The corners of Jordan's mouth twitched.

"Which is something you could also do on your family's ranch for free."

"Don't argue with me." Paige held out a dust mask. "If you're going to help, you ought to wear one of these. But should Koda and Dixie even be in here with the mouse droppings?" she asked, gesturing to the two Australian shepherds standing next to him. They already seemed devoted to their new owner. "We can't put masks on them."

"I haven't seen any evidence of mice in here, so I don't think we need to worry about it. But I'm not sure there's any point to cleaning when I'll be doing construction."

"You want to get employees onboard before you can get the wall built. That means cleaning unless you ask them to do it themselves. Either way, you're just making excuses to get me to leave. You already said you were going to put up plastic sheeting to protect the side being occupied during construction."

JORDAN SHRUGGED, WONDERING how Paige managed to outthink him so often. She was smart and determined to help. He had to believe it was her crusader instincts, backed by genuine heart.

She amazed him.

Over and over, every single day. After a massive effort the day before, here she was, ready to start again. With a smile. She'd even recognized Dixie and Koda and remembered their names.

"I'm glad there isn't a rodent infestation," she said a while later. "I forgot the bunkhouse was occupied until recently. But these things are awful." She poked one of the rusted bedsteads. "They must date back decades. Are you sure those alleged mattresses aren't filled with straw?"

He continued working. "I'm guessing they're surplus supplies purchased by my great-grandfather, the same as in the foreman's quarters. They must have been a bargain at the time, but that time is long gone. I put an order together this morning for new furniture and bedding and appliances. A store in Bozeman will deliver this far for free if the purchase is large enough. So don't worry, I have every intention of providing a proper living space for my employees."

"I know. Saul couldn't have realized how bad it was."

"I'm sure he didn't," Jordan said awkwardly.

He hadn't been trying to criticize his grandfather. No one could accuse Saul of living a life of luxury in contrast to his ranch hands, but he hadn't offered incentives to keep them on the payroll, either. Come to think of it, that might be one of the many reasons people had been reluctant to apply for work at the Soaring Hawk. Stories would have circulated about the thin, musty mattresses, along with squeaky springs, worn-out blankets and other inadequate living conditions.

"Where's Beau?" Paige asked.

"Up at the house. He seems to have instantly connected with my grandfather and vice versa. I spoke to Claire Carmichael about it last night. Beau isn't trained as a service animal, but she says he'll know to get help if needed."

"That's nice. He just won't get much exercise with Saul."

Jordan nodded. "I've already taken that into consideration. Beau can work with me part of the time and spend evenings and nights at the main house." He reached down to give Dixie and Koda attention, knowing he needed to work on bonding with them. They wriggled happily. "By the way, I assume you're the one who suggested getting dogs to help work the Soaring Hawk. I appreciate it."

"Don't thank me. I probably would have made the suggestion eventually, but Anna Beth put the flea in Saul's ear, so to speak. He asked my opinion and I just confirmed Claire Carmichael is a great trainer."

Jordan was still having trouble calling Anna Beth anything except Sarge, but with Paige around, he'd probably get around to it. After winning over his grandfather, everyone else would be a piece of cake to her.

"He spent quite a bit on the dogs, didn't he?"

Paige nodded. "They're trained and ready to work, which makes them even more valuable. And Claire's reputation means her dogs are in demand. I wouldn't say they cost a fortune, but Saul must have put out a good amount. Maybe the equivalent of a purebred yearling colt or filly for each of them."

"I'm stunned. He's never liked spending money *except* on horses."

"That's because the Soaring Hawk barely survived the Great Depression," Paige explained. "His grandparents built the new house in the twenties and then the economy crashed. Suddenly there was a large mortgage to pay and no money. He was raised on stories about how they got by on what they could grow, or on game from hunting. Scrimping so they wouldn't lose the ranch. Shoes and clothes falling apart, never anything new. Saul and his parents didn't want the Soaring Hawk to ever be in debt again, so they refused to use credit and saved as much as possible. Crashing beef prices in the 1970s made him even more determined to have a reserve against the future."

Jordan wished he'd understood as a boy. It might not have made life easier with his grandfather, but at least he would have known why Saul was so cautious with money. Still, that meant replacing his mother's gravestone made even less sense. Why go to the extra expense?

"Bad timing for my great-grandparents to have a large mortgage when the Depression hit," he murmured.

Paige removed the faded fabric covering one of the windows, made a face and dropped it on a pile of old bedding. "Yeah, but you can't predict the future, and is it really living if you never take a chance?"

"Is that an argument you've used with Saul?"

"More or less." She scrunched her nose, the way Jordan had anticipated.

He checked the window and was pleased to see the putty sealing the glass was sound. Someone must have worked on it in the last few years. There also weren't any signs of leaks from the roof.

Thanks to the work day, prospects for the Soaring Hawk were far more promising than before. Jordan was even reevaluating his preliminary fall-market strategy, which had entailed a larger sell-off of the herd than normal. Doing that would have galled him since it meant a reduction of breeding stock, but he refused to keep animals that could die from neglect over the winter. Still, the situation was fluid and he'd keep weighing his options until a final decision had to be made.

A thumping noise grabbed his attention and he saw Paige hauling one of the thin mattresses toward the door. "We can clean easier if this junk is gone," she explained. "It's just stirring up more dirt. I think the stuffing inside is turning to powder."

"I'd rather wait to dispose of everything until the new furniture is here. What if there's a delay in it arriving?"

She dropped the mattress, coughed at the

dust cloud and turned around. "Rain isn't predicted for the next week and you'd have to air these out before they can be used. At the very least, put them in the sun to sanitize, freshen and beat the dirt out. If they're needed on a temporary basis, we'll haul them back inside. You can cover everything at night in case of a heavy dew fall."

Paige was right.

Again.

Besides, if necessary, he'd drive to Bozeman for the new beds and other items, even rent a moving truck if that's what it took. Jordan was willing to put up with the minimum for himself; he didn't want his employees to do the same. Besides, having the branding done was giving him latitude in how to prepare for a new crew.

Soon, all of the furniture was outside. It was a mess, the bed frames and dressers battered and dented.

They also took a look at the dining hall. The tables and chairs were usable, but Jordan decided to add couches and easy chairs to his furniture order, remembering Paige's suggestion to create a relaxation area for the cowhands.

"When is everything coming?" she asked

after he'd modified the purchase on his phone and they were cleaning again.

"They claim to guarantee delivery within forty-eight hours. I can store the order in one of the barns until needed."

Paige finished washing the last window. "Good. I'm going to do the glass on the outside. The grime is unbelievable. There'd be a nice view if they weren't so dirty."

Jordan followed her, carrying the step stool she'd been using. "I have longer arms. I'll scrub and you rinse with the hose."

It was a hot morning and the dogs were delighted to be in the open air. They romped with uncomplicated contentment, playing with each other and responding eagerly to attention.

Jordan gazed across the landscape before starting. Paige was right about the view; the length of the sturdy bunkhouse looked over the southern fields, the grass growing long and swaying in the breeze. The main ranch had been constructed on the high side of a wide valley leading up to the mountains. If he hadn't grown up in Montana he might have wondered why the windows didn't look toward the hills with their stands of evergreens and the mountains beyond, but he knew the reason. *Wind.* The bunkhouse had been built so that the smallest wall took the worst of winter storms sweeping down from the Rockies.

Jordan soaped the first window, stepped down to let Paige rinse it off and moved to the next.

"By the way," he began, trying to be casual, though it wasn't his strong suit, "is something bothering you?"

"Such as?"

He gave her a look from the corner of his eye. Apparently she wasn't going to make it easy to find out if she was unhappy that he'd kissed her, or if something else was going on. Because he was certain she had *something* on her mind.

"I'm not sure, to be honest," he told her. "You're the people person, not me."

"You don't give yourself enough credit. Everybody thought you were a terrific leader yesterday. You wouldn't have gotten job applicants otherwise."

"I think you're deflecting."

"Yeah? How is this for deflecting?" She sent a spray of water over him. Koda and Dixie barked excitedly at the new game, darting back and forth.

"You—"

Jordan and Paige, trying to wrestle the hose away from each other, tumbled to the grass laughing. Both managed to get squirted before she let go of the nozzle and the water stopped.

He rested his weight on one elbow and brushed a damp strand of hair from her cheek. She was so beautiful, with a heart to match. All the things he'd warned himself a thousand times that he couldn't risk damaging by getting involved. But at night he was starting to see her in his dreams. He'd never allowed himself to remember dreams before and now he couldn't keep them out of his head.

"What is going on here?" asked a stern voice.

Jordan rolled onto his back and looked at Sarge. She was obviously trying not to smile.

"We were just washing the windows."

"Uh-huh."

PAIGE SQUIRMED UPRIGHT and wiped a drip of water from her chin. "And I thought there was a bee on Jordan's shoulder. I was trying to shoo it away. We slipped and fell."

"A likely story."

"That's the only one you're going to get," Jordan said.

He looked so relaxed that Paige could hardly believe her eyes. For a heart-stopping moment she'd even thought he was going to kiss her again, but Anna Beth's arrival had squashed the possibility.

Which was good.

Really.

And maybe she could convince herself of that if she thought it often enough.

"Sorry, Anna Beth, did you need something?" Jordan asked, sitting up.

"Sure do. I'd like to cook for the new employees when they come on board."

He patted Dixie, who had cuddled up to him, a great big doggy smile on her face. "Isn't dealing with my grandfather enough?"

"Hardly. You claimed he was a challenge, but he's just an ol' pussycat at heart. Come on, you know I dislike having time on my hands and it would give me a better taste of Western living."

He gave her a narrow look. "You said having too much time on your hands was the reason you wanted to paint the house."

"Cooking would be a break in the routine. Besides, painting won't keep me occupied forever. You know I need to stay busy. I've given it some thought. We could feed everyone up at the kitchen, but you probably don't want Saul and your employees in the same room, so the dining hall would be best. I could freeze meals ahead, all sorts of things."

Jordan looked at Paige and she shrugged, secretly amused. She was sure Anna Beth would be pleased to have a new project, but her goal was to help him keep cowhands on the payroll, not to save herself from boredom.

"I appreciate the offer, but you'll have to let me know if you change your mind," he said. "There's a chest freezer in the dining-hall kitchen. I can order another one if it doesn't work or isn't big enough."

"That's great. I'll take a look." She eyed them for another long moment, a smile still playing on her face, then turned and walked back around the end of the bunkhouse.

Paige leaned against the wall; her clothes were already drying in the warm air. "She's right that you shouldn't feed everyone up at the house. Saul's good intentions might not hold up if everyone is in the same room for meals. Half of the dining hall can still be an employee lounge."

"True. I won't be hiring twenty or thirty ranch hands, like in the old days, so there's enough space for both purposes."

"Ah, the old days. Life must have been interesting when they had that many cowhands on ranches. I suppose mega ranches still have that many or more employees, but none of the spreads around Shelton are that big."

Jordan sat next to her. "I don't think traditional ranching has changed much, except now cows are trucked off ranches when they're sold in the fall. None of those 1800s marathon John Wayne cattle drives."

She laughed. "John Wayne cattle drives?"

"Yeah. Chisholm Trail kind of drama. Tension. Jealousy. Feuds."

"Thank goodness we don't have anything like *that* any longer," Paige said in a droll tone. "Though your father might disagree about the feuds."

"True. I've never understood why my grandfather hates my dad so much."

"I don't think he still feels that way. Some fathers have a hard time letting go when their daughters grow up. To be honest, my folks wouldn't have been too happy if I'd dated a guy like Evan Maxwell. He had quite a reputation before he met your mom. People still tell stories about him racing through Shelton in his truck, or the time he left a three-year-old bull in the bride's dressing room at the church before a wedding."

Jordan stretched out his legs. "Saul was always saying something negative about Dad when we lived here. My father may have messed up after Mom died and was wild before they met, but when I knew him, he was a good guy who worked hard running the Circle M, and even harder to make her happy."

"I'm sorry. Things haven't been easy for you."

"Not your fault."

"Okay, but can I offer another bit of advice?"

He gave her a look from the corner of his eye. "Sure."

"Never talk Chisholm Trail to a Shelton County cattle rancher. It's all right to mention the Bozeman Trail, but never the Chisholm. That's a Texas thing."

Jordan chuckled and before she knew it, he was kissing her. A deep, soul-stirring kiss that made Paige feel as if fireworks were going off inside her body.

When he finally lifted his head, he gave her a lazy smile. "I don't really care about the Chisholm *or* Bozeman Trails. But you're cute when you say stuff like that."

Her mouth was dry. "Uh, cute doesn't sound great. We aren't in grade school."

His expression turned sober. "You were still in grade school when I finished my SEAL training."

Paige made an exasperated sound. "Sheesh, you're only nine years older than me. Stop making it sound as if you're the old man of the mountain and I'm a baby. All anyone can do is make the best life possible."

"The years are less important than what I've seen and done."

"Nobody *ever* has equal experiences. Besides, anyone growing up on a ranch knows the harsh reality of life and death."

She ran her fingers down his arm to the scars she'd seen the first day they'd ridden together. He'd also taken off his shirt while they were erecting some of the temporary pens, so she knew there were others. A *lot* of others.

It was awful to think he'd gone through such terrible experiences, but he'd survived, like Mishka, and he was a good, decent person.

"That's from a fire in Kabul. On my first mission," Jordan said as she traced the scars. "I got off pretty light. Several members of the team didn't fare as well. See? I'm not even a safe person to know."

"That's something else we disagree about. I've never felt safer with anyone." Paige scrambled to her feet and held out her hand. "Right now, I'm going to keep cleaning windows. Coming?"

Jordan brushed her fingers with his, but rose under his own steam. She wished she knew the future and whether her feelings toward him were a distraction from other issues, or a heartbreak in the making. The age difference was obviously a huge issue in his eyes.

Or an excuse.

Okay, they had widely varying past lives, but that was true of many successful couples. Wasn't it more important that they both shared the same values and believed in the same things, like caring about animals and ranching and the land? She was jumping ahead of herself, but they also both loved children. If that wasn't a sound foundation for a future together, she didn't know what was.

CHAPTER TWELVE

On Monday morning, Saul carefully descended the main staircase, holding the railing with one hand and his cane with the other. Beau went down beside him, but not close enough to get underfoot.

"Good boy," he said.

The dog yipped.

It was pleasant having him in the bedroom at night. Saul had slept alone since Celina's death, but Beau had come in the last two evenings, settling with a contented sigh on a rug at the end of the bed. Saul hadn't realized how much company a pooch could be. Perhaps he'd call Claire Carmichael and see if she had another dog he could get for Jordan, otherwise he'd feel guilty that Beau was becoming attached to someone else.

He didn't need more guilt.

At the bottom of the staircase, he looked up and let out a discouraged breath. They seemed to get higher every day and going down wasn't any easier than going up.

Anna Beth kept telling him that he'd be better off using a bedroom on the ground floor, along with getting his hip replaced. He was considering both, though not because of her. He wouldn't improve without an operation, and if he had it, they might not let him climb stairs for a while. There was also no guarantee he could ride again after a hip replacement, though the doctor had said it was possible.

Horses had been his constant through the years. Riding, chasing cattle, being out in the open range, letting the wind blow across him. A man could be lonely, but not feel it as much while riding his horse.

Still, none of that mattered right now. Jordan would be moving into the house tonight and Saul felt like a little kid anticipating a treat. This was another opportunity to get things right, or at least better than before.

Anna Beth was polishing the long table in the entryway and he frowned. "You've scrubbed this house to an inch of its life and you're working on that old thing again?"

"The wood needs extra attention after being neglected for so long. Any objections?"

"No, but it can't be worth much."

"If it's worth something to you, then it's worth taking care of."

Saul gazed at the table. He remembered putting his schoolbooks there, and his mom keeping a basket on the end to collect Christmas cards. The table had also held countless vases of wildflowers in the summer and branches of bright yellow leaves in the fall. The "feminine touch," she'd teased his father. They'd loved each other as much as Saul had loved Celina.

"Yeah, I guess so," he muttered. "My mom called it a console. It came from her folks as a wedding gift. The table was old then, sort of a family heirloom."

"That makes it extra special. My pop didn't have anything worth keeping when he died except a few pictures and his old pocket watch, but I got great memories and that's what counts the most. Bet you do, too."

Saul nodded. He had good memories when he was willing to think about them…or when Anna Beth prodded him into it. "What room is Jordan going to use?" he asked.

"I fixed the upstairs bedroom on the southwest corner of the house, the one with the best view of the barns. He said if anything happens in the middle of the night, he can take a quick look out to assess the situation, then go down to handle it. Does that happen very often?"

Saul sat on a chair and patted Beau as the dog leaned against his leg. "Sometimes. Coyotes will harass the horses and cattle, especially when there are young foals or calves. We have to keep watch for 'em. But there were more problems in the old days, before so many bears and the wolves got killed off around here. We still see bears, but not that often."

"Seems like there should be a place for all."

"Yup," he agreed, though it wasn't a view shared by many ranchers. Those other ranchers hadn't known Great-Grandmother Ehawee. She'd loved the wildness of the land and animals. "Is Jordan having dinner with us?"

Anna Beth shrugged. "Your guess is as good as mine. I'll tell him that I'm serving steak. Maybe that'll get him here."

Saul's mouth watered. Anna Beth knew exactly how to broil the meat to medium rare, the way he liked his best. Funny, he didn't see her as a housekeeper. Surely housekeepers weren't this opinionated and could be fired.

She was annoying, like a burr under a horse's saddle, but there was one thing she had in common with all the women Saul had ever cared about—she had genuine heart and a whole lot of grit, which she needed to put up with him. He also looked forward to seeing her each morning, something he couldn't have imagined feeling the day they'd met.

"Go out to the porch and I'll get your breakfast," she said briskly.

"Maybe I could eat with you in the kitchen."

"OH. ALL RIGHT." Anna Beth hid her surprise.

Cooking for Saul was easier than she'd thought it would be since he wasn't on a restricted diet, other than caffeine. Still, she tried to keep meals nutritious, a difficult task with a man who'd eaten canned and frozen convenience foods for years and didn't see any real need for fresh fruits and vegetables.

Not that Jordan was much better.

Anna Beth shuddered when she thought about the MREs Jordan relied on so often. She'd viewed them as a necessary evil while deployed, but had never voluntarily consumed one when options were available. Jordan, on the other hand, had kept them stocked at his base apartment instead of regular groceries. He appreciated good food, but usually opted for something easy.

She gave Beau his dog chow before making a fluffy cheese-and-green-pepper omelet for Saul, topped by leftover chili. “Do you want toast?” she asked as she put the plate in front of him.

“This is more than enough. What about you?”

“I’m having oatmeal.” She sat at the table with her bowl.

He snorted. “Health food.”

“Healthy food,” Anna Beth corrected him. “If you ever have great-grandchildren in the house, their mother isn’t going to appreciate you being sarcastic about oatmeal.”

“Then you think Jordan will have a family someday?” The hopeful tone in Saul’s voice made her sigh.

“He says not. But isn’t one of your other grandsons an expectant father?”

“That’s right. Wyatt is an excellent young man.” Saul ate another bite of his omelet. “It’s just that Paige would be a wonderful wife for Jordan.”

“I agree, but that’s up to the two of them. Don’t worry, if Dakota accepts your challenge, you'll still have another shot at getting her as a granddaughter-in-law."

Saul scowled. "This isn't about that. Not exactly. I want the best for Jordan. Surely you see that Paige is the best."

Anna Beth looked at him carefully. She still hadn't entirely made up her mind about Saul. As a marine she'd dealt with absolutes, but people were different. Having warm feelings for a man and being confident of his motives were two different things. At least he wanted to mend fences with his grandsons and was willing to make gestures like buying the Australian shepherds to help.

Of course, she'd heard a few of the ranchers mutter that purchasing a few herding dogs was the least Saul could do after allowing the Soaring Hawk to get so run-down and counting on his grandson to fix the problem. But they didn't understand what a huge step the dogs had been for Saul. He'd given it real thought, too, ordering a supply of quality food to have ahead of time for them and setting up a vaccination and exam schedule with the veterinarian.

"You aren't the only one who wants what's best for Jordan," she said finally, "but people have to make their own choices."

Saul seemed to lose interest in the last bits of his omelet. "Getting older is hard. You can see your mistakes, but you don't know if there's enough time to fix them. Or *if* they can be fixed, and you're so tired, you don't know where to start."

"That sounds like a confession. Aren't you the one who declared that old men get set in their ways when I told you it's never too late to change?"

"I've said a lot of things. Besides, no confessions from me are needed. I'm sure you already know all there is to know about Jordan's childhood."

Anna Beth gave Saul a wry smile. "He rarely talks about the past. But I'm curious how *you* turned out to be such a cantankerous soul."

A parade of emotions crossed Saul's face. "A whole lot of stuff happens to make up a person." He pushed his plate away. "But lately I've been wondering if it could be from having life too easy when I was young."

Too easy?

That was the last thing she'd expected to hear. She was learning about the challenges involved with ranching and it didn't sound like a picnic at the best of times.

Saul nodded, looking serious. “My family had one of the top spreads in the county. Beef was in demand and we had quality stock. I sailed through agricultural college, hardly needing to crack a book. While I had to register for selective service, I never got a draft letter. Basically, I was cocky, popular with women and knew I'd always have a place on the Soaring Hawk and eventually inherit.”

He fell silent and Anna Beth waited. Paige had done the hard part, wearing Saul down with food and patience; maybe now he *needed* to talk about the past.

“After college I came back and the sweetest girl in Shelton County fell in love with me,” he said finally. “We got married, had a daughter and I figured a solid gold future was ahead. Working with my folks and building the ranch even bigger, a house full of kids and a wife I adored. Everything was rosy. My idea of perfect.”

“That sounds nice.”

“It was. Then my mother and father died during a flu epidemic in the late sixties. Not from the flu. Mom had pneumonia and Dad was driving her to the hospital in Bozeman when a truck ran 'em off the road. Not long after, Celina was diagnosed with leukemia.

The truth is, I didn't know how to handle the bad times. Life was easy until it wasn't."

"That's true of most people."

"Not Jordan and my grandsons. They never had anything easy and a good deal of that can be laid at my door."

Anna Beth stirred her oatmeal, sad for him. Saul had handled his hard times by closing down and becoming a bitter curmudgeon. But she didn't believe he'd intended to be cruel, and he seemed to regret his choices more than anyone she'd ever met. No wonder Paige was gentle and kind to him; she'd seen his heart beneath the rough, weathered exterior.

"Your daughter's death wasn't your fault," Anna Beth murmured.

"Wasn't it? The Circle M was smaller than the Soaring Hawk. Getting by must have been a struggle. I could have helped. Maybe they couldn't afford the medical care Victoria needed, or she had to work too hard, lending a hand on the ranch. She was close to her mother's age when she passed. That just isn't right. It isn't right that Jordan is working so hard, and now I got Paige to work along with him. What was I thinking?"

The pain in his face made Anna Beth feel

terrible; for good or bad, she cared about Saul more than she'd ever cared for a man. "Paige is strong-willed—she'd speak up if it was too much for her. Sad things happen. They can't always be prevented."

"Yeah, but I'll never know if I could have made a difference for Victoria. Maybe by letting her know how much I loved her, or by giving them money. It was easier to blame my son-in-law all those years for her death, instead of facing those questions. It made me tough on the boys, and toughest on Jordan. I wish more than anything that I could undo the past."

Anna Beth was honored that Saul had confided in her. Her instincts said that the past had to be confronted before he or Jordan could move forward, but she didn't know if it would work. Paige and Mishka seemed to be softening Jordan's heart, but would it be enough for him to forgive his grandfather?

Saul didn't need her getting soft and sentimental on him, so she squared her shoulders. "You should explain to Jordan."

He snorted. "My behavior was inexcusable. How can I hope he'll forgive me, when I can't forgive myself? And why would he believe I've changed?"

"I believe it."

She finally did.

Anna Beth had spent years looking into soldiers' eyes and assessing them. Years of dealing with adversaries, not always knowing who was simply pretending to be on your side and having to make life-and-death decisions with limited information. She was as certain as a person could be that Saul regretted his mistakes and was looking for redemption.

"You know," she said slowly, "I'm not sure how much faith Jordan has in the future. For himself, at least, but let's combine our efforts and see if there's anything we can do to nudge him into seeing the possibilities."

Saul's eyes widened. "Really?"

"I don't say anything I don't mean. *Old man.*"

He chuckled. "You must have been a handful when you were a marine recruit."

"I still am," she assured him. "More than you can imagine."

He cocked his head, still smiling. "Actually, I can imagine quite a bit."

JORDAN HAD HOPED to avoid eating with his grandfather while staying in the ranch house, but Sarge came out to the barn after Paige left for the day and crossed her arms over her chest.

"I'm fixing a proper meal for your first night. Rib eye steak, twice-baked stuffed potatoes and a chocolate rum cake with extra rum on top," she announced. "The least you can do is come eat it on a timely basis."

"I have work to do."

"Which you can do better on a full stomach. I would have asked Paige to stay, but I knew she wanted to get home to Mishka. Maybe tomorrow night."

Pain throbbed in Jordan's head. He'd thought Sarge understood his concern about getting too close to Paige.

"Look, Sarge, I'll find a way to thank Paige for all she's done, but please, no invitations to dinner or anything else. I may have said you could run the house the way you wanted, but that doesn't include interfering with my life."

"Your grandfather told me the same thing, the morning I arrived. More or less. I do what I do. You know that."

Jordan did know it, but still he wanted her to understand his concern. "I'm serious. It's important to limit the time I spend with Paige. I can't prevent her from coming over because of the contract I signed with Saul, but socializing is something I *can* avoid."

Sarge rolled her eyes with exasperation. "You weren't avoiding her yesterday when I found you practically in each other's arms, or did I misunderstand the situation?"

The scene she'd stumbled on had kept Jordan awake the few hours he'd given himself to sleep, along with remembering the kiss he'd shared with Paige afterward.

"You didn't misunderstand, but that's why I need to be more careful."

"You're being ridiculous. I kept myself from falling in love for over fifty years, most of them spent around some very hunky marines. You can certainly manage to avoid falling for a pretty rancher's daughter."

He glared, frustration boiling out of him. "I didn't say I was falling in love."

"Of course not. But what's wrong with being friends? Paige is generous and has a sound head on her shoulders. I'm sure she'll make room in her life for you."

"You weren't talking about friendship. She's an idealistic do-gooder who leads with her heart. I *don't* want to be the one who hurts her." It was just hard to remember his resolution when Paige was close to him. She represented warmth and love and the sweet temptation of hope.

Sarge waved her hand. "You can't protect the whole world. Besides, Paige is stronger than you give her credit for being."

"I don't want to discuss this any longer."

"Then think of something else to talk about over dinner. Be at the house in one hour, or I'll cook your rib eye to the texture of shoe leather and serve it on your pillow."

She turned crisply on her heel and Jordan glared again. Sarge said and did what she thought was best, but that didn't mean she was always right. Come to think of it, Paige had the same habit of being outspoken and taking action without being asked.

Paige.

He groaned.

How could he have kissed her again? The interlude of laughter and relaxation outside the bunkhouse must have unhinged him. He couldn't remember a single carefree moment like that in all the years since his mother's death.

Pure, simple pleasure.

Jordan pressed his fingers to his temples, headache pounding now in earnest. What had his first commanding officer said?

Navy SEALs and long-term relationships don't get along. So keep those engagement rings in your pockets, boys.

The commander had been going through a divorce at the time, proving he had firsthand experience at messing up relationships. But the last Jordan had heard, Delvaney was retired and had gotten married again. Apparently he hadn't taken his own advice. Maybe he'd discovered that it was pretty lonely without someone who cared whether or not you came home at night.

Jordan sat on a bale of hay. As a SEAL he'd kept things simple. Who would have thought being a rancher was so complicated?

One of the black-and-white cats was giving himself a bath, unconcerned by the tension in the air. Jordan scratched under his chin and received an enthusiastic purr in return.

The cat family was falling into patterns. Marmalade spent a chunk of his time in the main house trying to become a lap cat, Oreo and Gus hung out in the horse barn chasing horseflies and mice, while Bo and Frances had discovered the calving barn and its diversions. Bo and Frances were the least sociable of the six when it came to people.

Lady G still preferred the foreman's quarters. She'd be pleased when the two cowhands moved in, however temporarily. Two people meant twice the number of hands for neck scratches, but he'd have to warn them she didn't allow belly rubs. If Melody James and Carmen Melendez weren't cat lovers, he'd bring Lady G up to the house at night, no matter how his grandfather felt about it. He couldn't let her keep employees awake with her complaints.

Dixie and Koda sat happily nearby while Gus batted at Koda's ears. The cats and Australian shepherds were getting along as if they'd been raised together.

Jordan massaged the back of his neck. Riding with Paige, rounding up cattle and moving them was different than working side by side with her in close quarters. More intimate. He still had a feeling that something was on her mind, but his efforts in getting her to open up had been unsuccessful.

Maybe tomorrow.

She'd made it clear she was coming over, despite his protests, claiming that prepping the dining hall would be easier with two of them. She'd also pointed out that his own quarters needed more cleaning. She knew he'd done little more than remove the mouse droppings and douse everything with chlorine bleach since moving in. There weren't enough hours for niceties.

Right now Jordan's plan was to have three of the employees start Wednesday morning. The two who wanted to compete in the rodeo had been given the following Monday as their first day on the job. The rodeo opened Friday evening and went through the weekend, so they wouldn't have been available for much work, regardless. He wouldn't have felt right refusing to let them compete since they'd already entered, but it also wouldn't set a good precedent to immediately give three days off when the other cowhands were working.

In the meantime, he'd assign the new employees to mowing for hay, assuming they knew how to operate the old equipment. He could ride out and check on their progress periodically while building the dividing wall in the bunkhouse.

The plan should work. If the new people were any good, the way Paige seemed to think, they'd be worth waiting for.

Paige.

Everything kept coming back to her. Jordan looked down at his wrist, remembering the way she'd stroked his burn scars. The scar tissue was less sensitive than the rest of his skin, but he'd felt every tiny movement of her fingers. He still felt it, as if her touch had been imprinted on him.

He'd deliberately taken off his shirt when they were working on the branding pens, thinking that seeing his various scars would remind her of the violence he'd experienced.

Instead of being repulsed, she'd touched him. Gently. Soothingly. As if regretting he'd felt a moment of pain. A woman like that was one in a million. But he hadn't changed his mind about getting involved.

He just had to resist a while longer. Once he had employees on the payroll, he and Paige wouldn't be spending much time together. She'd still visit Saul with Mishka, but it would be harder for her to justify working alongside him.

Dixie let out a short whine and bopped her head up under his hand. It was her love-me request and he gave her a good rubbing all over.

Koda was next. He was gallant toward Dixie, giving her a chance for attention first, but wanting his share. Jordan didn't skimp on responding to them—he knew that being bonded was an important way they'd work together as a team.

Paige's dog, Finn, had demonstrated how much a herder could do, and now Jordan had three of his own. He was itching to get out with them and test their skills with the cattle.

Maybe he could offer Dolley Madison to Paige as a way to thank her for bringing Finn and the other border collies from her family's ranch, along with helping in so many other ways. She was fond of Dolley and the Thoroughbred adored her in return. Dolley might even be carrying Tornado's foal, making her more valuable.

The mare would be a good gift. Not repayment—that was impossible—just a gesture of appreciation and friendship.

And if he kept telling himself that friendship was all he wanted, he might even start to believe it.

CHAPTER THIRTEEN

"I'M AFRAID WASHING isn't doing any good," Paige said as she scrubbed a wall in the bunkhouse dining hall on Tuesday morning.

Jordan threw his sponge into the bucket. "Agreed. It'll have to be repainted."

He sank onto one of the chairs and scowled at the stubborn stains. They'd done the kitchen the day before and had spent the early morning cleaning the dining hall while Sarge worked on the foreman's quarters. He'd hoped window cleaner and an application of bleach would spiff things up temporarily, but it wasn't going to be nearly enough. They could scrub all day and nothing would make them less offensive. Even the grease marks weren't getting better.

Paige sat next to him. "Painting wouldn't take much longer and I prefer it over cleaning. But we might want to put primer on the worst places."

"Good idea." Jordan looked at her from

the corner of his eye. He was more and more convinced that something was bothering her. Maybe he could help. He nudged her shoulder with his own. “Look, I don’t know *how* to be subtle. So what’s going on? Don’t say it’s nothing because I can tell you have something on your mind.”

Paige leaned over and rubbed both Koda and Dixie around their necks before straightening.

“I’m probably making a big deal out of nothing,” she said finally. “I received an email from the adoption agency. They attached a request from Mishka’s uncle, asking how she’s doing. That’s all.”

“I thought he gave up his rights. You found her at an orphanage.”

“Technically.”

“Technically?” Jordan didn’t like how that sounded.

“I guess *legally* is the right word. Her uncle felt he didn’t have any choice because her health problems were so extensive. Mr. Gupta’s family died in a flood right after Mishka was born. He tried looking after her, and then brought her to an orphanage when it was clear she wasn’t going to improve without specialized medical care. Care he couldn’t provide.”

"And to make her eligible for adoption, he had to give up his rights. Legally walk away from her."

Paige nodded. "Yes. Adoptive parents are required to travel to India and I'll never forget the first time I held Mishka. I was already in love with her picture, but here I was, halfway around the world, and this wonderful child was going to be my daughter. At the same time, I was terrified she wouldn't survive. I would have done anything to get her out of that orphanage."

"Are you worried about something you said or did there?" Jordan asked. His fondness for Mishka was tangled by his emotions toward Paige, but he knew one thing—he was prepared to start a war for them if needed. He didn't like feeling that way, but he couldn't deny how much they'd both gotten to him. "I know people in the State Department and other agencies who might be able to help resolve any questions about the adoption, though I can't see you doing something that put the legalities into jeopardy."

"There was nothing I *could* do. They don't let you just take kids. There's a process that has to be followed. It might sound heroic to sneak a child out of an orphanage because you're worried about them, but not a sick baby in another country. Besides, they weren't villains, they were decent people doing their best."

"Then what's the concern?"

Paige released a painful breath. "Before I ever heard of Mishka, her uncle learned there were American doctors in the area providing emergency care. My sister was one of them. Mr. Gupta went to Noelle and asked if she could find someone she trusted who was willing to adopt his niece. The orphanage must have been keeping him updated, because he knew that every adoptive parent shown her profile had passed on taking her. Maybe they thought Mishka's condition was too serious, but at that point he'd become desperate for her to have the possibility of a new life and family."

"So your sister arranged the adoption."

Paige shrugged. "I'm not sure how much she did, or even if what she did made a difference. Open adoptions are rare in India. But Noelle had contacts and could have told them I wouldn't turn down a child who needed me. All I know is that a few days later, I was told we'd been matched. Normally it takes a while for everything to go through, but Mishka's condition was serious and the adoption went faster than usual. Don't get me wrong, they were trying to give her good care—she just needed so much and they were overwhelmed."

Jordan gave in to temptation and put his arm around Paige, pulling her close. She was shivering, despite the sultry air in the dining hall.

"Now you're worried that her uncle will claim there's an irregularity to the adoption."

"In a way. It's unlikely any rules were broken or bypassed since they're very careful, but knowing he'd talked to my sister makes me wonder if he might argue that he didn't really abandon Mishka and the adoption should be invalidated."

"Then why did you reply to the request?"

Paige dropped her head back to look at him. "How did you know I've written back? I haven't even told my family about the letter, much less about replying. They're going to be so upset. I was sure they'd react badly, which would alarm me even more than it already has."

"I knew you wrote back because it's the sort of thing you'd do. You care about him, too."

Her eyes softened. "I do care. Mr. Gupta loved Mishka enough to give her up because he knew it was the only way to get her the help she needed. He lost everything. His brother and the rest of his family, his home and income. Then his niece. If he doesn't hear how Mishka is doing, it's like he's lost her all over again."

Jordan had seen people forced to make terrible choices in the midst of war and disaster, or devastating poverty. So he understood how someone could love a child and still leave her at an orphanage; it had been a chance for Mishka to receive the medical help she needed. Maybe her only chance.

"You may hear nothing from him," he said.

"I realize that. I just hope if he knows Mishka is happy and healthy, he won't do anything to upset her life. Isn't that what a loving uncle would do in these circumstances?"

"You know, you're really special," Jordan said slowly.

She gave him a puzzled look. "What makes you say that?"

"Because you have faith in people. It's great, except for the part where you could get hurt." His own stomach was twisting at the thought of how devastated Paige would be to lose her daughter, yet she'd responded out of compassion, rather than fear.

And now she'd trusted him enough to confide something she hadn't told anyone else.

He pulled her into a kiss, reveling in the sweet taste of her mouth. When he finally lifted his head she had a dazed expression in her eyes.

"Where did that come from?" she whispered.

"Uh, I was making up for the kiss I missed on Sunday because of Sarge's untimely arrival outside the bunkhouse."

"Except you kissed me after she went to check on the dining-hall kitchen."

"I still needed to make up for the first one I missed. The second one was a different kind of kiss. Couldn't you tell?"

"Hmm. Maybe I need to do more experimenting. Or was this one just a pity kiss?"

Jordan stroked her hair. "You don't need pity. I told myself to put distance between us, but I'm not doing too well with that, am I?"

"Do you hear me complaining?"

He shook his head. Paige was dangerous. She'd made him look at what his grandfather had chosen—the loneliness and isolation, pushing people away who could have made a difference. Cold, empty years, filled with nothing except the ranch. Saul must have had opportunities to change his life. He could have let people help when his wife got sick, but he hadn't.

Now Jordan was comparing his own choices with his grandfather's and not liking what he saw.

"You should keep me at arm's length and tell me I'm a hypocrite," he said, but his voice lacked conviction.

PAIGE LAUGHED. ONE of Jordan's hands was on her rib cage and the other on her shoulder. She liked them exactly where they were. "We're all hypocrites to some extent. We tell ourselves one thing and do another. We'll say this or that is a problem, then don't do enough to fix it."

"Sometimes that's called picking our battles."

She sighed. "I'm reluctant to point this out, but our battle right now is the dining hall. Shall we go buy the paint? Anna Beth can sign for the delivery from the lumberyard if it comes while we're gone. It would be best to leave now, before the city workers start closing streets for the chili cook-off. Essentially, the whole downtown becomes a street fair."

Jordan had a wry expression. "I could have gone for everything myself if I'd known a trip to Shelton would be necessary."

"You also ordered a load of fence posts, so you would have needed to drive in more than once. This will work out for the best."

Paige slid off the table, away from Jordan's touch, though there was nothing she'd rather do than sit there with his arms around her. She felt better having someone know about the reply she'd written to Mr. Gupta. It was also nice that Jordan hadn't declared she'd taken an unnecessary risk. When it came down to it, *not* responding was also a risk. Emotions were complex. Mishka's uncle might react badly if he didn't hear anything back.

Still, the reasons she'd written and sent the pictures were very simple—Mr. Gupta loved his niece and deserved to know how she was doing. How could she justify causing him more anguish? He might even wonder if Mishka had died if he didn't hear back. The agency would be careful not to release Paige's name or location; now she would just have to hope for the best.

Before they left, Jordan stopped to tell Anna Beth they were going to the hardware store and let her know they weren't taking the dogs. The Australian shepherds were new to the Soaring Hawk and he didn't want to bring them into town, especially since so many visitors had arrived for Shelton Rodeo Daze.

"I'm planning to paint in here, too," she said. Her sleeves were rolled and she wore rubber gloves that reached to her elbows.

"Don't worry about it. These quarters are temporary, the bunkhouse and dining hall aren't."

Anna Beth frowned. "Your own living space is temporary? You're testing my patience, Jordan. But I'm not going to argue. I have enough paint left from doing Saul's bedroom and the upstairs hallway to spruce the place up. I'll take care of it today and you can move the new furniture in tonight or tomorrow."

"Maybe we could use the leftover paint for the dining hall instead and save a trip into town."

Her eyes narrowed. "Unless you plan to continue living in the main house, I'll do what I want with that paint."

The iron tone in her voice made Paige

struggle to keep from laughing. Jordan had paid for the painting supplies and he topped the retired marine by at least twelve inches and a hundred pounds, but he was outmatched; Anna Beth didn't allowed him to get away with a single thing. She was the same with Saul, who might grumble about her being his jailor, while clearly enjoying their sparring matches. It was fun watching their relationship progressing.

"I'm moving back to the foreman's quarters once the bunkhouse is divided," Jordan returned sharply.

"Then you'd better get to the hardware store and not waste any more time. I'm not letting anybody move in here until it looks better, whether it's you, or some of the ranch hands."

He growled something beneath his breath and turned around.

Paige followed him to his truck and got into the cab. "It's okay," she said. "You're still on schedule."

"I know, I just hoped to do better than provide minimally habitable accommodations. I even tried hiring a handyman for a few days, but everyone is either busy with Shelton Rodeo Daze or haying." Jordan stopped and looked at her. "Sorry. Needing the bunkhouse in order means I'm going to finally have cowhands. That isn't a problem—it's an opportunity I wouldn't have had without the work day you organized."

"No need to apologize. You're probably just extra tired because it was your first night in the house. Did you sleep at all?"

He snorted. "I can sleep anywhere."

"That doesn't mean you slept last night." Paige wiggled her toes in her boots. Jordan had fiercely rejected the idea of staying in the main house the day he'd arrived at the Soaring Hawk, and she didn't know if anything had changed in the intervening weeks to make a difference in his feelings. Sometime she thought he was softening toward Saul, and other time he acted as if his grandfather was still a stranger.

"Okay, it was awkward and brought back some unpleasant memories," Jordan admitted. "But I didn't sleep badly. I had a lady keeping me company."

Paige stared. "What?"

He tossed her a grin. "Lady G. She has a thing for the foreman's quarters. I've been leaving the window open for her to go in and out, or else she makes too much noise.

Last night she figured out how to get into the house. Don't ask me how, the only open windows were on the second floor. I woke up with her snoozing on my chest as usual. She's quite determined."

"Lady G has a thing for *you*, not your quarters," Paige said, trying not to feel envious.

"I'm just a soft spot to sleep."

Paige doubted an inch of Jordan's body was soft; he was all muscle and determination.

"You know, it's okay if Lady G loves you," she said. "She's a cat. She isn't going to ask for more than food, neck scratches and a little company, and will repay you with purrs, warmth and pest control."

Jordan started the engine. "Some people contend that cats are incapable of love."

Paige fastened her seat belt, irritated. Couldn't Jordan even accept a cat being capable of loving him? "And I contend those people don't truly understand cats. Let's go."

"I DON'T WANT to just sit here with everybody else doing something," Saul grumbled as Anna Beth walked up to the porch.

"Then come down and keep me and the dogs company while I work," she told him.

He got to his feet. By the time she'd fetched

the paint and other supplies, he was looking around the foreman's quarters, almost as if he'd never seen them before.

"Can't recall the last time I was in here," he said, sitting on one of the two remaining pieces of furniture, both chairs similar to the one he used every day on the porch. The three Australian shepherds were lying nearby, though Koda and Dixie had their gazes fixed on the open door, probably waiting for Jordan to return. "I always did the ramrod job myself. But when Celina and I were married and my folks were alive, we'd come in here for a bit of privacy."

Anna Beth popped the lid from a can of paint, gave the contents a stir and poured some in the tray. "Privacy on the narrow little bed Jordan hauled out of here? Didn't the squeaky springs give you away?"

He chuckled. "Not *that* kind of privacy. We mostly talked about the future. Oh, I had huge plans. I was going to breed and train horses, not just cattle. Everybody in the ranching world would want to buy them. Arrogant to think I was the only one who could match the right dam and sire for certain traits."

"You never know."

"I was a young man, talking big to his

wife. Now I'm interested in my grandsons. Funny how one minute you're looking at all those years ahead, the next they're gone and you don't know what happened."

Anna Beth shook a finger at him. "Stop saying that kind of thing. We've still got years ahead. Both of us. You're in good health except for your bad hip, and you can get that fixed."

"Then stop calling me *old man*."

"I will when you stop acting old," she returned tartly.

She began running the roller over the walls. Jordan wanted his employees to have a good living space and she liked being able to help in a variety of ways. Heck, she'd already made several dishes for the cowhands and stowed them in the old chest freezer. There was plenty she could do, provided she could work around his pride. Lord, the man was just as mulish as his grandfather. Now he was insisting he'd pay her extra for the cooking, which was ridiculous. She didn't have enough to do as it was.

As a marine, she'd requested assignments where she could accomplish something tangible. Maybe that's why she and Jordan got along so well. He'd fought when necessary, but had viewed his SEAL team missions as a way to save lives. Deep down, he was as much a softie as his grandfather. Neither would have been as deeply wounded by the losses they'd experienced if their hearts were as impervious as they liked to pretend. In Saul's case it had led to bad choices, but at least he was trying to make up for them now.

"A hip replacement won't fix my arthritis," Saul said, sounding glum. Perhaps that was the reason he didn't think the surgery would be worthwhile, but relieving part of his pain could help with managing the rest.

"It might not be as bad if you weren't walking funny," she pointed out. "Limping puts your whole body out of whack. I learned that firsthand when I broke my leg on maneuvers in Afghanistan. After using crutches for a couple of weeks, my back hurt worse than my leg."

"Afghanistan." Saul scratched his chin. "Do you know that I've never gone farther than the Montana state border, while you've been everywhere?"

"Not quite everywhere, but I've met my share of people. One thing I've learned, folks aren't that different, no matter where we live or what language we speak."

"Why didn't you ever get married?"

She blinked at the question. "I've had my share of proposals and propositions, I just never found someone worth the compromises I'd have to make." She dipped the roller into the tray again.

"That doesn't mean you couldn't still meet someone and fall in love."

Anna Beth didn't know if Saul meant anything by his comment, but liked that he wasn't saying something silly about her being too old for the hearts-and-flowers routine.

"Possibly," she replied. "Marriage would be a new adventure. Kind of fun to think about." She immediately questioned whether she'd said too much, then dismissed the concern. If Saul was interested in a real relationship, he wouldn't get hung up on words, and if he did, he wasn't the man she thought he was.

A warm breeze blew through the open windows and door, carrying the scent of paint away and bringing new fragrances. With it came a contentment Anna Beth hadn't experienced since retiring. She'd seen Jordan as family for nearly twenty years, but now she had Paige and Mishka, along with Saul, even if nothing happened between them.

She'd met other people, too. Three women at the work day had invited her to join their exercise group and Margaret Bannerman had suggested they get together for lunch on a regular basis.

Life was good.

Saul began asking about her postings and she told him a few stories about the places she'd seen. For someone who'd spent decades on bad terms with most of his neighbors, he could carry his half of a conversation quite well.

"Will you miss the warm climate in Southern California when freezing weather arrives?" he asked after she described a year spent in the subtropics, where the temperature never seemed to drop below seventy degrees. "Our winters aren't for the faint-hearted."

"I know about cold. I grew up in Maine near the Canadian border. Southern California is nice, but there are too many people for my taste, and all that sunshine and sand gets to you. *Bleh*."

"Some folks wouldn't agree."

"Most folks aren't me."

She regarded Saul for a long moment. For a woman who'd traveled and met people all over the globe, she didn't have much experience with love. It was also the last thing she'd anticipated when Jordan invited her to become his grandfather's housekeeper.

Just then Anna Beth's stomach complained and she realized it was close to lunchtime, so she stuck the roller in a plastic bag to keep the paint from drying.

"I'm going to make us some grub. Sandwiches okay with you? They're the quickest."

"Sure. But before you leave, let me see if you have paint on your nose," Saul said, standing up.

She made a disgusted sound, but went over and presented her face for inspection. "Nope, no paint," he announced.

And dropped a firm peck on her mouth.

SAUL WAS HAPPY that Anna Beth looked pleased, rather than insulted by his kiss. Courting a lady after nearly fifty years wasn't easy. He barely remembered what it had been like to be a young man, considered a highly eligible bachelor. A few women had come calling after Celina died, but he'd slammed the door in their faces. The thought of marrying again had repulsed him.

One of the many ways he'd been a fool over the years.

"Er, um, do you want to eat here?" Anna Beth asked. "I can bring down a tray."

"Why not?"

She left and he sat again. He wished he could continue with the painting and surprise her, but it wouldn't help if he fell and broke his bad hip.

Or worse, broke his *good* hip.

Anna Beth would give him an earful if he did either. Yet the possibility brought a fond smile to his face—that woman would scold a grizzly bear for tracking up her porch steps and then give it a mop to clean up the mess.

The marines must have loved her.

Saul gazed around at the empty ramrod's quarters. *Foreman*, he reminded himself. Walking down, he'd anticipated a rush of sorrow since he and Celina had used it as their private place, but the memories here were happy. It was nice that Anna Beth didn't seem to be bothered when he talked about his wife, but maybe he should ask, just to be sure.

Paige had once said that people who've lost someone they loved, honored them by going on and loving again in the future. He thought that must be true.

Anna Beth and Celina were as different as two women could be, but Anna Beth was *here*. She wasn't comfortable and would never go along with something just because he wanted it. She was also smart, interesting, had a sense of humor and was strong enough to tell him whatever she had on her mind.

Sometimes a man needed someone to tell him the truth, particularly when he had a talent for behaving like an unreasonable clod.

CHAPTER FOURTEEN

"NANA HARRIET OFFERED to make curtains for the Soaring Hawk crew quarters and dining hall, so let's go into the Bibs 'n' Bobs store," Paige said after they'd gotten the painting supplies and were loading them into the cargo area of Jordan's truck. "It's just across the street and they carry fabric."

"Curtains?" Jordan repeated skeptically. "The men will think curtains are fussy."

"I'm not talking about calico and ruffles, though just because you don't care about how things look, you can't assume all guys feel the same. Once upon a time *somebody* put curtains on the bunkhouse windows."

"Probably to stop cold drafts from rolling off the glass. And who said I don't care how things look?"

Paige snickered. "Anna Beth described your apartment at the navy base. *Spartan* would be an understatement, and you only gave your quarters on the ranch a minimal cleaning."

"Hey, Sarge doesn't own much stuff, either. We aren't sentimental. Our places came fully furnished, there wasn't a need for more. She may have put out a few decorative blankets from the Southwest for color, but that's all. Too many belongings make it difficult to pick up and go."

"That doesn't explain why you didn't scrub the foreman's quarters better. They were empty for ages and needed serious elbow grease."

Jordan closed the tailgate. "I sanitized, but the ranch takes priority."

"Oh, please, I don't want to hear anything else about your agreement with Saul."

"This isn't the place to talk about it, anyway. My first concern is taking care of the animals. They can't be neglected."

The sincerity in his eyes made Paige's heart melt. It was clear that whatever had happened in the past with Saul, Jordan truly cared about the cattle and horses on the Soaring Hawk. Her questions about whether ranching was in his blood had long since vanished.

But when it came to people, he was pretty dense. Contrary to what he thought, Anna

Beth was quite sentimental. She'd embraced the antiques left in the Soaring Hawk ranch house, caring for them as if they were made of gold. Several of Mishka's drawings had been framed and hung in places of honor. A set of Depression glassware, long relegated to the top kitchen cupboards, was now sparkling clean and displayed in the built-in china closets in the dining room.

Paige's grandmother was sentimental, too, in her own way. She might be uncomfortable with clutter, but her condo glowed with artistic handmade patchwork quilts in vibrant colors and patterns. Glass art paperweights, given to her over the years by the family, were prominently displayed. And she was delighted when Paige surprised her by transmitting new photos of Mishka to her electronic picture frames.

"It's okay to also take care of yourself," Paige said. "I might even argue that it helps you take better care of the Soaring Hawk."

"Sure, and maybe I'll be able to do that once I have employees. I'm not complaining. Having the branding done is huge."

He looked so earnest that Paige wanted to hug him.

What would he do if she claimed she owed

him a kiss, rather than the other way around? His excuse earlier had been exactly that, an excuse. She was pretty sure he had feelings for her that went beyond friendship, but she didn't just want kisses, she wanted all of Jordan. Forever. Which wasn't reassuring since she didn't know if his opinion on *forever* had changed.

At least he hadn't gotten weird when the neighbors teased him about wooing her. His sense of humor might be stunted, but it was getting healthier. And his rare smiles and laughter were well worth waiting to see.

"Come on, let's get the curtain fabric," Paige urged before she could give in to temptation. "Something has to be done about the bunkhouse windows. We can get a neutral color, identical throughout. Your employees should be offered the same accommodations across the board, which includes the window treatments. If they want to change something, they can ask, but this will be faster than ordering and installing something else."

"Fine, but I can't let your grandmother do the sewing."

"Yes, you can. Nana Harriet was unhappy we didn't have her cook for the work day. This will make it up to her."

His aggravated expression made Paige bite her lip to keep from grinning. She was pushing things again, but this was part of getting the bunkhouse ready for habitation. And the more Jordan got caught up, the more he'd be able to think about personal matters.

Besides, she wanted to show him that people cared, even people who weren't ranchers to whom he'd feel obligated to offer a reciprocal day of work.

JORDAN SURRENDERED, KNOWING Paige would just come up with another counterargument.

Aside from paying the bill, his presence was superfluous as she made her selections at the shop. She consulted a sheet of paper and asked the clerk to cut the fabric into specific lengths. Curtain rods were next, but the store seemed to carry something of everything, so that wasn't a problem. She chose spring rods, saying they were the fastest to put up and take down—no installation required.

Thinking about it honestly, Jordan knew he couldn't have asked employees to live in the bunkhouse without something over the windows. If nothing else, he would have had to cover the glass with paper. Window coverings hadn't occurred to him, but Paige had not only remembered they were needed, but she'd also come up with a solution.

"Okay, what's bothering you *now*?" she asked as they left the store.

Jordan closed his eyes for a second. "For Pete's sake, stop reading my mind. All I did was hand over some money. I should have ordered blinds or curtains when I got the furniture. Instead I didn't even think about it. Now it's going to be taken care of with a minimum of effort on my part."

"Honestly, you haven't been on a ranch in over twenty years, and yet you expect to be perfect? That isn't reasonable. As it is, you've done as well or better than most experienced ranch managers would have done."

Some of the tension unwound in Jordan.

He was supposed to be concerned about Liam Flannigan's approval, but Paige's opinion had become the one that counted.

"Do you want to drop the fabric off to your grandmother now?" he asked.

She smiled brightly. "That would be great. I didn't think I'd be able to get to Bibs 'n' Bobs until tomorrow, so this will give Nana Harriet a head start."

At the retirement complex, Jordan carried the packages into the condo where Paige hugged her grandmother and introduced them. Harriet Bannerman was a striking woman, with silver hair, intelligent hazel eyes and a pleasant, no-nonsense manner. He instantly liked her.

"Did you get the fabric?" she asked.

"Yes, we just left Bibs 'n' Bobs."

"I can hire someone to do the sewing," Jordan interjected. "Or pay you. I don't want to impose."

Mrs. Bannerman gave him a stern look. "You aren't imposing, young man, I offered. I wouldn't take a dime for doing my part. Goodness sakes, it's nice to do a small task in memory of your grandmother. I taught high school for a couple of years after getting married and Celina was one of my best students. She was so sweet and kind to an inexperienced teacher. Very endearing. You must come for a visit when you aren't as busy and I'll tell you about her. I also have pictures to share."

"I appreciate the offer, Mrs. Bannerman." Jordan wished he could hear her stories right away. His mom had kept a photograph of his grandmother on the wall in the bedroom, but it was the only one he'd ever seen of Celina Hawkins.

Then another thought occurred—was that photo still at the Circle M? Jordan still hadn't gotten over there, so he had no idea of what his father had left behind.

"Please, call me Harriet," Mrs. Bannerman said, breaking into his thoughts. "Or is that too familiar for a former navy officer toward a more mature woman?"

"Courtesy is always required, ma'am."

"Hmm. I think you'll do."

Do?

Jordan glanced at Paige, hoping she'd interpret, but she was sorting out fabric and spools of thread from the shopping bags. It was probably just what an older person might say when they believed someone had been suitably polite.

"The windows are all the same size, but these are the measurements," Paige said, handing her grandmother the sheet of paper she'd consulted earlier. "The fabric is already cut in the right lengths for the panels, including the extra inches you wanted for the hems and top."

"You didn't have to do that," Harriet scolded.

"The clerk at Bibs 'n' Bobs took care of it. Mom told me your electric scissors weren't working right and I thought this would be easier. Oh, she's ordered a new pair, so don't buy one for yourself."

"I'll call Margaret and thank her. I should be able to run the curtains up quickly. Give me until tomorrow afternoon. Now, scoot."

As they were briskly ushered to the door, Jordan decided Harriet Bannerman would have made an outstanding admiral.

He gestured around the retirement complex as he and Paige got into the truck. "Why does your grandmother live in Shelton instead of at the Blue Banner? A lot of the ranches here seem to be multigenerational, with everyone living and working together."

"Nana Harriet grew up in a city. Adjusting to the isolation of a ranch was challenging. After my grandfather was gone, she decided this was the best compromise between staying near the family, and having a more active social life. Not that Shelton is anything like Denver."

"She seems strong-willed."

Paige laughed. "That's an understatement."

Jordan averted his gaze as he drove by the cemetery for the second time that day. For the most part he'd made peace with the past, but it continued to bother him that his mother's headstone had been replaced. Mostly because it suggested his grandfather wasn't quite as regretful of his actions as Paige believed.

He flexed his fingers on the steering wheel as they neared the Circle M Ranch road. Checking on the house could wait; another few days or weeks wouldn't make a difference. Still, he and his brothers had gone on faith that the property agent was as trustworthy as his reputation.

"By the way, would you mind if we stopped at the Circle M?" he asked. "I should see if everything is in good order."

"No problem."

Jordan turned onto the overgrown track, going slowly so the cans of paint wouldn't bounce too much in the back. The Circle M was closer to the county road than the Soaring Hawk, but it was still a while before they drove over a small hill hiding it from the world. He braked and gazed at the cluster of buildings he'd once called home, a rush of memories pouring through his mind.

He finally drove forward again and parked near the house.

"I haven't been here since county employees came and took us to Saul's house," he murmured. "We were able to stuff some clothes into a pillowcase, not much more. Saul never let us come back, even to see our father. *Especially* to see Dad."

"No wonder belongings have little meaning for you." Paige put her hand on his forearm. "It must have been awful. I know Saul regrets the way he handled everything, but that can't be any consolation now."

Jordan sighed.

Maybe he'd have to tell her the truth.

"I hate to disillusion you, but if he truly regrets the past, why did he replace my mother's headstone at the cemetery? Instead of saying 'Victoria Hawkins Maxwell, Beloved Wife and Mother,' now it's just her name with no message. Saul is the only one who could have done that. It's as if he was trying to erase what she meant to us."

Sadness filled Paige's face. "Seeing that must have been a shock. I don't know what he intended, but I probably know when it happened. Soon after Saul and I became friends, vacationing tourists got drunk and went four-wheeling through the cemetery. A number of the historic and modern stones were destroyed. A few could be repaired, but most had to be replaced."

Revulsion filled Jordan. "The town must have been horrified."

She made a helpless gesture. "Shelton was in an uproar. Violating a grave touches on so many emotions. That's why there's a sturdy fence around the cemetery now, with cameras linked to the dispatcher's desk at the sheriff's station. But since families are responsible for maintaining stones, they would have contacted Saul and asked what he wanted to do about any markers connected to the Hawkins family. You should ask why he chose what he did. It isn't something we've discussed."

Jordan had noticed the extensive security around the graveyard. It had seemed unusual, but vandalism explained everything. While beliefs varied around the world, most cultures seemed to have the customs and rites that honored the dead and were deeply offended when those customs were disrespected.

"I was unhappy when I saw the new stone and will probably order a different one," he admitted. "But I haven't spent the last twenty-one years angry at Saul. I had to let it go. Maybe I should leave this alone, too."

Paige shook her head. "Dakota and Wyatt will probably feel the same if they come back.

Besides, this would be a chance to get everything out in the open with Saul."

"I'll think about it. Do you want to go inside?"

She nodded and they got out.

The porch steps were worn, but not falling down, and he unlocked the door. Though the interior was dim, he could see the outline of furniture. A bright beam suddenly illuminated the space. It was from Paige, using the flashlight function on her cell phone. He took out his own phone and did the same.

"I wonder who replaced the roof," she mused, breaking the silence.

"We have a property agent in Bozeman. He inspects twice a year and arranges for necessary work."

"Oh. I hoped that maybe—" Paige stopped.

"Yes?" Jordan prompted.

"Nothing."

He released a heavy breath. "If you were hoping my father was involved, I've stopped believing he's still alive. Dad sold the Circle M's cattle and left Shelton before I graduated high school. He paid the property tax for a number of years, then the payments stopped. My assumption is that he got sick or had an accident. Dakota hired a private investigator to search, but nothing came of it."

PAIGE DESPERATELY WISHED she could heal the emptiness in Jordan, but that was something he'd have to do for himself.

What would it be like to have your childhood house sitting abandoned like this, finally to return and see it after so long? Everything looked as if Evan Maxwell had simply walked away. She couldn't imagine how she would respond in Jordan's place.

There was a newspaper and cup on the table between the couch and an easy chair. Also a capped whiskey bottle with an inch of amber liquid at the bottom. A bookcase on the wall still held books, along with figurines and photos. Paige blew dust from an old-fashioned wedding photograph. From the little she could discern, the clothes were probably Edwardian; perhaps the happy couple was Jordan's paternal great-grandparents. Next to the frame was a ball and handful of jacks with chipped red paint.

She felt if she listened really hard, she would hear the echoes of three young boys and their parents, along with other generations going backward in time.

If ghosts existed, surely this was the kind of place they would be found.

By the couch, Paige looked down at the yellowed newspaper. The date was from almost twenty-three years earlier. She extended her hand and then froze. There might be a clue in the paper about why Evan Maxwell had left, a trigger perhaps, but Jordan and his brothers deserved their privacy.

Jordan disappeared into the back of the house and she could hear him moving from room to room. To avoid intruding, Paige went out to the porch and sat on a bench to wait. A trip down Jordan's memory lane was the last thing she'd expected today.

She was on her own emotional roller coaster, wondering how Mishka's uncle would react to her letter, at the same time knowing she'd fallen in love with Jordan. There was no way she could cut Saul out of her life, but if Jordan didn't change his mind about love and the future, her heart would break whenever she visited his grandfather.

Stop, she ordered, annoyed with her train of thought. She was borrowing trouble, as Nana Harriet would say. Nothing had been decided or even fully voiced aloud, although she was certain Jordan had feelings for her.

Jordan Maxwell was one of the good guys.

He must have been a great commanding officer, and fiercely looked after the welfare of his fellow SEALs. He'd do the same with his crew at the Soaring Hawk. Anna Beth had even mentioned Jordan was in contact with a friend who was leaving the Navy Construction Battalion, suggesting his buddy start a contracting business in Shelton and offering to let him operate from the Soaring Hawk while getting established. His first job would be putting new bathrooms in the bunkhouse, along with doing other updates. "Two birds with one stone," Anna Beth had laughed. He'd both be helping a friend and improving conditions on the ranch.

A few minutes later the boards on the porch creaked and Jordan sat next to Paige.

"It's beautiful here," she murmured after a long silence. "I love that it's in the middle of rolling land and trees, but you can still see the Rockies rising up through the hills."

"Dad used to worry about the stand of evergreens behind the barns, thinking they'd be a problem if a wildfire got started, but he never got around to cutting them down."

"We have black cottonwoods around the

Blue Banner. My father worries about the same thing."

They sat for a while longer until a sigh came from Jordan. "I'm wasting time."

"No, you aren't. I told you, taking care of yourself is important. Coming here is what you needed to do today. Painting the dining hall doesn't have to be done before the cowhands move in. If necessary, we'll just put the cans of paint and rollers in a prominent location so they know it's on the agenda."

"I'm sure they'll be greatly reassured."

"They know the Soaring Hawk is rundown and you're working to fix it up. What will reassure them is having brand-new furniture, including quality mattresses and new bedding. The new washer and dryer will make them happy, along with the couches in the dining hall. And I don't need to tell you how much they'll enjoy Anna Beth's food."

"I had no idea she could cook this well. We always went for pizza or burgers or something."

Paige noticed Jordan was holding a framed photograph and took a closer look. "That's your grandmother."

"My mom kept this in the bedroom. After what Mrs. Bannerman said, I started wondering if it was still here. That's the real reason I wanted to stop by. I don't understand how my dad could leave everything behind this way. I know he tried to sell the ranch, without any luck. But to just abandon the place?"

"Maybe he was trying to get his head together and planned to come back."

"Except he didn't. We're lucky the house didn't fall down after he left."

"Jordan, it took over twenty years for you to return, even though you and your brothers own the Circle M. The only reason you're here *now* is because of the agreement with Saul."

He gave her a sideways glance. "I thought you didn't want to talk about the agreement."

"Because you use it as an excuse to push me away," Paige blurted out, then winced. "Sorry, that was uncalled for."

She got up, only to have Jordan catch her hand and pull her back to the bench.

"What? You're right, we should go," she said.

"Not yet. Look, I'm sorry I let things get to this point. You're the most incredible woman I've ever met, but that doesn't necessarily mean we belong together."

Paige was both sad and angry as she looked

into his face. He hadn't proposed or said he loved her, but he thought she was incredible? Of course, he'd also said they didn't *necessarily* belong together. So maybe he wasn't completely denying the possibility of a future.

"You didn't 'let' anything happen—your grandfather basically shoved me in front of you," she reminded him.

"Saul was matchmaking, but we both know I'm the wrong man for you, and the wrong father for Mishka."

Paige rolled her eyes. "Actually, nobody knows that. You're the only one who even thinks it. Just because I haven't gone through the same experiences as you have, it doesn't mean I'm not strong enough to deal with whatever the future throws in my direction. I told you before, children who grow up on a ranch are well-acquainted with reality. We know that you just have to put your head down and keep going through the hard times. If I wanted easy, I wouldn't have adopted a child from such a long way away."

"I know."

"Good, because I want you to try looking at yourself through my eyes. The man I see is very different from how you see yourself."

"You have no idea of how many people I

couldn't save," Jordan said swiftly. "I'm not a hero."

His fingers were clasped on the picture of his grandmother so tightly that his knuckles had turned white.

"You said that before. But to me, a hero isn't someone who's superhuman. It's easy to be heroic when you can't fail. A real hero is someone who just tries to make a difference. Believe it or not, it's possible to save the world, one person at a time."

JORDAN GAZED INTO Paige's eyes, wanting her to be right. Was there such a thing as being realistic and an idealist?

He was starting to think it was possible.

Paige had an inner course she charted, based on love and hope. But she wasn't oblivious. She was aware of the darker side of life. Yet despite all of that, she still had a faith in human nature he'd long since lost. How else would she have gotten through to Saul?

Jordan thought back to that day near the branding pens, when he'd wondered if she could work a miracle in him. Perhaps the question was whether he was willing to embrace the miracle she offered.

Change wasn't easy.

He'd spent his life defining himself as a cynical loner who tried to do the right thing, all the while believing the world wasn't going to ever get better. But Paige didn't believe that. She'd adopted Mishka and the two of them were bright beams of hope who just wanted other people to be happy.

"Will you promise to think about it?" Paige asked.

He looked at her, his heart crowding his throat. "Yeah, I promise."

CHAPTER FIFTEEN

A WEEK LATER Saul sat on the front porch, hoping Anna Beth would finish her housework, then come and sit with him. Or that he could go in and help.

Shelton Rodeo Daze was over, not that it made much difference on the Soaring Hawk. The ranch was too far off the main road and away from town to see congestion from the traffic and crowds. He just wished he hadn't forbidden his eldest grandson from competing all those years ago. At least he'd finally realized it was wrong to keep the boys so isolated and had allowed Dakota and Wyatt to do more with their friends.

There were many things to regret, yet it was better to have Jordan here and be trying to make up for the past.

Anna Beth had gone to the carnival on Friday morning with Paige, Mishka and the rest of the Bannermans. They'd invited Saul to join them, but he'd known he couldn't manage with his leg. That hip replacement was looking more and more attractive.

Though he hadn't gone with them, they'd returned with tri-tip sandwiches and coleslaw to eat with him as if he was part of the family. Then Mishka had insisted on sharing her cotton candy, something he detested, but willingly ate to make her smile.

Jordan hadn't accepted the invitation to attend the carnival, either, and had worked all day instead with the crews mowing and baling hay.

Haying was Saul's favorite time of the year and he was enjoying the sweet scent of cut grass in the sun as it blew toward the house. The pastures were thick with growth this year, benefiting from the early, wet spring. There should be plenty to feed the herds when the snow got too deep. Jordan's determination to cut every inch of grass possible, at the peak of its nutrition, proved that he understood the importance of preparing for the winter.

Saul frowned at himself. Who was he kidding? Jordan needed experience, but he was already a fine cattleman. Hardworking and willing to learn. From the little Saul had seen of his grandson with the new cowhands, they seemed pleased to have him as their foreman.

Still, something wasn't quite right. It wasn't the ranch; the problem was between Paige and Jordan. Paige was trying to be her usual cheerful self, yet there was an undeniable tension between her and Jordan. They'd seemed to be growing close, but now they were barely speaking.

Saul sighed, his chin sinking to his chest. It was hard enough living with his old mistakes, now he was wondering if he had new regrets. Taking Paige and Mishka to his heart meant he could hurt them, too.

The porch steps creaked and he looked up.

"Sorry, I didn't mean to wake you," Jordan said. "I was going out for a ride."

"I wasn't asleep, just thinking."

Jordan looked toward the paddock, then seemed to make up his mind. "In that case, can we talk?"

Saul nodded, uneasy about the intent expression on his grandson's face. "Of course. Please sit down."

Jordan sat on the edge of a chair, his body ramrod-straight. "I have to be blunt and I'm sorry if it upsets you. I want to ask about my mother's headstone at the cemetery. It's different than the original. Just her name, instead of saying 'Beloved Wife and Mother.' Paige told me the cemetery was vandalized and the stone probably needed to be replaced, but why did you change the inscription? Do you hate my father so much that you needed to erase what she meant to us?"

This wasn't the question Saul had expected.

It was worse.

He lifted his shoulders; he couldn't run away from the questions or the pain he'd caused. He had to face what he'd done, and he'd obviously erred on replacing his daughter's headstone, too. Odd, the things that could trip you up when weren't thinking.

"I'll understand if you don't believe me," he said slowly, "but it had nothing to do with your father. Most of the family stones were smashed. The Hawkins plot was one of the hardest hit. They may be long gone, but it was as if their lives had been spit on. A real kick in the gut."

Jordan nodded. "Paige was upset when she told me what happened."

"Not surprising. Her grandfather had just been buried. The vandals drove through the flowers after the service and threw 'em around. She's the one who went over and checked for the family when they found out."

"How awful. She didn't tell me about that."

"Paige does her best to focus on the positive." Saul rubbed the end of his cane. "The thing is, I didn't deliberately change your mother's stone. She wasn't in the family plot and I'm ashamed to say I didn't know what was inscribed. She was my daughter and outliving your own child is a terrible thing. I, well, I could never bring myself to look at the final evidence she was gone."

Jordan didn't seem angry, just thoughtful. "I see."

"I got a letter afterward, saying which stones needed to be replaced and asking what I wanted to do."

"What about cemetery records? Surely they could have used those instead?"

Saul shook his head. "No one had imagined something happening like that, so they'd never recorded what was on the stones. Just where the plots were, and who was buried there. They had to rely on families. Cost wasn't an issue. They caught the vandals and they were paying for the damage. I didn't want to think about it, so I told 'em to just put the names and the years of birth and death."

"On all the stones being replaced."

"Yes. I ought to have done better by Victoria and everyone else. The truth is, I've felt so guilty about your mama, I rushed to finish the paperwork to keep from having to think about how I'd failed her."

"Failed her? Because you'd cut her out of your life."

It wasn't quite a question and Saul shifted uneasily. Telling Jordan everything was easier said than done; his grandson already had every reason to hate him.

He cleared his throat. "Partly. I should have understood Victoria falling in love, even if I didn't think much of her choice. But after she died, I started wondering if I… If I might be responsible. Since I couldn't face that possibility, I blamed my son-in-law."

JORDAN STARED AT SAUL. "What are you talking about? Mom died of heart failure."

"I know, but the Circle M is a small spread. She and your dad had to work awful hard to make a living there. Maybe if I'd helped, she'd be alive today. The Soaring Hawk's finances were stable by that time. I could have sent ranch hands over or given them money to help out. Or just been there for her. But I was standing on my pride. She'd married a man I didn't approve of and I wouldn't back down."

Jordan knew he could let his grandfather continue stewing in guilt, but that wouldn't be right—Paige had made him see that. Besides, his intense feelings for her were helping him understand how losing somebody you loved could lead to bad choices. His grandfather wasn't the only one who'd made mistakes; his father had done the same.

"No one is to blame," Jordan said slowly. "Mom had a viral infection that damaged her heart. Dad took her to Helena, then San Francisco, where she saw a top cardiac specialist. They told her she needed a transplant, except she had a rare blood type and the chance of a donor heart was practically zero. Even so, she was always upbeat. I don't know, maybe she believed anything was possible. She's the one who kept our spirits up when she was sick, being hopeful and smiling so much."

Saul sagged in his chair. "Are you sure?"

"As sure as anybody can be. She was healthy before she got sick. Not run-down or anything. It was just one of those things that doesn't make sense. We all took it hard."

"I should have talked to Evan when it happened. Maybe I could have helped, instead of taking you away from him. That was wrong of me."

A wry humor caught Jordan by surprise. "Hey, don't go looking for something else to blame yourself about. Dad chose to dive into a whiskey bottle. That wasn't your fault. He was supposed to take care of us, it's what Mom expected, and instead he fell apart. The county probably would have made the same decision about taking us away from him, sooner or later, without you getting involved."

"Perhaps." The emotion in Saul's face was another revelation. "I know you won't believe this, but you mean everything to me."

"Even though I look like Evan Maxwell?"

His grandfather heaved a deep breath. "I don't deny it bothered me. Your resemblance to him was a reminder of my guilt, but I also worried you'd turn out the same. As fate would have it, you're the most like me. Isn't that a kick?" His grandfather chuckled. "Can't say I envy you. Do yourself a favor and don't make my mistakes."

"Nah, I'll make my own. That's par for the family, right?"

"I suppose." Saul shifted in his chair. "Why don't we replace the gravestones at the cemetery together? I should put something personal on your grandmother's marker, too. And we might find something to show what was on the others. I remember there was a poem on my great-grandmother Ehawee's stone. Something about the wetlands and such. I don't know if cemeteries are the way of her people, but she wanted to be buried next to her husband."

"I think that's a good plan."

The silence that fell was comfortable and Jordan relaxed. His days had remained hectic. With the new employees on board he'd also needed to evaluate their skill with the haying equipment. Melody James was excellent. She had experience with aging machinery, so he'd given her the lead in the pastures being mowed, allowing him time to build the dividing wall in the bunkhouse more quickly than anticipated. The two hands who'd competed in the rodeo were now working as well.

Staying in the main house wasn't proving as difficult as he'd thought, but now that the bunkhouse was fully functional and his quarters were available again, it would be best to move back.

As for Paige, she'd continued coming over, but she'd kept things light between them. She was meeting with clients for the next couple of days, along with visiting her grandmother and the people involved with her Connections Project.

Jordan already missed her. He wanted her with him, every minute of the day and night.

Maybe Paige *did* see him as he was, flaws and all, while also seeing who he wanted to be.

"I called Claire Carmichael to ask if she has more dogs available," Saul said, breaking into Jordan's thoughts. "Beau got attached to me and that isn't what I intended. Unfortunately, she won't have any available until next spring at the earliest. I told her we wanted one, or possibly more. Said I'd ask what you prefer."

"It's all right about Beau. I'm glad he's fond of you," Jordan assured his grandfather. "As for how many more dogs, I'll know better when I've worked with them longer. Another consideration is that Dixie may have puppies in the next few months. I saw Finn frisking around her the other day, so I think she's gone into heat."

"I hadn't thought of that." A pleased smile grew on Saul's face. "Puppies would be interesting."

Jordan agreed. He watched the sun drop

lower on the horizon. Curiously, he felt no impulse to pack his duffel bags and rush them down to the foreman's quarters. Instead he kept thinking about Paige and what she'd said about saving the world, one person at a time.

He'd been too focused on the people he couldn't save, instead of remembering the ones he'd helped. It was one of the reasons he'd disliked being called a hero. Yet he could live with Paige's definition of heroic, maybe because *she* was the bravest person he'd ever known.

Paige had loved Mishka from the beginning, even knowing the struggles her daughter would face. As for the message she'd sent to Mishka's uncle? Jordan didn't know if *he* could have written that letter, yet she'd had the resolve to do what she thought was right.

And somehow, she loved an obstinate, battle-scarred SEAL.

Jordan knew Paige loved him with a certainty that wrapped around his heart and made feel safer than he'd ever felt. In fact, he was a complete fool for pushing her away.

Suddenly restless, he got to his feet. "I'm glad we talked, Saul. I'm going to go for that ride. I'll see you tomorrow."

SAUL WATCHED JORDAN saddle Tornado and ride out with Dixie and Koda. He sent Beau after them to get some exercise.

Beau yipped to catch Jordan's attention, who looked down and acknowledged the dog. Saul wasn't concerned. Though it was evening and the sun would be setting in an hour or two, horses had excellent night vision. He'd often ridden at night when he had something to work out in his mind, or to just get away from the demons that greeted him when he tried to sleep.

Things might be better tonight. He still had two grandsons to bring home, but at least his eldest grandchild may have forgiven him.

"Is everything all right?" Anna Beth asked, stepping out onto the porch. "I didn't want to intrude."

"You wouldn't have been intruding. Jordan and I talked. He doesn't blame me for his mother's death, which is more than I could have hoped for."

"That's good to hear."

"Yeah. You were right about being honest with him. It's been a long time since I felt half this good."

"In that case…"

Anna Beth grinned, making Saul think

about the kisses they'd shared over the last week. She reminded him of the old saying that there might be snow on the roof, but a fire still burned on the hearth.

Falling in love again at his age was a surprise. Yet in some ways it was easier and more peaceful, because they'd gone through so many storms and knew what was important. She didn't even mind hearing about his wife, saying Celina had been a precious part of his life.

"In that case, what?" Saul asked, returning her grin.

"I was thinking we could celebrate."

"Oh. And how do you suggest we celebrate?"

"By getting married."

Saul regarded her with delight. He'd given marriage some thought, too. But not because he'd been lonely, and not because he needed someone to take care of him. He loved Anna Beth, and he wanted to spend whatever time he had with her. There were still possibilities ahead.

"It's a lucky thing I'm modern enough to appreciate a woman proposing to me," he told her.

"Good, because I think a wedding ring

would look nice on my hand. And it turns out, *I'm* old-fashioned enough to want one."

He returned her smile, wishing he had already had a ring in his pocket to give her. "Tell you what, I accept your proposal, but only if you'll give horses a try."

She narrowed her eyes. "Then you have to get your hip replaced so we can ride together. We don't want our great-grandchildren deciding we're wimps."

"Do you really think we'll have great-grandchildren here to see that?"

Anna Beth leaned over and gave him a kiss. "We can only hope."

PAIGE HADN'T PLANNED to be at the Soaring Hawk the next morning, but she drove over when she got a text from Anna Beth, saying she had news.

"Engaged?" Paige excitedly repeated when they told her.

"That's right," Anna Beth affirmed. She was sitting on the porch next to Saul and they were holding hands like a couple of kids.

"I'm thrilled. What, um, did Jordan say?"

Anna Beth rolled her eyes. "He was shocked. I reminded him that I might have been a marine, but I'm also a woman."

"I'm sure he didn't mean anything by it."

"Of course, he didn't," Saul said firmly. "Jordan is just dealing with a lot right now getting the Soaring Hawk in shape. I've never seen anyone work as hard, not even me. He'll get used to the idea real quick."

Paige shared a smile with Anna Beth. Saul was staunchly in his grandson's corner. It was odd to have his reliance shifting away from her, but she didn't mind. They would always be friends. What bothered her was the sensation that *Jordan* was slipping away from her, a day at a time. Maybe she'd pushed too hard, or said the wrong thing that day at the Circle M.

"I had to do the proposing," Anna Beth said out of the blue. "Sometimes a woman has to do what she has to do."

Paige blinked. "*You* proposed?"

"That's right." Saul chuckled. "I like a woman who knows her mind."

Hmm.

Paige wondered if she'd have to do the same thing. She may have all but proposed the other day, but she might have to spell things out even more clearly for Jordan. Her heart lifted. She had over ten months ahead, when he couldn't refuse her company. After all, she was Saul's "observer," though she was fairly sure the whole concept of Jordan having to prove himself had been forgotten.

"I couldn't be happier for both of you," she told the couple. "When is the wedding?"

"We have an agreement that I'll have my hip replacement, and Anna Beth is going to learn to ride a horse, but we aren't going to wait for the surgery, are we?" Saul asked, turning to his fiancée.

Before Anna Beth could answer, Paige stood up. "I'll leave you to negotiate. I need to get ready for my first appointment. See you tomorrow."

She left feeling encouraged. If Saul and Anna Beth were working out their differences, surely she and Jordan had a chance.

AFTER TWO DAYS without Paige, Jordan was lonelier than he'd expected to ever feel.

Like it or not, she'd become more necessary to him than eating. She was staying away because of him, something that made him feel worse because he should be offering emotional support while she waited for a response, if any, from Mishka's uncle. The last time they'd spoken about it, she'd said her parents still didn't know since she didn't want them to worry. The chance of anything going wrong was low, but she was all too aware of the unexpected challenges life could throw at her.

It was one of the many ways he'd underestimated Paige since they'd met. She'd talked about a ranch kid learning to put their head down and move forward through the hard times; he had no doubt she would do it with a smile.

She was the strongest person he'd ever known, but it had taken him a long time to understand.

"Boss, do you want us to shift to mowing fields farther north, or go west?" Melody asked as they finished baling the latest field of hay.

"Go east. We're at the Soaring Hawk property line," he said. He was itching to mow the Circle M's lush grass, but the property was currently considered an inactive ranch and he had to check on the tax implications of putting the land back into use.

"Sure thing, boss."

"I've sent Gaffney up to check on the herds," he told her. "I'd ask you to go for a break from haying, but nobody knows this old machinery better. I need you here too much."

Melody gave him a quick, pleased smile and returned to work.

Haying was a cyclical process. Melody understood and was doing an excellent job of keeping the mowers going, along with juggling the other steps to getting the hay baled. Jordan didn't want to take the responsibility away from her.

Once again he was reminded of something Paige had said, this time about a good commander delegating. He might be the foreman, but recognizing talent and rewarding responsibility was one of the keys to success no matter what work was being done. He'd known that as a SEAL, only to forget it in Montana.

With the crew in other fields, Jordan began forking bales of hay to a flatbed truck, jumping on and off to stack them properly. Some of the hay would stay in the fields; some had to be stored at the main ranch for the horses and cows when they were calving.

"Jordan."

At first he thought he'd imagined Paige's voice, but when he looked up, he saw her riding Dolley Madison across the field.

He wanted to grab her into the deepest

kiss she'd ever received, but kept his fingers wrapped around the pitchfork.

"Hey, Paige. Thought you couldn't come today."

She dismounted and pulled a folded piece of paper from her pocket. "I had to show you something. Here, *look*."

Tears were streaking down her face, but she was smiling. He thrust the pitchfork in the ground and unfolded the paper.

Dear lady,

I do not know your name, just that my niece is now in your care. Thank you for sending kind words and pictures to reassure me. I am comforted to know my brother's daughter is healthy and happy, and most of all to know she is loved. Perhaps one day, when she is grown and ready, I may hope to see her again. Until then, my gratitude will grow each day because you have a heart big enough to include me. This is already more than I had ever wished.

As Jordan looked up from the letter, Paige threw her arms around his neck, crumpling the paper between them.

"Isn't that wonderful? I just got the email and had to come over and show you. You're the only one I can celebrate with until I tell everyone else. Now I can, and the family won't get all frantic."

"It's incredible," he agreed, his own relief exploding through his veins.

The message had humbled him. Paige's heart was that big. Big enough to understand the choice a man had been forced to make, half a world away, and to lovingly send him a message of comfort and reassurance.

When Paige tried to step away he tugged her back into his arms. "Uh-uh," he said. "I'm not letting you go."

"Oh?" Her eyebrows lifted.

"Yeah. I'm absolutely, wildly, head over heels in love with you, Paige Bannerman. I can't wait any longer to ask if you'll be my wife and let me help raise Mishka. She already asked me to be her papa, after all. It's only right that I do it properly."

Paige smiled as she rose onto her tiptoes. She cupped her hands around the base of his neck and gave him a long, lingering kiss. They were both breathless as she drew back an inch.

"It's about time. I was ready to propose like Anna Beth," she said against his mouth.

Laughter welled from Jordan's chest. Life had taken some strange turns. His buddy would soon become his grandmother. He was going to be a father. And best of all, Paige was going to be his wife.

"Then you love me, too? I suppose I don't need to ask, but I really want to hear you say it."

"I love you. Completely, wholly, without reservation."

He kissed her again, knowing that whatever came, she would be the light he'd always needed.

* * * * *

For more Western romances from author
Julianna Morris and
Harlequin Heartwarming,
visit www.Harlequin.com today!

COMING NEXT MONTH FROM

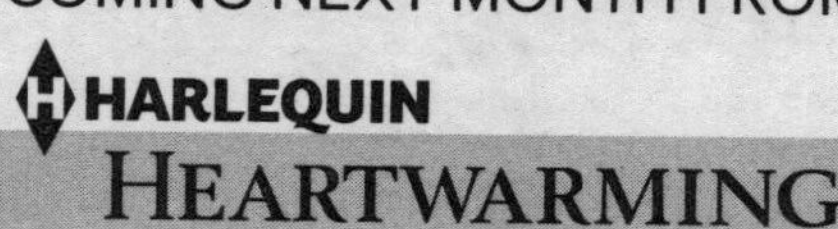

#427 THE BRONC RIDER'S TWIN SURPRISE

Bachelor Cowboys • by Lisa Childs

After weeks of searching for his runaway wife, rodeo rider Dusty Haven gets a double shock when he finally finds her. Not only is Melanie Shepard living at his family's ranch—she's pregnant with their twins!

#428 HER COWBOY WEDDING DATE

Three Springs, Texas • by Cari Lynn Webb

Widow Tess Palmer believes a perfect wedding beckons a perfect life. Roping cowboy Carter Sloan in to plan her cousin's big day might be a mistake—unless she realizes this best man might be the best man for her.

#429 AN ALASKAN FAMILY FOUND

A Northern Lights Novel • by Beth Carpenter

Single dad Caleb DeBoer hires Gen Rockwell to work on his peony farm for the summer. When she moves her daughters to the farm, the two families become close—but a startling secret threatens everything.

#430 THE RUNAWAY RANCHER

Kansas Cowboys • by Leigh Riker

Gabe Morgan found sanctuary as a cowboy in Barren, Kansas. But he can't reveal his true identity—even as he falls for local librarian Sophie Crane. How can he be honest with Sophie when he's lying about everything else?